Hearts *racing.*
Blood *pumping.*
Pulses *accelerating.*

*Falling in love can be a blur...
especially at 180 mph!*

So if you crave the thrill of the chase—on and off the track—you'll love

HART'S VICTORY
by Michele Dunaway

*Kellie was an enigma, much more so this morning—
when Hart had been told that she wouldn't date
anyone but him.*

Sue had almost choked with embarrassment, and seeing Hart's
subsequent confusion, she'd explained the whole "joke."

Hart had found the entire paradox intriguing. Kellie, who hated
him, was "holding out for Hart Hampton." Funny thing was, he
was very taken with her. The more time he spent with her, the
more he wanted to get inside her head and see what made her
tick.

Inviting Kellie and Charlie to the track next weekend was simply
the right thing to do. He was Hart Hampton and he knew what
he wanted when he saw it. She would never come to him; he
had only convinced her this time because of Charlie. But he was
determined that she discover he wasn't what she thought him to
be.

Hart Hampton was no joke.

Dear Reader,

Start your engines, for Kellie Thompson and her son, Charlie, are about to go on the ride of their lives when NASCAR's most popular driver, Hart Hampton, takes a personal interest in both of them. I know that's my ultimate fantasy, that Mr. Right is not only a hot NASCAR driver, but that he's also kind, caring, understanding and down-to-earth. In fact, the drivers I've met are just that and their significant others the sweetest women in the world.

The idea for this story came from my own daughter, who got to ask a question similar to Charlie's at a January 2006 charity event in Nashville. She was tired and cranky from a long day's excitement, but she stumped one of the top drivers of our time. As I drove the six hours back to St. Louis, *Hart's Victory* began to take shape in my mind. When I did the research, my daughter tagged along, getting to do fun things like meet her favorite driver, tour the inside of a race shop and see the inside of a hauler. Seeing her wide-eyed excitement drove home how special this sport really is.

I hope you enjoy *Hart's Victory*, which marks my fifteenth novel for Harlequin, a major milestone for me. Thanks for being with me on the adventure of a lifetime, and as always, feel free to drop me an e-mail through the link at my Web site, www.micheledunaway.com.

Enjoy the romance,

Michele Dunaway

//////// NASCAR

HART'S VICTORY

Michele Dunaway

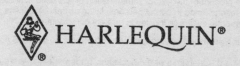

HARLEQUIN®

TORONTO • NEW YORK • LONDON
AMSTERDAM • PARIS • SYDNEY • HAMBURG
STOCKHOLM • ATHENS • TOKYO • MILAN • MADRID
PRAGUE • WARSAW • BUDAPEST • AUCKLAND

ISBN-13: 978-0-373-21782-3
ISBN-10:   0-373-21782-X

HART'S VICTORY

MICHELE DUNAWAY

In first grade Michele Dunaway wanted to be a teacher when she grew up, and by second grade she wanted to be an author. By third grade she was determined to be both, and before her high school class reunion, she succeeded. In addition to writing romance, Michele is a nationally recognized high school English and journalism educator. Born and raised in St. Louis, Missouri (hometown of several NASCAR drivers), Michele has traveled extensively; the cities and places she's visited often become settings for her stories. Described as a woman who does too much but doesn't know how to stop, Michele gardens five acres in her spare time and shares her home with two young daughters and five extremely lazy house cats. Michele loves to hear from readers. You can reach her through her Web site, www.micheledunaway.com.

For C. M., who continues to touch people's lives;
and for Alison. This one's for you.

ACKNOWLEDGMENT

Thanks to Clarann Gafrarar, Susan Benedict
and Val Perkins, who took me in and shared
their racing stories; to Chuck Gafrarar, Brandon Mudd,
Jamie Rodway, and to those drivers, wives and
staff members who graciously answered my
research questions; and to my agent, Jessica Faust,
who helped make this dream book reality.

CHAPTER ONE

"AND FOR THOSE OF YOU just joining us after the commercial break, fighting for the checkered flag are Kyle Doolittle in the Manifest Ford and Hart Hampton in the Number 413 Elementals Chevy."

"Those two have dominated the track today, Gus. Between them, they've led all but sixteen laps and have swapped the lead ten times."

"It's been a tight race, Malcolm. Both have had superb restarts. But this has always been Hart's track. He won here in 2003, 2004 and 2006. Hampton's hungry; he's been dry on wins since Daytona."

"And Hampton's Number 413 car starts to make its move, passing low inside as Doolittle goes high on Turn Three."

"Doolittle's car's loose! If Hampton can hold the low groove, he's going to take home his second win this season. Wait! Doolittle's scraped the wall. Sparks are flying! Doolittle's off—and directly into Hampton. They're giving each other donuts."

"They seem to be locked. Doolittle's managed to get an edge. He's pulling ahead, but his back panel just clipped Hampton's nose. Now Hampton's loose! He's backward...and into the wall!"

"He's catching car 510, Ronnie McDougal, on the

rebound. They're now spinning into the infield grass. Wait! Hampton's caught McDougal wrong. He's airborne...and has landed on McDougal's hood. He's rolling off! Whoa, he's landed upside down."

"A vicious tumble. The caution flag waves at Richmond, freezing the drivers in place with two laps to go."

"Definitely not Hart Hampton's day."

"WELL, THAT ends that," Anita Wertz said with a resigned sigh. She reached over and ruffled her fifteen-year-old grandson's thin tufts of brown hair. Both had been watching the stock car race on television for the past several hours. "Sorry, sport," Anita told Charlie, her own disappointment evident as her favorite driver found himself knocked out of the race. "Looks like Hart's not going to win this one and break his streak of bad luck."

"Hart was so close," Charlie Thompson said wistfully as cameras focused on Hart Hampton's wrecked car. Hampton waved once to show he was all right. "I'd even worn my lucky shirt."

Charlie glanced down at the green T-shirt emblazoned with a picture of Hart and a huge 413. When she'd moved in with her daughter, Anita had gotten Charlie hooked on the NASCAR NEXTEL Cup Series and Hart was his favorite stock car driver.

"Hart needed this win, Grandma. He's already too far behind in point standings if he's going to have a chance to make the Chase. This might send him down to twentieth."

"I know," Anita said. She rolled her shoulders, her own racing attire moving as she shifted her sixty-three-year-old body. "But fate's like that sometimes. Maybe it's not Hart's year. The race winner will probably be Kyle Doolittle if he doesn't run out of fuel."

"I know," Charlie replied. He frowned for a brief moment, then brightened. "I guess there's always next week."

"That's the spirit," Anita said. Back from a commercial break, the newscasters were discussing the crash. Behind them, cars still raced under the caution as officials cleared the debris from the track. "You shouldn't worry. It's still early enough in the season for Hart to make a spectacular comeback."

"IT'S NOT OVER yet?" Kellie Thompson asked as she entered the living room and glanced at the twenty-seven-inch TV. The only view she had was of race cars going around single file as they waited for the restart. "Hey, what's wrong? Why the long faces?"

"Hart crashed and is out of the race," Charlie told his mother as he retrieved the glass of water and cancer medication she'd brought in. His attention remained glued to the events unfolding on the screen, the movement of taking his medicine rote. "He climbed out of the car on his own, but they're putting him in the ambulance now."

The television was now showing repeat footage of the accident. Kellie cringed, unable to imagine how anyone could have walked out of the crash—the car had done a complete roll onto its roof. She credited Hart's survival to his car's strong roll cage and NASCAR's safety standards, including requiring the track's soft walls—all explained in great detail by Charlie.

Still, just the force of watching what looked like a movie stunt had her shuddering. Unlike Anita and Charlie, Kellie wasn't impressed with the challenges the drivers endured every week. In fact, NASCAR wasn't really her sport.

But, ever since the new season had started in February, watching stock car races had become a sit-down ritual in the

Thompson household every weekend, no matter what day or time the race occurred. Kellie hadn't minded, for if Charlie was well enough to watch racing that meant it was a good day, better than most.

Kellie shoved her son's medical prognosis into the far recesses of her mind. The unspoken rule was that any long-term thoughts of her son's mortality and other depressing topics related to his leukemia were banned on race days. Race time was respite time.

"That looked like a nasty crash," Kellie said, attempting to join the conversation.

"They've just announced that he'll be okay," Charlie replied, pale blue eyes so like her own remaining fixed on the television screen as he spread the news. All remained silent while they watched the caution lift. Kyle Doolittle crossed the finish line first, followed by Mike Turnfield, who came in second instead of fourth because Hart and Ronnie's crash had opened up the field.

The cameras followed Doolittle's victory lap as he carried the checkered flag, fist raised triumphantly through the driver's side window. Kellie used the moment to assess her son.

While "officially forbidden" to worry today, she still couldn't help but notice that Charlie seemed a little paler than usual. The last round of chemotherapy treatments had been particularly harsh on his body; Charlie had needed several weeks in the hospital to recover. Of course, she could pretend to be optimistic and pretend that perhaps his skin color was just an odd reflection of the incandescent light. It was after eleven p.m.

But as much as she'd like to say that Charlie's skin color was from staying up late or from a lack of Myrtle Beach sun, Kellie was a realist. She knew the truth, no matter how much she wanted to deny those facts or wish that her reality were different.

While survival rates for blood disorder cancers had more than tripled because of modern medicine, Charlie would never be like other boys. He'd been diagnosed at age seven with an acute myelogenous leukemia. He'd never played sports, played a musical instrument, or enjoyed other things boys his age did. He'd never attended school with much regularity, instead receiving homebound instruction for the past two years. He'd suffered through chemotherapy treatments, remissions that didn't last and bone marrow transplants and platelet transfusions that helped, for a little while.

In the past six months, her son had dropped much-needed weight and the result was that he'd turned pencil thin. His wire-framed glasses appeared too big for his face. His brown hair, often absent from chemotherapy, had returned thin and downy, but the strands were weak and broke easily. The evidence covered his pillow every morning.

"So are you both excited about next weekend?" Anita asked suddenly, as if sensing her daughter's inner turmoil and stress. Kelly gave her mother a small, sad smile that Charlie, still focused on the TV, missed.

Anita had moved into Kellie's small bungalow three months ago, just in time for the season's start at Daytona. That had been about the time when things with Charlie had taken a turn for the worse.

Although, right now, you'd never know his condition from the large smile crossing his face.

"You bet I'm ready for next weekend," Charlie said. He gazed over at his mom, his smile suddenly wavering. His blue eyes flickered once as he assessed her.

Kellie knew what he saw. She was thirty-five; her blond

hair was twisted up unglamorously in a hairclip; and she wore a faded sweatshirt and blue jeans. "How about you, Mom? You excited?" Charlie asked.

"Yes," Kellie said, determined not to rob her son of any of his current joy. She'd been against the idea of going to the weekend camp for chronically ill children, but now that the date had nearly arrived, she gave Charlie a wide, reassuring grin. As he smiled back at her, her conscience eased slightly.

At this time, making Charlie happy and keeping him healthy were her main goals. Anita had finally convinced Kellie to apply to the camp for a family weekend. The camp, founded in memory of a deceased stock car driver, was race car-themed and specialized in kids with chronic and life-threatening illnesses. Race fan Charlie had been thrilled, even more so when the acceptance letter had arrived.

"We'll have a great time," Kellie said.

"I went to the Web site and I can't wait," Charlie said. "Do you know that a lot of the buildings look like you're at a race track? I even printed out some directions. It should take us about four hours to get there."

"Impressive," Anita said with an approving nod. "I thought you only used that laptop I gave you to play video games."

Charlie made a face. "Funny, Grandma. You know I also use it for my schoolwork. Hey, I just thought of something. Maybe we'll meet some of the drivers. They do drop by. I saw the pictures on the camp's Web site."

"They'll be racing at Darlington next Saturday," Anita pointed out.

"Oh that's right." Charlie's expression soured slightly. "You know, if I were going to be there for a week-long camp, there'd be one NASCAR-themed night and I'd learn how to change a tire."

"I'm sure there will be plenty of other things to do," Anita said.

"Yeah, but I'll miss the race. You'll have to tape it. I hope Hart wins. One minor accident won't keep him from driving next weekend."

"That's for sure," Anita replied. "Those guys drive under all sorts of conditions. Pulled muscles, injured shoulders…"

"We're going to have fun," Kellie inserted, not wanting to hear about how heroic the drivers were. "Besides, with it being a family weekend, this way I get to go to camp, too."

"True," Charlie said. "And we haven't had a vacation in forever."

"Exactly." Kellie nodded. Vacations had been pretty sparse as she had to make her late husband's assets and insurance stretch to pay Charlie's medical bills. Since Charlie had another treatment scheduled during the camp's cancer week later that summer, a weekend trip had been their only option. Charlie also turned sixteen in few weeks, making him too old for the regular sessions. The great thing was that, once accepted, attending the camp was free. "What activities were showcased on the Web site?" Kellie asked.

"Archery. Horseback riding. Fishing," Charlie said.

"So there you go. Plenty of things to keep us very busy," Kellie stated. She sat down in the armchair. The television cameras were now focused on Victory Lane and a reporter was busy interviewing a wet Kyle Doolittle. His team had showered him in soda pop once he'd climbed out of the car.

"They should interview Hart at some point," Charlie announced. The group continued to watch, until the programming ended and a movie came on. However, no word had come forth from Hart's camp about his status.

"I'll check the Web sites later," Charlie continued. "Don't

worry, Mom. Your future husband's fine. The reporters would have said something if he wasn't. You won't need to go looking for anyone else."

"That's good because I'd be way too upset," Kellie replied with a heavenward glance of her blue eyes. Trust Charlie to bring up the family joke he had created last fall when some well-meaning person had asked Kellie when she was going to start dating again. Charlie had observed his mother's discomfort and announced that his mother was holding out for Hart Hampton. Although she could have handled the charged situation herself, Kellie had always appreciated her son's "rescue" as his answer had defused the tense situation.

"I think Dusty Burke is pretty cute," Anita observed, naming a rookie driver.

Charlie laughed. "Yeah, but he's too young and married. Mom's better off with Hart. He's more her type."

Right, Kelly thought. The type that didn't know she existed. "I'm sure he'll show up at my door someday," Kellie said, completing the family joke, even though this time it slightly pained her to do so.

No one liked being a widow. Occasionally Kellie felt a little freakish. Widows aged thirty-five were something of an oddity. Add to that Charlie's illness, and dating was simply not an option at this time in her life. And where was it written that a woman had to have a man to be complete? Her first go-round hadn't exactly been a picnic in the park.

Of course, how could she worry about her own needs when she had her ill son to care for?"

As for Hart Hampton, Charlie couldn't have picked someone farther from Kellie's type when he'd said she was holding out for Hart Hampton. She was a homebody—Hart was well, everywhere. His face and that famous smile of his graced everything from slow cookers to acetaminophen boxes.

Television and print advertising showed him wearing boxers, and little else but a tight T-shirt and his famous smile. Race fans adored him, having voted Hart most popular driver last year, despite Hart's failure to make it into the top ten in points. Hart's supporters were rabid—if Hart was going to be at an event, organizers were assured a success, if not a complete media circus, as fans clamored for autographs and waited in line for hours.

The press played Hart Hampton as a "down-home" boy, a second-generation race car driver trying to live up to his dad. Although Hart wasn't ever photographed out partying, he'd admitted jet-setting in interviews—Kellie had peeked at all those racing-related publications her mother devoured. In the race of life, Hart was known for changing women like tires, usually swapping them every two to three months when the newness wore off. So Kellie didn't believe the media hype. Hart Hampton made too much money and suffered too much adoration for her to believe he was a "simple" Southern man.

Of course, letting herself dream about Hart Hampton sweeping her away was occasionally fun, especially after a particularly hard day. Although she was quite capable of saving herself, sometimes she needed to pretend a hero would someday carry her off and solve all her financial and medical worries. Like waiting for Charlie's full remission, a girl should never give up hope or stop allowing herself to fantasize.

Her short break from reality over, Kellie stood and headed into the kitchen. With his immune system weakened, Kellie kept the house spotless and she needed to finish cleaning the kitchen before turning in for the night. As she passed by the hallway mirror she paused. Once, long ago she'd been slim and stylish, even after Charlie's birth. Now, beneath the sweat-shirt she wore, she had mother's hips, tiny stretch marks and the extra five pounds that every average American female carried. She'd aged and accepted that she wouldn't pass for a cover model again, not that she ever had.

Nowadays, she chose one-piece bathing suits, not string bikinis. Her makeup, when she wore it, came from the pink case of the beauty consultant down the street. The last time Kellie'd had a pedicure? She glanced at her naked toes and knew she could never compete with media images of beauty. Not that it mattered. Whenever a man did find her attractive, once he learned about Charlie, he hit the road.

As for Hart Hampton, he was handsome. Fascinating. But his lifestyle was as far from hers as the planet Mars was from Earth. He was also probably an egotistical person who only thought of himself. Well, that and racing. She'd bet the man didn't even do his own dishes. And hers were calling.

Reality won and Kellie banished Hart Hampton to where he belonged—in her mind as a silly fantasy and family gag.

HART HAMPTON was ticked. Angry. Furious. There were much worse words he could use, but ever since his father had washed his mouth out with a horrible-tasting soap at age five, Hart never cussed.

Still, he could think of quite a few foul things he wanted to say right about now. He stood in his office, which was a separate five-room building on his seventy-acre estate west of Charlotte, North Carolina. His office contained trophies, memorabilia and family photos, but what concerned Hart right now was the woman standing in front of him wearing an oversized Carolina Panthers sweatshirt and tight jeans.

Hart glared at Cynthia Jones, his fifty-six-year-old

office/business manager and technically his boss. She was also his aunt and forty-five-percent owner of Hampton Racing, which meant that his loving aunt Cynthia figured she could take liberties, such as telling Hart exactly where he could, and couldn't, go.

"What do you mean I'm not going to be at Darlington this weekend?" Hart repeated, working any angle to make Cynthia reconsider her earlier decision of sidelining him from the race track. "I like Darlington. It's one of the few places where you race the track more than the other drivers. I could win Darlington. Lead some laps. Earn some desperately needed points."

"You scraped the wall there several times last year," Cynthia said, hands planted on her hips. "And I'm not risking more stripes on the car."

Hart bit his lip, for a moment wishing he could stand up, pace and let his five-foot ten-inch frame dominate his aunt by at least the one measly inch he was taller. However, sitting in his leather office chair right now was probably better—and safer. He hadn't yet returned to a full hundred percent following his crash at Richmond.

Richmond. Hart tried to stop berating himself for that, but not mentally replaying the accident fifty million times was hard. Thinking about the race made him angry. While NASCAR had made racing much safer, drivers still often bumped each other as they jockeyed for position.

Hart hadn't been far enough forward when Doolittle had bounced off the wall, and the impact had sent Hart's front end spinning. And then somehow he'd landed on McDougal's hood, and rolled over—out of the race and his top five finish.

"Stop thinking about the crash," Cynthia commanded. She'd known Hart since his birth and knew him far too well. "Sometimes it all boils down to fate."

"Yeah, and crappy driving on my part," Hart said grumpily. He'd been making far too many errors lately. Thankfully, McDougal had been okay—the infield hospital had seen him and released him. Hart, however, had suffered a lovely post-race excursion to the hospital. While the staff doctor had thought overnight observation might be best, Hart had managed to get himself released and cleared to race.

But none of this solved the problem of the following weekend and the five-hundred-mile race he was going to be sitting out. Hampton Racing had the cars. The crews were ready. But management had decided to sit Hart out and place NASCAR Busch Series driver Ricky Senate behind the wheel. And Hart wasn't happy.

"Cynthia, it's bad enough we've got to substitute Ricky next weekend, but I'll live with that—this time—since he's gaining Cup-level driving experience. But you're killing my standing. I have to at least start the race to earn my driver points."

"No," she said flatly, shifting position.

"Listen, I'm going to be at the track. Other drivers are there with their teams. One raced in pain after suffering burns when he wrecked in that non-NASCAR race a few years ago. Remember that? Then in the weeks following, if he couldn't finish, a sub went in. Same with Anderson when he separated his shoulder. He started the races, too."

Cynthia's arms remained folded across her chest. She didn't plan on capitulating. Still, Hart had to try.

"How can the car's main driver not be at the track with his team and his substitute? What will people think, especially when Billy Easton and Mitch Bengal are still driving their own cars?" Hart continued, throwing out the names of Hampton Racing's other two NASCAR NEXTEL Cup teams.

Cynthia simply arched a brow. "Your teammates didn't

wreck. You did," she pointed out. "And that's exactly why you shouldn't be there. I don't care that NASCAR cleared you to race. I don't care that this is something probably any other owner or team wouldn't do."

She uncrossed her arms and then refolded them across her chest. When she made that movement it always reminded Hart of his father, Cynthia's older brother, who'd retired from racing five years ago. Carl Hampton's name was as revered as much as any of NASCAR's other dynasties.

"My dad would have been at the track," Hart stated. People often said he looked like his dad: same dark brown hair, same green eyes.

"Don't think this is just because I'm your aunt," Cynthia said. "Although I admit that this time family plays a major part of it. Your parents both agree with me, and our ninety percent to your ten makes this is a business decision. You're Hampton Racing's best driver and we're not ready to lose you in any capacity. I know this is hard, but driver points aside, it's the best decision for the long run."

Hart tapped his fingers on the leather armrest. Cynthia and Hart's dad had founded Hampton Racing, a legacy that would eventually pass to Hart as he was the only child and had no cousins.

"Trust me on this. Besides, I don't want them to be thinking about you," Cynthia said suddenly.

"Them?" Hart queried.

"The media. If you're at the track, they'll want access to you. Hampton Racing can't ignore requests for interviews. And while we can put a positive spin on things, I don't want the media finding out what your personal physician said. We have to tightly control the press surrounding you from this point forward."

"I'm fine," Hart said as his head started to pound. Since Cynthia was here, he refused to rub his temples or the back of his neck, lest he show any weakness. While a headache wasn't enough to keep Hart out of the driver's seat, his doctor had warned that another accident this close to the last one could make matters worse.

The medical explanation had been long and confusing, but in layman's terms, Hart had rattled way too much stuff upstairs over the years and not just from racing. The bungee jumping, parachuting and four-wheeling hadn't helped. His personal physician had said that another blow to the head, even just falling around the house, could knock him out for the entire season—especially if he lost consciousness or his memory.

That was definitely a risk he couldn't take, especially as he had been crashing a lot lately, more so than normal. Usually lucky with the Number 413 car, it was as if his muse had left him. Hart wasn't necessarily that superstitious. While many other drivers avoided things such as peanuts and the color green, Hart embraced both. Still…

He frowned. Maybe he did need to take some time, at least one weekend, off the track to heal like his doctor suggested. While Hart would fall in driver points and the NASCAR NEXTEL Cup standings, Hampton Racing would still get the owner points. But to not even be present at the race and in the pit, that was unthinkable. He opened his mouth to speak, but Cynthia beat him to it.

"Here's how we're going to handle this. I thought that you would go to camp for the weekend."

Hart blinked. "I'm going camping?" he asked.

"Yes." Cynthia pushed a silver hair off her face. "The camp for chronically ill kids you always donate to."

Hart knew exactly what camp she meant.

"I participated in their fundraiser in Nashville back in January," Hart reminded Cynthia. "But why do I need to go to camp instead of the track?"

Her mouth thinned, as if his constant questions were starting to annoy her. "Because I don't want you at the track. And you love this organization."

Hart arched an eyebrow at her, asking silently if that didn't just prove his point. "I do, but I still want to go to Darlington."

Cynthia exhaled a long sigh of frustration. Having no children of her own from her marriage to Hampton Racing's president, Liam Jones, she'd practically been more Hart's second mom than an aunt.

"No, and that's final," Cynthia said firmly. "Liam and I both agree with this. If you're at the track, you'll want to give Ricky advice. That's your crew chief's job, and the last thing you need to do is second-guess Wally, especially when it's not your rear out there driving. And with you absent, the press will interview me. You know how good I look on camera."

"You don't," Hart said, taking her bait like she'd wanted him to do. Because she was five foot ten and still had what she called her "basketball build" from her college playing days, Cynthia hated being on television.

"So there you go. My point exactly. The newshounds aren't going to want to put me on TV for longer than a second unless Hampton Racing places in the top five. Unlike you, I'm not sexy enough."

Hart made a face at her. His status as a sex symbol bothered him. It was about racing, not underwear. Still, every driver, including Hart, knew that the money to run a racing team came from sponsors, endorsements and merchandising. And racing teams needed millions.

"When I am interviewed, this is what I'm going to do,"

Cynthia continued, ignoring her nephew's scowl. "I'm going to say that you're fine, you'll be back in a week, and that you're spending the weekend volunteering. Your volunteerism shows that you're active, which will completely take the edge off your crash and speculation that you're all washed up."

"I'm not washed up," Hart insisted angrily. One idiotic blogger had just posted something to that effect yesterday on one of the fan Web sites. Hart was still ticked.

"Of course you're not washed up, but since your Daytona win, you haven't placed higher than fifth. At Bristol you didn't even make the top twenty."

"You're the one killing my points. Are you sure you're not getting a kickback from some of the other car owners?" Hart asked.

"Stop it," Cynthia said, rolling her eyes skyward. "Go to the camp. I've already got your schedule rearranged and you'll stay in your motor home. They're expecting you at five."

"Aren't you efficient," Hart said, conceding only because his head now pounded with a massive migraine. Maybe his aunt was right, and surely a bunch of kids would be quieter than the roar of race engines and squeal of burning tires.

Besides, he'd hate to be standing on the sidelines like an unused wheel. He'd done that once, and had felt like an animal with its leg caught in a trap. He'd been stymied. Frustrated. Even more so than right now. "I guess I have no choice."

Cynthia smiled now that the matter was settled. "No, and this is the best thing for everyone. I told you earlier to trust me. Have I ever been wrong?"

"There was that time when…" Hart began.

"Yes, well, I'm not perfect," Cynthia said quickly. "And that was a rare foible. I'm at least ninety-seven percent in my statistical correctness."

"Whoopee," Hart said. He raised his finger in the air and made a small circle.

"Such a smarty-pants. You get that from your dad. By the way, are you planning on signing while you're over here? Your mom and I laid out about three tables' worth in there before she left for the airport."

"Yeah," Hart said. His office building included a room where he had tons of fan-mailed-in items to sign. He tried to knock out a lot of signing autographs at one sitting so that his fans only had to wait about four months to hear back from him. Although his parents and his aunt controlled Hampton Racing, Cynthia's husband Liam oversaw the day-to-day operations, freeing up his wife and sister-in-law to meddle in Hart's life. And meddle they did—giving advice on everything from women to endorsements.

Of course, there were benefits. Hart never saw his mail unless his mother and his aunt felt the letter was worth a personal reply. They'd become fantastic screeners over the past ten years he'd been racing professionally. They handled all the mundane details of his life, such as hiring his household staff, managing his investment accounts and paying his bills. This freed him up to focus on fun and racing. A hands-on driver, Hart lived at his race shop. He helped build engines. He assisted in the fabrication of his car bodies. He was determined to be the best, no matter what the effort and no matter how hard the work.

Had there ever been a time he hadn't planned on being a race car driver? Probably not. Hart had grown up with racing in his blood.

Hart's father Carl had made his money the old-fashioned way—by inheriting it from his father. But Carl had had little use in the family's coat hanger manufacturing firm in St.

Louis. He'd sold the company at the first opportunity, relocated and sunk his entire fortune into founding Hampton Racing twenty-five years ago.

The gamble had paid off. Hampton Racing now owned two truck teams, five car teams, and three of those NASCAR NEXTEL Cup contenders. Since Hart was a ten-percent shareholder, he technically owned a part of his team and his car. Most drivers didn't—they were hired to drive by the car's owner. Still, like many of his peers, Hart was paid a salary to drive and kept about half the race winnings.

"I'm going to get out of here and leave you to your autographs. Call me if you need anything. Since your parents are touring Europe for the next few months, I don't want them worrying. They deserve this vacation," Cynthia said.

"I know," Hart replied, and seconds later he heard the front door close. He leaned back and sighed. Then he simply listened: a clock ticked, the fan on his computer blew.

There were times, such as now, that he actually preferred the silence, at least for a little while. The brief solace meant that, for a moment, no one was demanding anything from him.

No one screamed his name, no one asked for his autograph, no one wanted to be with him just because he was Hart Hampton, earner of over fifteen million last year.

Hart closed his eyes, letting himself enjoy the blackness. His headache ebbed away. Finally he opened his eyelids, letting those green orbs of his focus on his surroundings. His office contained many items of sentimental value, all strategically placed by the decorator he'd hired when he'd built the building.

The decorator had been young and sexy, and Hart had enjoyed a brief one-month interlude before she'd started to make demands. In his world, racing was top priority. Females who dated him often pretended to understand that, at least at first. Truth was that usually they really didn't, and, once they started making requests for more time or more attention, Hart found himself with an immediate urge to move on. Racing was as essential to him as breathing. Nothing was more important.

His father had felt the same way, and while his mother hadn't loved racing, she had understood her husband's passion. She and his father were perfect together, the ultimate complement of beauty and the racing beast. They'd had one child, Hart, who had been a fixture each weekend in the motor home as his father built Hampton Racing and carved out a legacy of NASCAR NEXTEL Cup Series wins.

Hart sighed again, an exhale that really didn't have any real purpose except to let the surrounding four walls hear his frustration. Okay, maybe not frustration. Perhaps simply a longing for something that he didn't have. He felt…melancholy. He frowned. Was that the word for what he was feeling? And if so, why was he so blue?

Probably because as a driver he was still missing the elusive wins he craved. Unlike his father, Hart didn't seem to have the magical touch that brought pole positions and consistent wins. So far, Hart had failed to achieve what he'd set out to do.

That irritated him. Gone was the kid who'd once bagged groceries for minimum wage because his father insisted he be a self-made man instead of a pampered child. Gone was the high school boy who'd raced whenever his schedule allowed, often missing things such as the prom or football games. In that boy's place was the jet-setting superstar whose life was cars and driving, and the lifestyle that came with.

Hart liked to think he was still humble, but the paradox remained that it was hard to remain humble when you were Hart Hampton, celebrity, used to having people screaming your name and handing you anything you wanted.

Cynthia was right. He'd hit a funk, and his current mood had affected his driving. Maybe a weekend off would allow him to come back recharged and reenergized. He could focus on racing, and why he loved it. He now understood what his father had said: "Racing is your life and you want to win, but once you do win, the expectations quickly change and the pressures increase."

Hart's fans expected him to win, and the need to win had overtaken Hart's desire to race. Racing wasn't only about the 180 miles per hour and the checkered flag thrill. He now worried about points. He worried that his car wouldn't pass inspection. He worried about his image, about his merchandising and about pleasing his sponsors. His family had benched him from an upcoming race. He'd have to battle uphill to regain the lost points, although this early in the season it was probably doable. He'd have to crunch numbers, run scenarios. The headache returned and Hart stood to clear his mind.

He entered a room that was set up with stacks and stacks of items for him to autograph. Hart grabbed a permanent marker and began to sign *Hart Hampton, #413* over and over, holding the black thin-tip marker like a paintbrush so as not to wear out his wrist.

Everyone wanted a piece of what they saw as Hampton magic. For a second, Hart wondered if there really was such a thing. Heck, if there were, he wouldn't be recovering from a wreck. He'd have points, and already have that NASCAR NEXTEL Cup Championship, which so far had eluded him.

He wanted to join his father. He also wanted join NASCAR's iconic legends and earn his own place in the history books. Heck, Hart figured he'd settle for even half of the current frontrunner's magic right now. He'd won the championship last year, when Hart hadn't earned enough points for a top ten finish.

Hart could see the writing on the wall—all it would take would be a few more lousy seasons and he'd be demoted from the NASCAR NEXTEL Cup Series to the Busch Series, which was basically NASCAR's second division. While Hart had occasionally still run a Busch Series race, he wasn't ready to go back full time at the expense of his Cup status.

As much as his uncle, aunt and parents loved him, Hampton Racing would replace Hart as a driver, no matter how popular he was with the fans. Hart had already lost ground to many of his teammates, who were outperforming him on the track. That had to stop.

And Hart had no desire to be downgraded until he was at least fifty. Driver Number 413 had to find his groove and get his luck back—and fast.

CHAPTER TWO

THEY'D BEEN WISE to come. From the moment they'd arrived at camp about an hour ago, Kellie could tell enchantment existed here. That magic had already transformed Charlie's face; he hadn't stopped smiling since he'd stepped out of the car. She'd checked his temperature before they'd left Myrtle Beach, and he'd been normal. Having leukemia meant Charlie could often run fevers, experience nausea and suffer overall body pain and muscle cramping.

Kellie heard the door to her and Charlie's half of the cabin thud and she turned from where she'd been sorting clothes. Two boys skittered to a stop in the doorway to the bedroom, both wearing baseball caps.

"This is Brad Muldoon," Charlie announced as he introduced the taller but younger boy beside him. "His family's staying on the other side of the cabin. His dad's going to take him exploring before dinner. May I go with them?"

"My mom's doing what you're doing," Brad said, pointing at the open suitcase. "Charlie's welcome to come with me." Both boys grinned at her hopefully.

"That sounds like a great idea." Kellie nodded, delighted that Charlie had already made a friend. At home, all his friends were cyberbuddies, just names and postings on the Internet of people he'd never meet. "Charlie, how about you meet me here before we have to go to the Pit Stop."

"Fuel Stop, Mom," Charlie corrected, giving her the official name of the dining hall. He rolled his eyes at Brad as if to say, "Mothers." "Let's go," he told Brad.

Feet scampered and the front door thudded again, indicating the boys had gone back outside. Kellie turned her attention back to making their part of the cabin home for the next two nights. She smiled to herself. Pit Stop. Fuel Stop. She might not have gotten the name right, but the dining hall was where the weekend's activities would officially start.

When she was wrong, Kellie admitted it. She'd been extremely skeptical and unsupportive about attending camp. Charlie's fever could spike at any time; his blood counts could rapidly change. But the camp had top-notch medical facilities in case of emergencies.

Her mother had refused to come, instead taking the opportunity to enjoy a weekend all to herself. Kellie knew deep down that Anita needed this break. Both women had put their own lives on hold as they supported Charlie.

But Anita had been right to insist Kellie sign the application—this place was great, everything a camp should be, as it was complete with buildings to delight any race fan.

The staff had worked to place families with similar aged kids in the same cabins, and each family was assigned a crew chief, which was a fancy name for the camp counselor who would help each family plan their day's agenda. Tomorrow would find parents and children traveling as a family unit to a wide variety of activities.

Charlie had already indicated he wanted to do everything, although Kellie had no idea how he'd work in all the camp's opportunities before Saturday night's closing dinner. She wasn't certain he'd even be up to the challenge, but so far

Charlie seemed to have a new lease on life, if only from excess adrenaline and excitement.

She heard a knock and went to greet her visitor, a woman who appeared to be about forty. "Hi, you must be Charlie's mother. I'm Sue, Brad's mom. It's nice to meet you." A leather headband held back Sue's short brown hair, revealing a round, friendly face. She extended her hand.

"I'm Kellie," Kellie said, shaking Sue's hand. "I take it you already met Charlie."

"I did," Sue said with a wide smile that immediately put Kellie at ease. "He's a lovely boy. Very personable."

"Thank you," Kellie said, her heart warming at the compliment.

Sue gestured around the room. "So are you like me? Have you stopped second-guessing yourself and decided that you were right in applying?" Sue asked.

"You know, I was just thinking that," Kellie said with a laugh. "My mother filled out all the paperwork. I wasn't very agreeable with her decision, but I bit my tongue and signed. I'm so glad I did."

"I know. There's such an uplifting feel to this place," Sue agreed with a nod. "It gives hope, and solidarity that you aren't alone. So where are you from?"

"Myrtle Beach," Kellie said. "I'm a teacher there, but I'm on a long-term leave of absence as of last December."

"I can understand that," Sue said empathetically. "I stopped working about three years ago. Brad has cancer, obviously, or we wouldn't be here, and it was too hard to work even part-time and still be with him at the hospital."

"My mother and I share a lot of the duties." Kellie saw Sue quickly mask a curious expression. "My husband died five years ago," she explained. "He was an overseas contractor in the Middle East. A roadside bomb. He died instantly."

"I'm sorry," Sue said with genuine compassion. "You have had a difficult time, haven't you?"

"Challenging," Kellie substituted, finding herself a little surprised that she'd owned up to her feelings. She never shared these things, much less with a perfect stranger. But Kellie felt an immediate connection and knew that Sue understood. "Charlie's such a great boy. He never whines or complains. He's always been mature for his age, and he has such an inner strength even when the treatments are rough and..."

"He's not doing well, is he?" Sue asked as Kellie's voice dropped off mid-sentence. "I'm sorry. I don't mean to pry. It's in my nature to be everyone's sounding board. Ed always tells me I shouldn't be so open, but I can't help it."

"No, it's okay," Kellie said, realizing that sharing solidarity with Sue was affirming. It meant Kellie wasn't alone. "I don't mind, especially since you're right. We're almost out of options and nothing's sent the leukemia into remission. He seems so healthy this weekend, but overnight everything can change."

Sue reached out and grasped Kellie's hand. "You're strong. I admire that. It's going to help you both pull through."

"Thanks," Kellie replied. Sue squeezed Kellie's hand once before letting it go.

"So isn't this place great? They really took the race stuff to the extreme," Sue said, changing the subject to something lighter. She glanced at her watch. "We should probably head to dinner. It's almost that time."

"I told Charlie I'd meet him here," Kellie stated. Camp meant no cell phones, so they'd turned them off and tucked them away.

As if sensing Kellie's worry, Sue said, "Oh, my Ed's great.

He'll figure out where we've gone and bring Charlie along if we aren't here when they get back."

But that was unnecessary, for Kellie and Sue ran into Ed and the boys on the way out of the cabin.

"Mom, this place is so cool," Charlie told her, and he began to tell her all that he'd seen as the two families wandered to dinner and sat together. Racing banners hung from the high, vaulted ceiling of the dining hall, and an almost tangible energy permeated the expansive room that put most hospital and college cafeterias to shame.

Before dinner started, the staff went over the rules and expectations, and then suddenly the camp director said, "And we're going to have a big surprise for you all after dinner. Something that we hope is really going to make this weekend truly memorable, something that wasn't scheduled until early this week. In fact, it's so rare, that all the other family weekend participants might get jealous."

"Tell," someone shouted, but the director simply grinned and gave the order to begin dinner.

"I wonder what it is?" Charlie asked as he began eating.

"Maybe a famous actor to play Zeus," Brad guessed. "This weekend's theme is ancient Greece. Maybe they found someone to come in. Aren't they filming a Civil War movie not too far from here?"

"I don't know," Charlie said.

"We'll find out what it is right after dinner," Sue said, passing Ed the pepper shaker without even being asked. Her glance at her son had Brad taking another bite.

"I wonder if we get to roast marshmallows at tonight's campfire?" Brad asked after he swallowed.

"That'd be cool to make s'mores," Charlie added. "I've never had real ones, only the kind Mom makes in the microwave. Do you think we'll wear togas at all, like tomorrow night?"

"Probably not," Ed said as he lifted his fork to his mouth and gestured at both boys to eat a little more.

Sue and Kellie shared a secret smile across the table. Their sons were having a great time. Dinner ended, followed by fifteen minutes of learning camp songs, the singing led by the counselors.

Then the camp director was back. "Are you ready for your surprise?" she asked, her voice booming through the audio system so loudly that it gave Kellie a little chill.

"Yes!" everyone screamed and the noise echoed off the ceiling. Kellie rubbed her ears and grinned. Charlie reached over and squeezed her hand. The anticipation was like being at a rock concert moments before the main act took the stage.

"Okay, let me first say that I'm more than a little bit excited about this weekend's special guest. When I learned that he agreed to come here, I screamed. Didn't I?" she glanced at the female counselor next to her, who nodded.

"Now, before I bring him out, I do have to tell you that he's agreed to give every family one autograph this weekend. Every family will be scheduled into their own time slot so that you can meet with him. So don't crowd him. Be respectful. Treat him as if he were just like everyone else."

Kellie glanced around the room. No one had any clue who the guest was. The room buzzed in expectancy, a humming noise as people whispered their guesses amongst themselves.

"Who do you think it is, Mom?" Charlie asked.

"I don't know. Obviously someone famous," she said. Both turned their attention back to the front of the room.

"Okay, without further ado, let me welcome our guest. In our midst this weekend, we've got a very special NASCAR driver."

"Probably someone retired," Charlie said as the crowd oohed and cheered. "Everyone's racing at Darlington." Beside him, Brad nodded, signaling his agreement with Charlie's assessment.

"Shh," Kellie said. Both boys fell silent.

"Our driver, though, isn't just any driver. He's won Daytona. Richmond. He was Rookie of the Year, and you voted him your favorite driver last year."

It couldn't be.

Kellie's face paled while next to her, Charlie's expression grew animated. No way. Only one man fit that exact description, and he wasn't retired. Far from it.

He should be at the track.

Yet, he was striding across the Fuel Stop floor right now, waving to the crowd. Beside her, Charlie shifted in his seat and rose to get a better view. "Mom, it's him! He's not at the track. Mom it's…"

But the applause drowned his voice out as the dining hall rocked with cheers. Even the camp director caught the fever as she shouted, "Ladies and gentlemen, please give a big round of welcome to Hart Hampton, driver of the Elementals Number 413 car!"

ALTHOUGH HART HAMPTON strode easily across the floor and expertly took the microphone from the flushed woman standing in front of him, his outer confidence hid a deep secret. Unseen by the crowd, he was terribly nervous.

Sure, he faced crowds of people every day on the track. He handled rabid fans who asked him to sign everything from their skin to their clothing. He charmed the media and easily dealt with having a microphone thrust in his face after a poor performance.

But these kids were chronically ill, although many didn't look sick. While a few were in wheelchairs, most appeared positively normal except for the baseball caps they wore to hide chemo-induced baldness. Hart had a momentary pang and determined to do his best as everyone clapped strongly. He took a deep breath. "How are you all doing tonight?" he asked, his typical opening line.

The answer was another round of enthusiastic screams, and Hart's nervousness ebbed. "That's great," Hart said, remembering the director's earlier suggestion to treat everyone as if they were perfectly healthy. Don't single them out, she'd advised. Here they are normal.

"I can't tell you how happy I am to be here," Hart said, his confidence growing. "Surprise."

"You can say that again," someone shouted.

Hart laughed, the microphone carrying the deep sound. "Yeah, I know, why am I here when I should be racing? Well, after that little roll last weekend, don't know if you saw it—" the group collectively groaned to indicate they had "—the general consensus from my team was that I should sit this one out. Now, I'm not the kind of guy who can stand on the sidelines doing nothing, so I decided to come visit y'all. I even brought one of my show cars here."

Cheers again erupted, and Hart totally relaxed. His aunt had been right. Just stick to the truth they'd decided to reveal, sign some autographs and lie low. The camp director stepped up at this point, a second microphone in her hand.

"As I said earlier, every family will have a chance to meet with Hart and get his autograph," she said. "But right now, before we go out to light our bonfire and sing campfire songs, Hart's agreed to answer some of your questions. If you have a question, raise your hand and I'll come out to you."

Hart watched as a little girl's hand immediately shot up. She appeared to be about five, and his heart twinged. Did she have cancer? Or was she just a sibling of a loved one who did?

The camp director lowered the microphone. "How old are you?" the girl asked, her voice resonating in the room.

"I'm thirty-two," Hart said.

"That's old," the little girl commented.

"Yeah," Hart replied, amused by her bluntness. Although thirty-two wasn't over the hill. Only on some days. Then again, how many children in this room would reach his age? For a moment, the thought that he'd led a blessed life humbled him. Some of the children in this room suffered from things he couldn't even begin to imagine.

The director moved on and Hart fielded a variety of questions. How much money did he make? A lot. When did he race? Every weekend. What was his favorite race? When he won Daytona for the first time. Daytona was everyone's dream track to win on; there was prestige for winning any race there even if it wasn't for driver points.

Hart discovered that questions weren't hard to answer; actually, the campers were much easier to face than the media, and thus Hart began to enjoy himself. The atmosphere was casual, especially after one precocious eleven-year-old girl asked if that was his rear end wearing Elementals boxers in the television ads. Hart had bitten his tongue, and then simply said, "Yes. It wouldn't be right if it wasn't." A few people had snickered.

"Time for the campfire, so one last question," the camp director announced and Hart watched as she approached an older boy, one of the few older children in the crowd. The camp catered to kids through age fifteen, and this boy seemed right about that age. He was a bit thin, and wore a Carolina Panthers T-shirt and a Florida Marlins baseball cap. He sat at a table with another boy his age and three adults Hart couldn't see very well from where he was.

"Hart," the boy began as he rose to his feet, "I'm Charlie. Except for winning the Cup Championship, what's the one thing you wish you had, but that you don't?"

Charlie sat back down, and Hart felt his brow begin to sweat slightly, like it did under his race helmet when the temperature in the car heated to 108 degrees.

"That's a good question," Hart said, using the answer designed to stall for a few seconds of thinking time. He stepped to the side so that he could see the people at Charlie's table better.

"You know Charlie, I usually try not to think about what I don't have. I've been so blessed from the beginning that I try to focus on what I do have rather than on what I don't have."

He paused; every face in the room was staring at him. Hart's gaze found Charlie to see if that answer had satisfied him. He learned it hadn't as Charlie leaned over and asked into the director's microphone, "But if there was something you were missing, what would it be?"

"Then the one thing I wish for would be…" Hart suddenly froze. He hadn't seen the woman before; she'd been blocked when Charlie had stood to ask his question. But Hart saw her now, and he had a pretty good view since he was only about thirty feet away.

Her blond hair was drawn back into a ponytail. She wasn't looking at him, and her profile revealed a short, cute nose and a chin that was in perfect proportion with her face. She laughed at something the woman across the table said. Hart studied the other woman for a moment. She had a round face and was heavier set. The woman behind Charlie was thin; her pale blue T-shirt showed him that.

She turned then, and her gaze caught his for a moment.

Blue eyes, Hart knew instinctively, although he was too far away to tell for sure. She blinked and glanced away, but the brief contact left him slightly rattled, as if he'd just spun out and was trying to regain control of his car.

He tried to remember what he was doing. Oh yes, answering a question. "Gosh, Charlie, your question is tough. But I will answer it," Hart said, still searching for the reason behind his sudden gut clench rather than what he wished for.

All around him families waited with expectant, smiling faces. Younger children had climbed into their parents' laps. Some parents had their arms draped around their children's shoulders, just a light, casual touch that let the child know how much he or she was valued.

There was no fame or fortune here in this room, just gratefulness for another day with those you loved.

"You all are inspiring," Hart told them, as he decided on his answer. "The way you care for each other, that's what I'd wish for. When I have my own family, I hope I can love them half as much as the love I feel in this room tonight."

"Aww," the crowd said, enjoying the warm fuzzy moment his words had created.

"So any prospects?" someone shouted loudly out of turn.

"Uh." Hart shifted his weight. His gaze trailed over to Charlie. It had been his question that had gotten Hart into this mess. Charlie caught Hart's glance and smiled. The woman— his mother, Hart guessed—stared at her nails as if she'd never seen fingertips before.

"I wish I could give you some hot, insider gossip," Hart said, watching the camp director come forward to free him from this mess. "But there's nobody special in my life right now. So, to wrap up this personal thread, I will tell you that one of these days I want to be a father. But first, I need to find a wife."

CHAPTER THREE

HART FIELDED two more shouted-out questions, thankfully no-brainers before the director rescued him and instructed the families to go out to the bonfire. Hart watched as everyone began to file out. He exhaled the breath he hadn't known he'd been holding. Thank goodness none of this question-and-answer session would ever reach the press.

Heck, perhaps it was a good thing he wasn't at Darlington, especially if he'd botched up a Q & A this bad. He'd just told everyone in the dining hall he needed to find a wife. If he'd made this statement anywhere else, his aunt, or even Hampton Racing's official spokesperson, would be wincing and fielding media mayhem. The press field day would be followed by a deluge of mail in the ensuing weeks as bags of letters came in with marriage offers. Instead, everyone was leaving, Hart's statement forgotten in lieu of the upcoming bonfire.

"Thank you so much for doing this. Will you be returning to your motor home for the night now?" the camp director asked.

The room had partially emptied, and if Hart went back to his motor home he could watch the Busch Series race on his plasma TV.

"I was thinking of perhaps attending the bonfire," Hart heard himself say.

"Oh, you should," she said. "The campers will love for you

to be there. I'll take you over in my golf cart. The camp has many golf carts, often used to transport campers who have difficulty walking."

"Thanks, but I could use the exercise," Hart said. "I'll meet you over there." He moved around her and exited.

The May night was warmer than average, and twilight had settled over the camp. Hart inhaled, smelling nothing but the fresh air of the camp's hundred acres.

Hart had always enjoyed being surrounded by plenty of trees and green space, which is why his home and office were in hilly terrain outside a small town about fifty miles west of Charlotte. Hart drove about thirty miles one way to get to Hampton Racing, a drive he didn't mind at all. North Carolina was home to most Cup race shops, many located just north of Charlotte and clustered near the towns of Mooresville and Concord. Some were farther north along the Highway 40 corridor, and many drivers lived on Lake Norman.

But not Hart. He'd opted for acres of woods and open fields instead of a water view.

He strolled along the camp's main path, still behind the crowd but catching up. Designed to resemble a race track, most buildings were situated along the oval roadway. Hart followed the curve around, passing the drive that led to where his motor home was parked. He said hello to a group of people and moved past.

Ahead in the distance, Hart could see campers gathered around the flickering campfire. Counselors were organizing their assigned families, readying them for the skits the director had told him about. The whole camp concept was worth seeing in person, something he'd never done before because he'd never had the time.

He could hear the refrain of a song as it began to build, traveling unimpeded on the still night air. Being a race car driver, wind was something he always noticed, as the wind could play havoc with a car on the track.

Hart passed another set of people, greeted them quickly, and continued walking, his gaze suddenly finding the people for whom he was searching. Just ahead of him was the teenage boy who'd asked the tough question, and to Charlie's left, his mother. *The blonde who hadn't even given Hart a cursory glance.* But he gave her one, noticing long legs clad in fitted blue jeans. He'd observed the lack of wedding ring on her left hand. Hart shoved his hands into his jacket, and quickened the pace.

THEY HAD ALMOST REACHED the campfire before Charlie's questions began. Kellie had expected them immediately, and then prayed he'd let what Hart said pass. But her son refused to provide Kellie with any respite.

"Did you hear that, Mom? Hart said he needs a wife."

"Charlie," Kellie began, warning evident in her tone. Her stomach churned. Surely Charlie wouldn't.

"My mom's holding out for Hart Hampton," Charlie told the Muldoon family. Kellie closed her eyes for a brief second. Of course her son would.

"It's our family joke," Kellie said quickly, shooting her well-meaning son an obvious glance. He raised his eyebrows at her in return and shrugged.

"What joke?" Sue said. She fell in step next to Kellie.

"Ever since my husband died, when people ask me when I'm going to start dating again, I tell them I'm holding out for Hart Hampton," Kellie explained. "It came out of something Charlie said once. Now we're rather quite flippant with it."

"Makes sense," Sue said. "It's probably easier than worrying about other people's perception of your marital status."

"Exactly," Kellie said.

"All that matters is that Hart's here and we get to meet him," Charlie inserted. He smirked at his mother.

"We will," Sue said with a benevolent smile. "But don't get your hopes up, Charlie. Hart meets lots of people. I doubt he can remember them all."

Kellie mouthed a thank-you over Charlie's head.

"He hasn't met my mom," Charlie insisted.

"You're right, he hasn't," Sue said. She winked at Kellie and Kellie's stress ebbed slightly. Thank goodness Sue had taken what Charlie said so lightly.

For that's all Hart was. A joke. One that she'd pull Charlie aside later in private and tell him not to share with anyone else, especially here where it made her look presumptuous or, worse, stupid.

Kellie tried not to sigh with frustration. She didn't want to burst her son's bubble. So how did you tell your son that the fantasy was better than the reality?

The reality was that tomorrow they'd meet Hart Hampton, get his autograph and be on their way. That would be all. She hoped Charlie wouldn't be too disappointed.

"Hey," a deep voice said. "I'm glad I caught up with you. I wanted to tell you, that was really good question you asked."

"Thanks," Charlie replied, turning and stopping so fast that his motion caught Kellie off guard. She almost stumbled, but quickly righted herself. The Muldoons, who were now a few feet ahead by this point, didn't notice anything amiss and kept walking.

"I didn't mean to make you think so hard," Charlie said.

"You were easier than the reporters I often face," Hart Hampton said with a laugh.

Kellie's insides felt as if she'd swallowed dozens of butterflies as Hart extended his hand and gripped Charlie's.

"So you're Charlie," Hart stated. "Are you studying to be a journalist, Charlie? You'd make a good one."

"No, I'm not planning on that." Charlie wore a dazed, starstruck expression as he released Hart's hand. Then he found the poise he'd had most of his life, composure that had carried him through his serious illness. "This is my mom, Kellie."

"Nice to meet you, Kellie," Hart said, his gaze roving over her.

Politeness had her answering him with a "Hi," but she kept her hands shoved inside her denim jacket. Up close, Hart Hampton was even more impressive. Pictures and video didn't do him justice. His green eyes were hypnotic. His chin had a slight dimple to it, and laugh lines graced the sides of his mouth, giving his full lips sexy, kissable appeal. She blinked and glanced at the ground. When she finally raised her gaze, he'd turned his attention back to her son.

"You have the makings of a good journalist," Hart told Charlie as the trio began walking again, Hart to Charlie's right and Kellie to Charlie's left. "Your question certainly got me thinking. It also got me to reveal more than I ever would have. My PR person would have been having a fit. Good job."

"Thanks," Charlie said. He wore an intrigued expression. "I've never thought about journalism. I'm not that great of a writer. I should be. My mom's an eighth grade English teacher."

Hart glanced around Charlie, but Kellie stepped out of his line of sight. "Really?" Hart asked.

"Yeah," Charlie said. "She took a leave of absence when her school started winter break. I have leukemia."

"I figured it was something like that if you were here," Hart said.

Kellie resisted the urge to roll her eyes. Few people who didn't deal with chronic diseases knew how to handle cancer, much less talk about the disease. So that's why it didn't surprise her when Hart effectively changed the subject. What did surprise her, though, was how Hart chose to do it.

"So tell me Charlie, aside from your health, what's the one thing you wish you had but you don't?"

Charlie stopped for a moment and glanced into Hart's eyes. With them facing each other, Kellie could see that Hart dwarfed Charlie by about ten inches, meaning that Hart was about five ten. She was five six.

Hart grinned and waved his finger at Charlie, a teasing gesture. "You see. It is a very good question."

Charlie broke into a wide smile as he realized Hart was playing with him. "Yeah, it is, isn't it?" he asked.

Hart reached up and gave Charlie a gentle high-five. "Tell you what," Hart said, "I'll give you until tomorrow to figure out your answer. You can tell me when you come by for your family session. Fair?"

"Fair," Charlie said, his expression incredulous at having been singled out by his favorite driver.

Kellie found herself clenching her fists. Hart's attention to her son was above and beyond what was necessary. She frowned. His interest would destroy the illusion. The fantasy. The joke.

"I've got one of my show cars here," Hart was saying. "You'll get a chance to sit in it tomorrow and you can tell me after that."

"Show cars?" Charlie asked.

"Those are specific cars that we bring to events like this. We build at least two show cars per year, usually from retired race cars that I haven't wrecked. These cars have engines, gauges and race seats, but they aren't made for the track anymore. They do run and are drivable, but not at 180 miles per hour."

"Oh." Charlie seemed impressed. "I didn't know there were different types of cars."

"Neither did I until I was about your age, and I grew up with racing. I always thought racing was driving one car around the track and praying you didn't hit anything. Even with the Car of Tomorrow, I could have up to fifteen in the shop back home, a lot of them built just to race on certain tracks. When we go to the track, we take a specific car and a backup in case we wreck during qualifying."

"Fifteen cars. Wow. I just want to turn sixteen so I can get my license and drive any old car. I think I'm ready to take the test, but Mom won't even let me get my permit until I'm officially sixteen."

"I remember those days. You know it's eighteen to get a NASCAR racing license," Hart said.

"I didn't know that, either," Charlie admitted. "I've been studying the driver's manual daily, though. I'm hoping that I'll be well enough for lessons in July. You have to let me then, Mom."

"So have you ever seen a race shop?" Hart asked when Kellie didn't answer.

"No," Charlie replied. "I'm new to the sport. My grandma's a huge fan and she hooked me late last year during the Chase for the Cup. We watch the races together every time they're on. She lives with us now, so it's a weekend ritual. I guess she's watching without me, though, this time."

They'd reached the campfire, and seeing Hart, the camp director waved him over. "Looks like I'm wanted," Hart said. "Remember, when you stop by tomorrow, I want you to tell me what your wish is."

"Okay," Charlie answered. "I will."

"See you tomorrow, then," Hart said, and he strode off. Kellie tracked his movements, her mind churning over what had just occurred. Surely Hart couldn't be serious? Of all the campers here this weekend, he had to single out Charlie? Because of a question?

"Can you believe it, Mom?" Charlie asked.

"No," she said honestly. The whole night had a rather surreal aspect to it.

Brad Muldoon and his family approached. "Hey, Charlie, were you just talking with Hart Hampton?" Brad asked excitedly.

"Yeah," Charlie said. He suddenly seemed a bit dazed again, as it dawned on him that he'd actually been holding a real conversation with his idol. Kellie reached out and put her hand on his forehead, but he jerked away. Luckily his temperature was still normal.

"You gotta tell me everything," Brad said. "I want to hear it all. That is so cool. How lucky are you!"

"Don't forget we're part of the skit," Sue called as the boys moved a few yards away.

"We'll just be right here," Brad said. Sue frowned.

"They're fine," her husband stated. He gave her a hug. "Let them go. They're boys talking racing. They don't need prying adult ears."

"True," Sue replied. "I forget that Brad occasionally gets to act like a regular kid."

"I understand," Kellie said. "It's like that with me, too. The illness makes them grow up so fast. Charlie is a fifteen-year-old who simply wants to get his learner's permit. Which, of course, I keep putting off until he's better. That's part of what he was talking to Hart about."

"We've got until December before Brad's even qualified for that," Sue stated. The two boys had bent their heads closely together. "I do wonder what they're talking about."

"Probably just Hart Hampton," her husband answered. "Relax."

The Muldoons' crew chief approached. "It's time for your skit," she said. "Are you ready to start your engines?"

"Yes, we are," Ed replied. "We just need to grab our son. He's right over there." Ed strode over to the boys.

The counselor turned her attention Kellie. "Are you part of their family? I apologize if I forgot to include you."

"No," Kellie said. "I'm not with them."

The volunteer frowned. "So did you get assigned a part in a skit? I don't want anyone left out."

"No, we're not in the skit, but it's okay. Charlie and I would much rather be spectators."

"If you're sure," the girl replied, taking the Muldoons with her as she moved away.

"So you and Brad look like you are becoming pretty good friends," Kellie said. She and Charlie had moved closer to the campfire. Night had fallen, and the fire threw an odd orange glow into the star-filled sky.

"Yeah, Brad's cool," Charlie answered. "Do you know he even believes in ghosts like I do, plus he likes country music."

"You two have quite a lot in common, then," Kellie said, impressed.

Charlie pushed his glasses back up the bridge of his nose. "We do. Like me, he's seen all those shows on the Travel Channel about the most haunted places in America."

"So is that what were you two talking about over there, just now?"

"We were discussing tomorrow," Charlie said quickly, glancing away. "That's all."

"And?" Kellie prompted. "There's nothing else you want to tell me?"

"Nope. Nothing really," Charlie replied, in voice a tad too high to have been totally honest. He shrugged nonchalantly. "We were just planning the activities we want to do together. Like fishing."

"That sounds fine and shouldn't be a problem, so long as your selections don't involve stalking Hart Hampton," Kellie said. "He's here to work. Autographs to sign. A car to show."

"Mom," Charlie whined in a chastising tone. "Don't be such a downer. All I have to do is tell him what I wish for. That's during our session. I'm not going to stalk him."

"He may not have been serious," Kellie warned.

"He was," Charlie insisted. He scowled slightly. "Just be happy he didn't ask you what you wish for. You'd have to tell him that he's your ideal man."

Kellie drew up short. "Charlie, you're almost sixteen. That's a joke. Our joke. We don't air family jokes. People aren't that interested and it comes across being pretentious or silly. It makes me sound like an idiot. He's not my man."

"Mom, stop stressing," Charlie said, deliberately ignoring her censure. "No one cares. The Muldoons thought it was funny. And life's too short for me to worry about what people think. I want to enjoy myself."

"You're right," Kellie said, his final words deflating any further argument. The last thing she wanted was to be reminded of how much time Charlie had, or didn't have. Impulse had her drawing her son to her for a quick hug.

"Mom! Public display!" Charlie protested.

"You just said life's too short," she reminded him with a wicked grin.

"Ugh, are you ever going to let me win one?" Charlie asked, referring to the minor match of wits they'd just had. "I thought I had you there."

"Never," she teased. "Mothers always win. It's in the rule book somewhere."

"Yeah, sure," Charlie said. He stepped out from her embrace, and she saw him as the grown man he was becoming. "Someday you might find out you're wrong about that rule book. Until then, let's just watch the skit."

Kellie wiggled her eyebrows. "Okay, Mr. Testy," she teased. "Let's."

Charlie sighed and rolled his eyes. "Fine. I love you." His words warmed her heart. One thing Charlie had never been shy about was telling her how much he cared.

"Me, too. And don't you forget it," Kellie said.

They focused their attention to where the Muldoons were currently singing an off-key version of "Take Me Out to the Ball Game" on the other side of the campfire. "They're pretty bad," Charlie remarked as they hit the Cracker Jack line.

"I think that's the whole point," Kellie replied. Since all the campers were now joining in, Charlie started singing as well. They stepped closer into the circle, and when Kellie opened her mouth to sing, she froze.

Was it her imagination, or was Hart Hampton watching her from his position on the other side of the fire? The flames flickered, and the rising heat and smoke made confirmation impossible. She couldn't tell.

But at that moment she was suddenly way too self-conscious. Hart Hampton was a fantasy, someone she'd never expected to meet, much less have him know she existed. He was a man far too attractive for his own good, a man who would probably sleep in a five-star hotel rather than on a single bed inside a racing-theme-decorated cabin.

He…he was something she could dream about, sort of like how Cinderella dreamed of her prince. Totally harmless, as long as he remained firmly rooted in her imagination. Kellie was a realist: dreams disappeared when morning came.

Unfortunately, Hart would not, and tomorrow she would face him again or suffer Charlie's extreme disappointment. They'd come on this weekend to relax and have fun, but instead every nerve in Kellie's body had tensed.

Men like Hart Hampton weren't supposed to notice women like her. His sudden interest was only because her son had asked him a really good question. That was all, she consoled herself. Hart was a celebrity. He'd date perfect, beautiful women, such as those Hollywood types with perfect faces who didn't exist in average-people America.

Kellie didn't purchase designer clothes; instead, she bought off the rack at the local discount chain since Charlie's medical bills took a big bite of her household income. She had to stretch the retirement fund, life insurance and accident settlement she'd received after her husband's death, making the money last as long as Charlie's care required.

Kellie sighed as she thought of her late husband. Although dating wasn't on her agenda, she'd resolved never to even consider anyone whose career involved travel. When she was ready to think about herself and her needs, she wanted someone basic. Stable. Someone nine-to-five. Someone who gave her peace and harmony. All those things certainly disqualified the wife-seeking Mr. Hampton.

He could simply remain a joke, or she'd have to replace him with rookie driver Dusty Burke, despite the huge age gap. Charlie would just have to go along with the change.

So, after chiding herself for being foolish over nothing, Kellie raised her eyes, determined to prove to herself that she could look at Hart Hampton and not feel like a silly schoolgirl.

She need not have bothered. Hart Hampton was gone.

CHAPTER FOUR

THAT ANNOYING NOISE early the next morning at 7:10 a.m. wasn't his alarm clock. The shrill tone sounding off at too many decibels next to his head was, unfortunately, his cell phone. He'd preset the ring tone, so without even glancing at the caller ID he knew exactly who was checking up on him several hours earlier than he normally woke up on a Saturday morning. He flipped the phone open and held the device next to his ear. "Good morning, Cynthia."

"Oh, good you're up," Cynthia said. "I wanted to catch you before breakfast."

"Yeah," Hart said groggily. The camp served breakfast at eight, and at that moment Hart's bedside clock flickered to seven-eleven. Hart leaned back against his soft burgundy sheets, stretching out his legs as if trying to touch the bottom of his queen-sized bed.

Despite being roused from slumber, he wasn't ready to give up the creature comforts of his down pillow. His event didn't begin until nine-thirty, so he'd set his alarm for eight-fifty-five. A quick shower, some chocolate-covered minidonuts and a diet cola from his kitchen, and he'd have been early to the meet and greet.

"I wanted to see how everything's going," Cynthia said, her voice jostling him back awake.

"It's going fine." Hart tossed his arm over his eyes. Upon returning to his motor home from the bonfire, he'd stayed up late and watched the last of the NASCAR Busch Series race and the highlight show that followed.

"Well, everything's just fine here," Cynthia announced. "Your car passed inspection, and Ricky's ready for tonight. He had a great practice session and qualified fifteenth."

"That's great," Hart grumbled.

"What do you have going on tonight?" his aunt asked.

"Watching the race on TV," Hart said, his tone still grumpy. "It's parents' night out. I'm kind of a fifth wheel after lights out."

"Oh," Cynthia said. "You can always go home once you're done. It's only a two-hour drive."

"I know," Hart said. "But Jerry's taken off on his motor-cycle for parts unknown, probably home, until Sunday morning and I noticed that you didn't ship my bike. So I'm sort of stuck here."

Jerry was Hart's driver, and instead of taking a helicopter or his airplane to camp, Hart had traveled in his motor home since the drive to the northern North Carolina town was under three hours. He'd napped most of the way, getting much needed rest.

"Well, look on the bright side," Cynthia said. "You've got a great motor home and you can simply relax like the doctor ordered."

"Uh-huh," Hart said, although after a while, a man could only watch so much satellite TV.

He heard his aunt exhale, meaning she was already running out of patience with him. Her stress level always shot up on race days.

"The simulator is already there. They called me to tell me they'd arrived."

Hart's eyes were closed, but he still winced. "You did not send the bimbo twins."

He could hear the indignation in his aunt's voice. "No, I did not. They were temporary hires sent from that promotion company for that one specific event. This is a family camp. Clyde and Clarissa drove up there this morning. If you get desperate tonight, ask to ride back with them."

"All right," Hart said, a bit more agreeable. One, he now had a way home, and two, the Hampton Racing employees who'd just arrived were superb choices.

Clarissa worked in Hampton Racing's front office and Clyde was one of the chassis fabricators. Both were in their late sixties and had been married for almost forty years. Both had been with Hampton Racing since the beginning, and Hart had known them forever. Clyde had his CDL license and had been Hart's first hauler driver years ago.

"So, before I go, it's all fine? No surprises?" Cynthia asked.

"None." Well, if he didn't count Charlie's mom, Kellie. She'd hardly given him the time of day, treating him last night as if he were one of the mosquitoes she'd wanted to repel. He hadn't liked that very much, or the fact that he hadn't been able to stop thinking about her.

"I'm glad you're having a good time," Cynthia said.

"Not as much fun as if I'd been there," Hart pointed out sarcastically.

"You're funny. Good try. Ricky's running well and the media's bought our story. Sally Jenkins from MRN practically gushed. I'll see you tomorrow night."

Cynthia said a quick goodbye and Hart closed his phone. He stretched and placed it on the nightstand. He then rested on his back for a moment and groaned. Going back to sleep was pointless, so he might as well get up, shower and see what was going on.

"So HOW IS HE doing?" Liam asked his wife as she came back into the bedroom. He shifted and tossed back the covers for her.

"He's surviving," Cynthia said. Amazing how after thirty-five years of marriage they could read each other's minds so well. Neither had anywhere to be for several more hours. "Thanks."

"You're welcome," Liam said. He set the novel he'd been reading on the nightstand. Liam always woke up at 6:30 a.m. and read for an hour, no matter what day of the year. "So he's fine doing the simulator?"

"I don't think he cares," Cynthia said. She climbed under the covers of the king-sized bed that took up the back half of their motor home. "Hart's got to recover from both the injury and this slump he's in."

"I fielded a call from Elementals yesterday." Liam casually mentioned one of Hart's top sponsors. "They needed some reassurance that Hart was fine. They also want Hart to film another commercial promoting their fall activewear line."

Cynthia winced. Sponsors could be so fickle and demanding. "You were wise not to tell me or I would have been even more stressed out than I already am. Did they settle down after your talk?"

Liam nodded. "I managed to smooth their feathers, but they definitely want a win in the next few races, or at least a top five finish. They're hoping to tie it in with the commercial."

"We all want a win," Cynthia replied. Even though it was May, she rubbed her feet on the sheet, as was her habit, so the friction warmed her toes. She leaned back against her pillows.

These past few years had been hard on her nephew. Some years had been up, others down. Hampton Racing had been her brother Carl's passion, and they'd all been shocked when he'd suddenly announced his retirement so that he could spend more time with his wife.

Carl had always been so dedicated and focused, racking up tons of Cup wins. But as he aged, his priorities changed, especially after Vivian's breast cancer. While she was in full remission, the fact that his wife had to have undergone treatment had shaken Carl. When it came to racing or his family's health, his family had top billing and Carl had retired.

For a moment Cynthia thought about her brother. She'd been the one to introduce him to the sport. Their parents hadn't been very enthusiastic, and Carl had entered racing late. He'd made up for lost time, though.

Just like big corporations couldn't always meet the analysts' predictions, perhaps racing, too, was simply cyclical. If someone was having the greatest year ever, that meant someone else wasn't. While most of Hampton Racing's drivers had done exceedingly well the past two years, Hart had instead been falling in and out of the point standings. They'd changed his pit team and his engine team, but all to no avail. He simply couldn't seem to eke out a win lately.

"I'm glad you don't race," Cynthia told her husband suddenly. "I'm glad you're in the office."

He glanced over at her, his expression quizzical. Liam had been with Hampton Racing as its president from the beginning. "You've never said that to me before."

"I know. I just think one driver in the family is enough."

"Hart's troubling you," Liam said.

She nodded. "Always. Sometimes I think he's more mine

than his mother's. She never quite understood racing the way we did."

"She married Carl when he was president of his family's coat hanger business," Liam replied. He'd been Carl's best friend since high school, which was how he'd met Cynthia.

"Vivian did kind of lose her cool when he sold the family company and invested in racing," Cynthia agreed. "She was always a little too high-class to get into the sport. She also didn't want to leave St. Louis. And then when I bought Hart his first go-cart…" her voice trailed off.

"Vivian eventually got over it and forgave you," Liam said with a smile.

"Sort of," Cynthia replied. "I often wonder if she wanted a bigger family, but racing always took priority. Hart was a handful. Still is. Now he's driving, and he has huge shoes to fill."

"Stop worrying." Liam reached over and patted Cynthia's hand. "We were right to bench Hart this weekend. Everyone needs a break now and then, and this will give him some time away, maybe even some time to assess his life without any pressure from us. He'll always have Hampton Racing, whether he's behind the wheel or simply being full owner when all this totally becomes his. He might not understand that now, but he will eventually."

"I hope so," Cynthia said. "The stakes are too high if he doesn't figure out what's going on and what he's going to do to get out of this slump."

Liam sighed. "The stakes in this business always are high. But Hart's battled worse. He's tenacious. He's a fighter. He likes the driver's seat too much to let anything compromise that. And you never know. Give him some time to see something other than the back end of another race car and he just might find what he's looking for."

THE MORNING DAWNED clear, sunny, and warm. An ideal day to enjoy the outdoors. "Our time is 10:45," Charlie told his mom as he read from the bulletin board outside the dining hall. The time slots for Hart Hampton had been posted during breakfast, and as Charlie moved aside, another family stepped up to view the list now that mealtime was over and the activity areas were opening. "I can't wait. Did you get a good look at his hauler?"

"I saw it," Kellie said. Covered with sponsors' logos, a huge Hampton Racing insignia and Hart's signature, the green semitrailer and custom green rig that pulled it had been hard to miss on their walk from the cabin to breakfast.

Someone had set up an open-air tent, and people had been rolling a green race car underneath when she and Charlie had passed by. Kellie glanced at her watch. They had more than an hour before their time with Hart. "Want to go shoot bows and arrows?" she asked. "After all, you're all clear today."

"I know," Charlie said. He adjusted his baseball cap. "It's a good omen, Mom."

"I agree," Kellie said, for even the thought of seeing Hart Hampton was not going to dim her mood today, not after an earlier stop at the camp's medical center had given Charlie the green light to participate in every activity the camp offered. Maybe the drugs were working, and maybe they'd turned a corner. Kellie crossed her fingers for extra luck.

The morning flew by, with Charlie managing to hit one bull's-eye. He also enjoyed a little catch-and-release fishing at the fishing pavilion before it was time to go to see Hart.

A family of six remained at the tent when Kellie and Charlie walked underneath. Hart was signing an autograph but he glanced up and smiled. "Hi, Charlie. Kellie," he added.

"Hey, Hart," Charlie said. He glanced at his watch. "Are we early?"

"Probably not." Hart gave his trademark grin to the autograph seeker. "Thanks for coming." As the little girl moved off, Hart turned his attention entirely to Charlie. "The simulator got a little backed up for a while, so that's why I'm running behind."

"Simulator?" Charlie asked.

"Yep. You get in, stare at that flat panel screen and you'll feel like you're actually driving. You work the steering wheel and the pedals and you'll hear your crew chief over the headset."

Charlie's eyes widened. "That sounds cool!"

"It is, actually," Hart said. "I get in there myself on occasion." The group of six thanked Hart and left. "Hey, it looks like you're up."

Hart gestured to where an older woman held the car door open, the number 413 emblem clearly visible on the outside panel. Hart's name was etched above the driver's window, and Charlie frowned. "The door opens."

"That's because a lot of people can't climb through the window like Hart here," the woman said, seeing Charlie's disappointed expression. "I'm Clarissa. I promise you it's a real car and the decals are all the same as they were then. We had to modify the door. That way I can get in to drive, too. Come on, in you go."

"Okay," Charlie said. He slid in and sunk into the low seat that sat almost on the floor. Charlie seemed to disappear, and Kellie leaned over to get a better view of her son.

"Can you reach the pedals?" Clarissa asked.

"Barely," Charlie answered.

"That's because this is Hart's old seat. He's taller than

you." Clarissa reached for a leather booster block and wedged the black, six-inch-thick pad between Charlie and the seat. Next she efficiently grabbed a pair of earphones, just like those seen on the race track.

"What you're going to do is watch the monitor attached to the dashboard. The seat's going to move, so you'll feel like you're actually driving on the track. After you hear the words 'drivers, start your engines,' give it gas. Don't worry if you hit the car in front of you when the race starts. The simulator's sensitive and most people bump into the car in front when they begin."

"Will I crash?" Charlie asked.

"You might," Clarissa said with a smile. "When I drove, I bumped off the wall and spun out into the infield. The steering wheel's pretty sensitive, just like it was when Hart drove this car."

Charlie glanced at the dashboard. "Where is the wheel?"

"On the top of the car. We attach it last. That makes it more realistic." She placed the headphones over Charlie's ears and he grinned, giving Hart and Kellie a thumbs-up.

"Good luck," Kellie called.

"He can't hear you," Hart said, his voice directly off her right ear. "Those headphones are pretty soundproof."

"Oh," Kellie said. She took a step away, out of Hart's proximity. Clarissa attached the steering wheel, and went around behind the car to a podium. Kellie quickly realized Clarissa had started the program after she saw Charlie's hands working the steering wheel.

"Can you see how he's doing?" Hart asked.

"No," Kellie replied. Hart had once again invaded her space, sending her awareness levels off the chart. She'd seen him on television wearing nothing but boxers and a T-shirt, but now, next to him, she found his tight jeans and polo shirt much harder to avoid and much more captivating.

"You could have gotten in on the other side," Hart said. "We retrofitted the car with a passenger seat and a monitor."

"I'll pass," she said. "Let him have his turn pretending it's real."

"That's fine. You can try it next."

Kellie shook her head and Hart frowned. "No?" he asked, arching an eyebrow. "You aren't going to do this?"

"I drive every day. It's really not that interesting." She tried not to wince at her crankiness. Hart Hampton's presence was doing something to her equilibrium. She felt out of sync, off-kilter. She certainly hadn't meant to sound surly.

"You'll enjoy this drive. I'm sure you've never been out on a high-bank oval, even if it is just a computer screen," Hart cajoled.

"No, I haven't," Kellie admitted. She tried to make her tone light yet firm. "And no, I still don't want to drive."

Hart crossed his arms across his chest and leaned back to study her. "You're not very impressed with me."

"That has nothing to do with driving your car," Kellie said, flushing under his scrutiny.

"You didn't answer my question," Hart said.

"You didn't ask one. You made a statement," Kellie pointed out.

Hart eased closer. "Ah, that's right. English teacher. Are you this picky with your students?"

She fidgeted. "Actually, yes. On occasion. If the circumstances warrant it."

"So you'd be one who corrects the kid who says, 'Can I go to the bathroom?'"

"Sometimes," Kellie said, smiling. "Don't all English teachers do that?"

"I think they're supposed to. Probably comes in the job description." The corner of Hart's mouth lifted as if he were amused. "So let's see if I ask this properly. *Are* you impressed with me?"

She dropped her chin as if looking over a pair of imaginary glasses. "You really want an answer to that?"

"I wouldn't have asked if I didn't," Hart said.

"Then, no," Kellie replied.

Hart blinked, those green eyes curious. "Really? That's rare. So, why not?"

She should have known that Hart Hampton would be used to people fawning over him. Charlie adored the man and they'd never met until last night.

"Okay, this is getting to be a weird conversation," Kellie said, trying to regroup. "I don't know you, and my opinion shouldn't matter. We'll never see each other again. Well, you won't see me. I have to see you on TV every weekend since Charlie loves watching NASCAR."

"Oh, come on. That's not an answer. Tell me," Hart insisted. "I'm curious. Women throw themselves at me. You're one that hasn't. I want to know why."

"Perhaps because I prefer men who keep their clothes on and don't flaunt themselves in public," Kellie said with a shrug that belied her inner tension. Well, he had asked, she rationalized.

"So you think I flaunt myself?" Hart arched a dark brow, as if daring her to continue. Already in for a penny, Kellie bit.

"You don't model for Elementals? 'Nothing touches my skin that's not Elemental'?" she shot back, mentioning the line from the ad.

Hart rolled his green eyes and shrugged. "It's promotion. They sponsor my car. They get to splash my image around.

Do you know how much it costs to run a race team and how much sponsors pay?"

"No, and I really don't care," Kellie said, stiffening. So much for not sounding surly. "Listen, I'm coming across like a shrew. Thanks for the interest in my son. Following your career has been a highlight to him this past year and I do appreciate that. He has it tough and you've provided a bright spot in his life. I apologize for my behavior. I have no right to judge you."

Hart shifted his weight, the polo shirt stretching across his chest. "I don't mind. It's actually rather refreshing not to hear the same gushing flattery from people who only want a piece of you. So it's been a really rough year?"

He'd thrown her with his statement and then his quick change of subject. "It's always rough when you have the disease he does," Kellie replied. "Life's not a party and I don't make him promises I can't keep."

Hart stared at her, a blank expression on his face, as if he were seeing her for the first time. She tried not to redo her ponytail, an action she'd repeat when she was nervous. She was acting so out of character, so unlike herself.

This was Charlie's favorite driver, and she was being a jerk. But for some reason, this man simply rubbed her the wrong way. Maybe he was simply too perfect. Too adored. Too good to be true. Maybe he had it too easy. Whatever it was, the energy between them hummed in the air, if that were possible.

"I'm not a bad guy," Hart said, if reading her mind.

"Charlie is not a toy."

He took a step back and held up his hands. "Isn't that being a bit harsh? I never said he was."

She resisted the urge to stomp her foot. "You asked him to tell you what he wished for. What are you going to do, be a genie and make his wish come true? He's not like normal children. He hasn't attended school, or had his heart broken by a girl, or suffered the indignation of being embarrassed when toilet paper gets stuck to your shoe or when you drop your books in the hall and all the kids laugh. You're his idol. Let's leave it at that. I don't want him disappointed. He's already had enough of that in fifteen years to last a lifetime."

"He's done," Clarissa announced, and Kellie jumped, wondering how much the older woman had overheard. Her poker face didn't reveal a thing, although she did glance at Hart for a brief moment. Charlie was currently removing the headphones, so Kellie knew he hadn't overheard her charged conversation with Hart Hampton.

Clarissa removed the steering wheel, opened the car door and let Charlie out.

"How'd you do?" Hart asked, his hand out for a high five.

"I got lapped!" Charlie said, slapping Hart's hand. Charlie's sheepish countenance failed to contain his excitement. "I was so afraid of wrecking after I scraped the wall on Turn One that I didn't go fast enough and everyone left me behind, only to come up on my rear end. At least that's what the crew chief said in my ear. I guess I was about to go a lap down."

"That sounds about right," Hart said. Kellie glanced around. Clarissa had disappeared and, amazingly, no one else was waiting.

"I thought we only got ten minutes," Kellie said, eager to get Hart's autograph and go. "We don't want to take up your time."

"I've got a short break scheduled. No one's up again until eleven-fifteen." Hart looked Kellie square in the eye, as if daring her to offer another excuse. At that moment, she experienced the full effect of this man, and she trembled slightly.

He was out of her league. Hart Hampton was a man used to being in control of everything, and right now that included her. She had no doubt he'd deliberately chosen their time slot, and his actions confounded her for she couldn't make sense of them. Why Charlie? Just because he'd asked a good question?

Like last night, no answer was forthcoming.

"Come on, Charlie, let's sit over here." Seeing Kellie's silence as acquiescence, Hart gestured toward a set of director's chairs. "I want to hear what answer you came up with. Kellie, are you going to join us?"

As Charlie was making a beeline for the chairs, what could she say? No? Hart had successfully checkmated her. Despite the temperature being eighty degrees, she shivered. She followed the men, who had already begun their conversation by the time she climbed into her seat.

"We're from Myrtle Beach," Charlie was saying.

"I've been there many times," Hart said. "That's where I started out racing."

"I'd like to race," Charlie said. "I'll be sixteen soon and I'm determined to get my driver's license that day."

"Ah, that's right. Still no permit," Hart replied.

"His treatments have precluded it," Kellie inserted a tad irritably.

Hart arched both eyebrows, and Kellie bristled. But Charlie noticed none of the tension. "Hopefully for your birthday," Hart said. "I was go-carting by your age."

"My leukemia means I bruise easy," Charlie said. "And chemo knocks me out. I've had a bunch of bone marrow transplants, but I can't get the disease into remission. So I watch and root for you instead."

"Just me? Or some other guys whose autographs I could probably get for you if you'd like them?"

"Oh, would you? My grandma loves—" Charlie said, mentioning another driver. "But she's come over to the Hampton Racing camp this season. We watch every race and yell for you. Unless you wreck or fall way too far behind. Then we yell for him."

"Does your mom cheer for me?" Hart asked, looking at Kellie.

Charlie wrinkled his nose, answering for her. "Mom's not really into NASCAR. She's been in a few car accidents—none her fault—and so she says she doesn't want to watch. Even though she was fine, they shook her up pretty bad. She's been rear-ended three times. What's the probability of that?"

"I don't know," Hart said. "On the track it's called bump-drafting. What tracks do you like best?"

"Grandma and I like the ones on the superspeedways best, the restrictor plate ones like at Talladega. Short tracks are okay and just as exciting, but I like the longer tracks best since the cars can spread out more and really get up to some good speeds."

"Have you ever seen a race in person?" Hart asked.

"No," Charlie said, shaking his head.

"Not even at the track in Myrtle Beach?"

"Nope," Charlie replied. "Grandma always says she doesn't want to sit outside in the hot grandstand, and Mom's not that much of a fan to ever consider going. I've always wanted to check it out, though."

"Well, that's got to change," Hart said. He glanced at Kellie as if to say, "Right?"

"I doubt that's possible," Kellie responded. "We take life

day by day." Her voice held a note of warning, and she wasn't surprised when Hart chose to ignore it.

"Everything's possible," he told her, that famous dimpled chin of his jutting forward. "What are you doing next weekend?"

"Watching the All-Star Challenge?" Charlie asked. "Grandma and I have it marked on our calendars. My diet is pretty restricted to keep me healthy, but on race nights we get to eat pizza. It's my weekly indulgence."

"I love pizza, too," Hart said. "And I'm glad you're planning on watching the All-Star Challenge because you're going to be watching it from my pit box. I have some extra seats that you can take."

"What?" Charlie's expression turned into one of a kid who'd just learned Santa Claus was real. "Are you serious? Mom?"

"I'm very serious," Hart said, ignoring Kellie's open mouth. "I get to be in the race since I won Daytona, and I want you to join me as my guest. That means you, too, Kellie."

"I…" Kellie started. Charlie's face practically glowed with unrestrained joy. She glared at Hart. "We can't possibly…"

"Of course, you can," Hart interrupted. "There's an infield hospital if you're worried about Charlie's condition and the need for emergency medical care. My aunt and uncle will be there, and I'll have them be your guides while I'm driving. Charlie, I bet my crew chief, Wally, will even put you to work. You could monitor the weather for us."

"Really?" Charlie asked. Kellie hadn't seen her son's eyes brim with this much excitement in years.

"Yep. Just be prepared, for it's loud, even with headphones. The noise is nothing like you hear on TV. It can rattle your bones."

"You're really serious?" Charlie confirmed once more, his excitement turning to unabashed awe.

"Absolutely," Hart said, grinning. "I already said I was, and I'm a man of my word. Give me all your contact information and it's a date. Bring your grandma, too."

"We'll be there," Charlie said. "Right, Mom?"

Kellie knew she had to be wearing a stunned expression, but that was far better than the fury that she trying to contain. How dare Hart just blow through her wishes? She wasn't a car to move out of the way. But Hart seemed oblivious to her anger, and he reached around and grabbed some official Hart Hampton merchandise. "What's your grandma's name?" he asked.

"Anita," Charlie answered. He watched as Hart autographed the color picture, "To Anita, with love, Hart."

"That's for her," Hart said as he passed the eight-by-ten color glossy over. "And this is for you." Hart autographed a picture for Charlie and then he took another picture from the stack and scrawled out a phone number that started with a 704 area code. "This is for your mom. That's my cell phone. That's should prove how serious I am. Very few people have that number."

"Thank you," Charlie gushed.

Clarissa reappeared and Kellie could see a family of eight approaching about a hundred yards away. "Our time's up," Kellie said, anxious to get out from under the tent.

"I guess it is," Hart replied. He glanced at her. "Why don't you and I talk later tonight and get all this set up for next weekend?"

"Charlie and I…"

"It's parents' night out, so I'm sure Charlie has plans to be with his new friends," Hart cut in smoothly.

"I do," Charlie said. "Brad and I are going to see the movie."

"So do you have a little free time in between your networking to meet with me?" Hart asked, and Kellie knew he'd trapped her.

"Fine," she stated. "I'll see you after dinner."

"My motor home," Hart said. "We can talk there."

Kellie gave an erratic wave of agreement and hopped off her chair. "Let's go, Charlie. We have some time to do a craft before lunch. Your grandmother would love a lanyard key chain."

"Sure," Charlie said. He stood and followed his mother.

HART WATCHED Kellie flee the tent, for that was really the only word for it, Charlie already ecstatically speaking in her ear as he followed.

Hart turned around. Clarissa had an odd expression on her face. "You just invited that boy and his mother to the race next weekend."

"Yeah, I did," Hart said, grinning. He was pretty proud of himself. "Did you see how happy it made him?"

"Did you see how angry your actions made her?" Clarissa asked gently. Around the shop, she was known as everyone's mom or grandma.

"I saw," Hart admitted with a sigh. Then he stood his ground. "But tough. That boy deserves a break. He's ill. She can stop being difficult for one weekend."

"Difficult?" Clarissa questioned.

"Can't you see that she hates me?" Hart said with a dismissive wave. "I come to this place and find the one woman who could care less that I drive a race car. She thinks I should keep my clothes on and turn away my number one sponsor. And her son, he's just a gem. I admit, I'm taken with that kid. Reminds me a bit of me at that age." His tone turned defensive. "If I can make him happy, then hey, I'll do it. Cynthia wanted me to have some good PR. Imagine how my aunt will spin that next weekend."

"What, off at camp, come home with a stray? These are not people you toy with," Clarissa warned.

"I'm not," Hart said, noting defensively that Kellie had said the same thing.

"Humph," Clarissa said. If there were more to her spiel, it would have to wait, for the next family had reached the tent. Hart plastered a smile on his face and turned to greet them.

He'd settle all of this silliness with Kellie tonight. Charlie deserved to be happy. So did Kellie.

It was three o'clock that afternoon before Hart realized that Charlie hadn't told him what he wished for.

CHAPTER FIVE

AT 6 P.M., Kellie knew she had to put a stop to this nonsense. All day she'd heard nothing but how wonderful Hart was, and how excited Charlie was to be viewing the All-Star Challenge from Pit Road. Kellie closed her eyes for a moment, shutting out the western sun. In twenty-four hours, her life had tilted on its axis and she wasn't quite sure if Hart Hampton was finished upending her world.

She approached his motor home, noting that the letters spelled out the make of the RV across the front. Hart's motor home was as long as a charter bus. A matching trailer was still attached, adding to the length. She and Charlie had seen a tour bus special on a country music video television station. Those buses had cost somewhere in the millions. She assumed Hart's motor home had to be the same.

A stool waited outside the door, which opened as if by magic, or rather, because Hart must have been waiting for her. He stood at the top of the stairs, wearing a different polo shirt and jeans than he'd had on earlier. She'd changed, as well, into a pair of knit sport pants and a short-sleeve sweater. She'd also showered and wore her hair long, straight down to her shoulders.

"Come on in," he said. Kellie reached for the support bar and climbed up. A movable wall divided the driver's area from the rest of the motor home. "Welcome to my weekend home. What can I get you to drink? Unlike the dining hall, I'm privy to the location of some libations on this bus."

"A diet cola is fine," Kellie said. Anything alcoholic might cloud her brain and weaken her resolve. As she followed him into what served as his living area, she couldn't help but be impressed. So this was how the other half traveled.

Hart's motor home was phenomenal. Wood gleamed, and because of the home's slide-out feature, his living area was quite spacious. A huge plasma screen TV was set into the wall section above the driver, and two other television screens were also popped out of their normal hiding places. All were tuned to the race.

"That's where I should be," Hart said as he passed the couch and went into the tidy kitchen area. He pointed as a reporter stood in front of Hampton Racing's pit. "There's my car and Ricky's going to drive it."

Kellie wasn't sure what to say, so she simply stood there as the young pretty female interviewed a young driver standing outside of the Elementals Number 413 car.

"So do you like my home?" Hart asked, changing the subject as he reached into a refrigerator and removed a soda can.

"It's nice," Kellie said as Hart passed the diet soda over. Their fingers touched briefly. Kellie took the can and glanced around the room.

Hart shook his head. "Again, you impress me by being so honest. Everyone else either gushes or fall all over themselves fawning over me. Personally, I think it's a bit overdone. Go on. Have a seat," Hart said as he retrieved a beer for himself. "Another one of my sponsors," he said as he held up the microbrewery brand.

"Beer and underwear," Kellie remarked as she sat on the

dark burgundy sofa. The room was done in dark, masculine colors, masterfully designed to coordinate while still feeling spacious. The room had windows, but they'd been covered with matching opaque shades.

"Beer and underwear." Hart shook his head as he removed the bottle cap. "You don't have to say it, I know what you're thinking. All I'd need to be complete would be to have a men's magazine sponsor me and put some bunny ears on my car. You're probably wondering, why couldn't I be sponsored by one of those home improvement companies? Or at least something more respectable, like candy or office supplies. But no, my two top sponsors are booze and boxers."

"Actually, I wasn't as concerned with that as much as I was hoping we could talk about next weekend. I'd like to see if there's a way you and I could agree to cancel Charlie's going."

"No," Hart said, shaking his head. He took a seat in a huge, comfortable recliner just a few feet away and kicked his feet up onto the footrest. He had an excellent view of all the television sets, but his attention was focused fully on Kellie. "I've invited Charlie to the track, and I'm a man who keeps his word. You agree that he's excited?"

"It's all he's talked about," Kellie said, sipping the diet cola.

"So how can you say no? He wants this."

She shook her head, willing him to understand. "Yes, but I don't."

"You'd break his heart by saying no."

Kellie set the can into a conveniently placed cup holder. "There's more to Charlie's medical condition than a broken heart. Charlie sometimes doesn't know what's best for him. He's fragile. Too much exertion can have him suffer a relapse. I can't risk that."

"You can't keep him in a bubble. He's almost sixteen," Hart pointed out. "You brought him here."

"Only because my mother filled out the paperwork and insisted I sign it. And this camp is prepared for kids like Charlie. It's designed for them. Charlie's special. He's been through so much."

"And so have you," Hart said. "Let me take care of him for a weekend. Let him live the fantasy. He can hang out with my team. We can have him sitting up on the pit box monitoring the local weather. If he's up to it, he can be in charge of my water bottle."

Kellie cocked her head slightly. "Those are jobs?"

"Actually, yes," Hart said. "Every guy in the pit usually has a role in helping me win my race. I even have a spotter up in the stands with a bird's-eye view so that he can radio me what's going on. When I'm driving, the only view I have is immediately in front and directly behind me. The only voices I hear are my spotter's and my crew chief's. Come on, Kellie. Let Charlie live a little. I'll be on my best behavior."

"I'm not even sure what that is," Kellie replied.

Hart opened both arms wide, his bottle wobbling in his left hand. "You're seeing it. Here I am, on a Saturday night, sitting in my motor home. If I don't fly home after a race, this is usually where you'll find me. My wild nights before a race will find me hanging out with some of the guys racing remote control cars or watching a movie. This is as exciting as it gets."

"Yeah, right," Kellie said dubiously. "You've been back-stage at rock concerts. You have a different girlfriend every month. How can I be certain I'm not intruding on her?"

"Because I'm not dating anyone and haven't been for a while. So my entire focus next weekend, besides winning, will be on Charlie, and on you," Hart said.

Kellie's eyes widened. "That sounds rather scary."

"It's not. You don't have to trust me or like me, but you should at least believe me. I'm a good guy despite the hype." He grinned and tapped his fingers on the armrest. She noticed he had large, proportional hands.

"What if I don't want this?" she countered.

He didn't seem fazed. "You should. Your son wants this. I want this. There's nothing to be afraid of. I don't know why you're so fearful of adventure. Let yourself go and live a little."

The air-conditioning must have been set low, for Kellie shivered. Hart was lounging in a chair and still his mere words tugged at her. Her life had enough drama in it just dealing with Charlie's medical problems. If she added the emotional turbulence of dealing with Hart... "You don't get what you want all the time."

"If I got everything I wanted, I'd already be a NASCAR NEXTEL Cup champion. But this is a good idea. Say yes."

"I still don't think I should," Kellie said. "It's like opening Pandora's box. Things won't be the same."

"And why would that be?" Hart parried. "What excuse can you give me that's valid enough for you to say no and deny your son's happiness?"

"My simple 'no' should be enough," Kellie insisted.

"And normally, as I have a great respect for people, especially women, your 'no' would be enough," Hart agreed. "But these aren't normal circumstances. Your son is ill. This may be his one and only chance to hang out at the race track, during the All-Star Challenge, of all things. You'd deny him that once-in-a-lifetime opportunity?"

Kellie bent her head and placed it in her fingers. Her head ached. "My life is simple. As peaceful as I can make it with Charlie being as sick as he is. My world is not this, this moneyed existence. How can he go back to watching races on TV once he's smelled the burning rubber?"

"I don't know," Hart said. "But he will. He can. Race fans do it all the time. Just think, this way Charlie will have a memory to take with him forever."

You don't understand! Kelly wanted to scream. She knew Charlie. The family joke, it would take on new life. Become real.

And it couldn't be real. So much that Charlie wanted was already denied him. Her life was a small house in Myrtle Beach. Hart Hampton could not enter the mix. But he had. He'd already upset everything.

Sensing her turmoil, Hart rose and moved to sit on the sofa beside her. "It's all going to be fine. Just believe."

"I can't," Kellie said, straightening. "You don't even know us. I know more about you, but then I know nothing at all. Like why my son? Why me?"

"Because," Hart said simply.

She craned her neck over her left shoulder to gape at him. "Because?"

"Yeah," Hart said. "You can fill in whatever blank you want. I crashed because. My life sucks because. I'm not at the track because. I've learned that it doesn't matter what comes after the because. There's always a reason, or an excuse. Some right, others wrong. Bottom line is that it all comes down to what you want. And I've decided I think this is a great idea. I like your son. He reminds me a bit of myself at that age. Maybe he might be a lucky charm who can help me get my winning streak back. All I know is that my brain tells me this is the right move, just like when it tells me to risk going topside into a corner instead of holding the inside groove down low."

"I admit, Charlie will love this. You've been more than

generous. But my mother won't want to go. She's had the opportunity several times before and just laughed and said she'd rather watch the race on TV in the comfort of her home than be out in the elements."

"One of the armchair fans. She's not alone, if the ratings are any indication. I can put her up in the Hampton Racing box, if that helps."

"That's really sweet of you," Kellie said, her resolve weakening. "But I still have a feeling she'll say no and it's going to have to be me. I'm really not a NASCAR fan. I usually only catch the tail end, when they wave the checkered flag. I don't want to be sucked into your world."

"And I respect that," Hart said. "It's another reason that I'm drawn to your family. You have no expectations. You don't want anything from me. Do you know how rare that is? How refreshing?"

"I suppose rare," Kellie said, looking at him. He was so near she could smell his aftershave. She bit her bottom lip, tugging at it with her top teeth.

"Very rare," Hart countered. "We'll have a great time. Charlie will be happy. And that's what you want most in this world, isn't it? Your deepest wish? That your son be happy?"

"Yes," Kellie said as her attitude toward him softened somewhat. "Yes, that's what I want."

"Then let me make him happy. Let me give him this." Hart covered her hand with his.

His hand warmed hers, calmed and convinced. It also hinted at something more, something dangerous. It made part of her long dead flicker and come alive.

"I'm not going to have a choice, am I?" she asked.

"No," Hart said. "This is the right choice, Kellie."

The TV suddenly roared to life; the race had started.

"Stay and watch it with me?" Hart asked. "I'll give you some pointers for next weekend."

"I'd better leave," Kellie said, withdrawing her hand from his. His touch had disturbed her equilibrium—made her remember she had her own needs. "Just tell me how this is going to work and what arrangements I need to make."

"You don't need to do anything," Hart said. "I'll arrange for a car to pick you up. Can Charlie fly in an airplane?"

"Yes." She nodded, her hair dancing on her shoulders.

"Good. I'll have a car pick you both up take you to the airport. You'll fly to Charlotte, and I'll have a member of Hampton Racing staff meet you and bring you to the track. Just tell me when you want to arrive."

"I don't know," Kellie said, honestly.

"Then I'll have you fly in Friday morning. I'll already be at the track, so you can meet me there. You and Charlie will stay with me."

"No! We can't stay with you," Kellie stated with determination. "You've already been very kind, but we'll get a hotel."

Hart smiled and patted her hand. "The hotels are booked and I didn't mean *stay with me*. My parents are in Europe. I'm going to have their motor home brought to the track for you and Charlie. It's like this one, only decorated differently, and you and Charlie will have it all to yourself. That way, if either of you decide you have to get away from the action on the track, you can escape. Hampton Racing also has a condo that overlooks the track, but I'd rather have you and Charlie infield. That's where the action is. Besides, my aunt and uncle are probably using the condo to entertain."

"Your parents' motor home is fine. Thank you for understanding." She again freed her hands, breaking the connection. She stood and reached into her pocket and drew out a folded piece of paper. "This is my phone number. You call me by Wednesday to confirm. If I don't hear from you by then, I'll assume you've changed your mind."

"I'll call," Hart said. He rose to his feet, hovering only twelve inches away.

"I'm going to leave now," Kellie announced, her skin prickling with awareness of this man. "I promised another single mother I'd be her partner for the spades tournament. I don't want to stand her up."

"I like spades. Sounds fun," Hart said. He moved aside so she could pass. She headed toward the door and he pressed a button to open it for her. "Thanks for coming by."

She paused and gave him one last look. "No, I guess I should thank you for making Charlie happy. I don't like this idea, but it's for my son and he's thrilled. I really do appreciate this opportunity you've given him."

AND WITH THAT she was gone, out into the night. Hart returned to his recliner and lifted the beer to his mouth. Then he sat the bottle down, untouched. He actually preferred to have something nonalcoholic. He stood, poured the remains of his beer out, and retrieved a diet cola from the refrigerator. His gaze landed on the can Kellie had left behind, and Hart went over and lifted it. She'd consumed maybe half.

He placed it on the kitchenette counter and tossed his body back into the recliner. Kellie was an enigma, much more so now than this morning—when Brad Muldoon had told Hart that Charlie had said Kellie wouldn't date anyone but him. Sue, Brad's mother, had almost choked with embarrassment, and seeing Hart's subsequent confusion, she'd explained the whole "joke."

Hart had found the paradox intriguing. Kellie, who hated

him, was "holding out for Hart Hampton." He'd deliberately asked those questions of Kellie during Charlie's simulator time to get a reaction. She'd been refreshingly honest and forthright. She wasn't that impressed with him.

Funny thing was, he was very taken with her. The more time he spent with her, the more time he wanted to get inside her head and see what made her tick. He wanted to get under her skin and see what reaction he could draw from her reserved persona. He asked himself if it was just because she was a challenge, and while he couldn't say what it was, he honestly could say he wasn't pursuing her because of that.

She wasn't dating anyone; Sue Muldoon had helpfully provided all that information the moment Hart had tactfully asked, and sworn that he'd never reveal that Sue had shared Kellie's secrets.

His cell phone rang. Cynthia. Hart flipped it open. "What are you doing phoning me?" he asked. "The race is on."

"Clarissa just called me and I happened to catch her message. She and Clyde are back in Charlotte and she told me that you invited some woman and her son to the track next weekend for the All-Star Challenge."

"I did," Hart said. The race broadcast had gone to commercial so Cynthia had his full attention. "You'll need to have my parents' motor home sent to the motor home lot for them. Can you get it slotted next to mine? Charlie has leukemia, so can you make sure the med center is aware of that? I want him in the pit during my race, so get whatever clearances you need from NASCAR. He's a few weeks shy of sixteen, so see what you can do."

"Hart, don't arrange PR stunts without telling me first," Cynthia said.

"It's not a stunt," Hart replied sharply.

He heard nothing but a long silence as Cynthia processed that. "Then what is it?" she finally asked. "Please don't tell me this is another pick-up scheme. It's bad enough that all the single rookies try to flaunt their prettiest girlfriends at the Charlotte races. Makes me feel like an old hag."

Hart cracked a wry smile. "No, I promise you it's not that, although she is pretty. But she hates me. Well, how about she dislikes me a great deal and doesn't watch racing unless she has to. Her son's the fan."

"Okay, you've lost me. Clarissa made it sound like you're enamored of this woman."

"I think I might be," Hart said, honestly. No sense in hiding that. Cynthia would see right though him next weekend the moment she met Kellie and Charlie.

Hart glanced at the screen. Kyle Doolittle and Ronnie McDougal were fighting nose to nose down the backstretch.

"So you like her?" Cynthia asked.

"I'm very intrigued. All I know is that I want her and her son at the track next weekend, and I want that as much as I want to win the race. I want to see her again, if only to prove I'm not the cad she believes me to be. And I do like her son. This will be the experience of a lifetime for him. He's great. You'll love him. You'll probably adore her. She's different from all the bimbos you always claim I date. Not that Kellie even thinks of me in a romantic sense. I told you she's not impressed with me, didn't I?"

"Hart," Cynthia said, and then she faltered.

"Cynthia," Hart responded, knowing his aunt was already running various weekend scenarios through her head. "It's all good."

"I hope so," Cynthia said. "We'll talk tomorrow. We've

decided to fly out tonight so I'll stop by your house early afternoon. Okay? I'm going to go back to the pit."

As Hart flipped the cell phone closed, a sense of quiet satisfaction stole over him, the same as when he'd decided to postpone his bachelor's degree for a full-time racing gig. Inviting Kellie and Charlie was simply the right thing to do.

He was Hart Hampton, and in this respect, he was exactly like his father. He knew what he wanted when he saw it. She would never come to him; he had only convinced her this time because of Charlie. But he was determined that she discover he wasn't what she thought him to be.

Hart Hampton was no joke.

CHAPTER SIX

THE CESSNA dipped low, dropping below the clouds on its final approach to Charlotte, North Carolina. Charlie Thompson kept his face pressed close to the rectangular window, but not so close that condensation formed. The things on the ground became increasingly clearer and bigger as the jet continued its descent. This was actually happening. He was almost there.

He hadn't believed that his mom was actually going to let him take this trip until about five minutes before he boarded the private jet. He knew she hadn't been too happy about Hart's offer. Charlie had seen the expression on her face the moment Hart had asked that morning at camp. And if his mom had really put her foot down and said no, Charlie knew both he and Hart would have respected her wishes.

He clearly remembered holding his breath, glad that Hart had been the one to push for this trip. Charlie had expected his mother to fight Hart on the issue more than she had, but then she'd given in, much to Charlie's delight.

Oh, his mom wasn't any more thrilled now than when she'd first heard the idea. She'd been pretty tight-lipped about the whole situation all week, like she was whenever the doctor gave her bad news that she didn't want to share right away. Although he hadn't had much actual classroom experience,

Charlie had had excellent homebound teachers. Because of increased one-on-one instruction and interaction, he knew he was more mature-sounding in his speech and thoughts than others his age. He also knew the toll his disease took on him and, in turn, his mother.

This trip would be good for both of them. Even the doctor had said so after his mom had called to check. Charlie's doctor was all about new experiences and living a quality life. Charlie's mom had researched his doctor and he was one of the best. And Kellie trusted him.

As for Hart, his motor home had been gone when Charlie and Kellie had walked to breakfast so Charlie hadn't seen him since last Sunday. On Wednesday, though, Hart had called. Pinching himself bruised, so when Charlie had heard Hart's voice on the phone, he'd actually danced around a bit as he'd realized this was real and not just some dream.

He and Hart talked for a few minutes about their respective weeks before Hart had asked for Kellie. The conversation between Hart and his mother had been even shorter, but the end result was that here they were, the only other person on the plane being Hart's personal pilot.

"We're getting really low," Charlie told his mom.

Kellie put her *Home and Garden* magazine down. She sat across from him in a plush oversized seat. She glanced out the window and then at her watch. "I guess we're about to land. It's around the time Hart said we'd arrive."

At that moment, the pilot came over the hidden speakers and announced that they were on final approach and asked that they buckle up.

"Now, Charlie," Kellie began as she reached forward to make sure his seat belt was secure.

"Mom," Charlie complained, tugging on his belt to show

her it was fine. "Don't start. Like last weekend, we're going to have fun. And the doctor said doing this is fine." He'd only unhooked the belt once, when he'd gotten up to use the bathroom. "I'm in no danger."

"I know," she said. She'd worn her hair down and applied some makeup. He couldn't remember when the last time that had happened. "I just don't want you to have too high expectations. Hart's going to be very busy this weekend. He's been generous in asking us here, as his guests, but this isn't a date or anything like that. No matchmaking. No trying to ingratiate ourselves with him and try to win his continued favor."

"Mom," Charlie protested.

She shook her head, the blond ends swishing around her shoulders. "No *but moms*. I know you. Let me make this perfectly clear. Just because Hart's invited us doesn't mean that we try to make the family joke real. Don't even bring that up this weekend. It's embarrassing."

"I promise," Charlie said. "But what if Hart likes you?"

Kellie sighed. "I think you'll see this weekend that that is a ridiculous notion. Even if I liked him like that, which I don't, we're not from this world. It's like visiting a theme park or being on vacation. We can't live there permanently."

AT THAT MOMENT the plane touched down, the wheels hitting the ground with a thump. Brakes squealed and several moments later the plane coasted to a stop. Charlie and Kellie remained seated until the pilot came out from the cockpit, opened the doors and lowered the stairs. Sunlight streamed in through the opening, and they followed the pilot out. A Chevrolet Suburban waited about ten feet away, right there on the tarmac. A woman stepped out of the driver's seat and approached them. She wore khaki pants and a white polo shirt embroidered with the Hampton Racing logo.

"Hi, you must be Charlie and Kellie." She held out her hand, and both Charlie and Kellie shook it. "I'm Cynthia Jones, Hart's aunt. Both of you call me Cynthia. Welcome to Charlotte."

The pilot came forward carrying two carry-on bags that he'd retrieved from the plane's underbelly.

"Ah, you've won my approval already," Cynthia said as the pilot loaded the luggage into the back. "You know how to travel light."

Cynthia watched as the pilot shut the Suburban's liftgate. "Thanks, Jake," she told him. "Hart won't be needing you until Sunday, so as far as I know you can park the thing and go home."

She turned to Kellie and Charlie and smiled. "Let's get you two to the track. We might get there in time for the last of the media interviews. If you want, one of you can sit up front with me. It'll make me feel less like a chauffeur, which, although I volunteered to do this, is not one of my regular jobs."

"Cool," Charlie said, climbing into back of the SUV. He turned around, noticing a third seat. Kellie climbed into the front. "This car is huge."

"We carry a lot of people and equipment back and forth," Cynthia told him. She fired up the engine. "On race weekends we have close to two hundred people at the track in various capacities."

"What do you do?" Kellie asked, her eyes wide as Cynthia expertly got them out of the airport and onto the city streets.

"A little of everything," she said. "Along with Hart and his dad, I'm an owner of Hampton Racing, so I have those responsibilities. That means media interviews, visiting with sponsors and their guests, being there for the drivers and crew chiefs, among other things. Mostly a lot of PR and face time."

"And you volunteered to come and get us?" Kellie asked. She glanced over her shoulder. Charlie had put his earbuds in and was listening to his iPod as he stared out the window, taking everything in.

"If this was important to Hart to have you and your son here, then it was important to me," Cynthia said.

"In other words, you wanted first dibs at checking us out," Kellie said.

Cynthia laughed, her good humor making Kellie a little less tense. "That, too. Ever since he fired the last guy, I serve as Hart's unofficial manager. He wanted to take more hands-on control of his sponsorships and such, so I stepped into help. As for his PR person, you'll meet Russ. On race weekends, Russ is responsible for maintaining Hart's schedule and getting him everywhere on time. He'll also be in charge of getting you where you need to be. You'll also have a schedule, and Russ will answer any questions you may have."

Kellie settled back against the seat and glanced out the window for a moment.

"You seem overwhelmed," Cynthia said.

"I am," Kellie admitted. "I have a schedule? I'm still trying to figure out why we're here."

"Hart wanted it," Cynthia replied simply. "He thought it would be a great opportunity for Charlie to watch a race in person. I happen to agree. When we announced our guests in the media center, the media thought it a great idea. We're always trying to draw attention to the camp."

"So long as no one flaunts my son," Kellie said. "I don't want this to simply be a PR stunt to make Hart look good. I won't stand for anyone using my son like that." She bit her lip. "Sorry. I don't mean to sound rude or ungrateful, but I wanted to make sure the air was clear before I meet Russ and he starts moving me around."

"You're wise to question, and I respect that you're not going to be passive about all this," Cynthia stated. She didn't appear too upset, and Kellie relaxed some more. "I can tell you that Hart's announcement was a new one for me. Hart's had visitors to the track before, but normally he leaves his guests to fend for themselves. He's never requested a separate motor home or for his schedule to be rearranged."

Meaning that Hart's previous visitors had probably all been females who'd shared his home-away-from-home and put up with his nonsense. A little annoyance flared and Kellie tamped that down as she focused on the last part. "Rearranged?"

"Hart wanted to make sure he had some free time to spend with you and Charlie, that is more than a few minutes between him running here and there. This is the All-Star Challenge, so there will be tons for him to do. Signings with fans, signings at the merchandise hauler, visits to the sponsor lunches and dinners, those types of things. He didn't consider the two of you riding with him in a golf cart quality time. So he requested we trim his schedule back to only the priority items, and Russ and I accommodated him."

Kellie fell silent as she contemplated that. Hart changing things for her sounded so surreal. The fact he was even bringing them here still didn't make sense. Celebrities didn't just make friends with those outside their "group." Did they?

Cynthia didn't seem like one who liked silence as she asked, "So you've never been to a race?"

"No," Kellie said. "I'm not the fan. My mother and Charlie are. They stay glued to the television and cheer for Hart while I get a few hours of free time."

"Is that rare?" Cynthia asked. The question was more out

of genuine curiosity, not just because she was trying to make conversation.

"With Charlie's illness, it is," Kellie replied. "I'm a single mother running a household, and there's always something to do. My mother moved in to help me out, and as part of the routine they eat pizza and watch TV. So race days are my time. I usually catch the tail end."

"And your mom didn't want to come?"

"She's thrilled to be having the house to herself and has booked the weekend solid with seeing her friends. So it's just me."

"Well, once you've experienced live racing, you either love it or hate it. If it hooks you, you're a fan for life. Russ will be your contact person. Ask either of us anything."

"Do I need to be wearing green?" Kellie asked. "I wasn't sure what to wear so my mother lent me her Hart Hampton shirt. I also have a seafoam green T-shirt. I figured that was close enough."

"You don't have to dress like a fan if you don't want to." Cynthia laughed. "Most of the people in the garage and the pits will be dressed like me. Hampton Racing polo shirts and chinos. I can get you one, if you like. The team will be the same. When he needs to be in the car, Hart will be in his uniform. If not, he'll wear jeans and a T-shirt or a polo. You can wear whatever you want so long as you have a closed-toe shoes, long pants and you aren't showing your midriff or wearing a tank top. Shoulders must be covered."

"I don't wear tank tops or show my stomach in public," Kellie said.

They were waiting for a stoplight and Cynthia turned to study her. "No, I didn't think you would." She seemed pleased with the fact, as if Kellie had passed some test. Kellie wanted to question Cynthia more, but right then Charlie shouted, "There it is!"

Kellie stared. Off in the distance, the grandstands rose majestically out of the flat ground. She'd never realized that race tracks were so huge. Of course they were, she chided herself. She'd done some Internet research. This track was 1.5 miles long. That meant it sat on more than two thousand acres of land.

Cynthia showed their passes, and soon the SUV dipped down through a tunnel and entered the infield area. Kellie tried to absorb it all as Cynthia began giving them some track facts. "You'll find our motor homes in the large lot behind the garages." She stopped at another checkpoint, showed her pass again, and then drove through. "You're sandwiched between Hart and Ronnie McDougal. Liam and I are actually over in the hookups. Why we pay thousands for those I don't know, but this race is all about status so we maintain ours. I'll show you where my motor home is later."

"Where does the team stay?" Charlie asked. He'd taken his earbuds out once they'd arrived at the track.

"Since we're in Charlotte, they'll commute from their homes. When we're out of state on race weekends, we get blocks of hotel rooms for them."

Cynthia parked the car next to a row of motor homes and Kellie glanced around. A portable basketball hoop had been set up down at the end of the lane. A few tricycles rested at the end of one home. A stroller sat next to another one.

"A lot of drivers have their families with them. Since we're so close to most everyone's houses, a lot of drivers will go home tonight, while others will choose to stay here. It all depends on the driver, his schedule and how he likes to prepare for a race. Some have routines they keep consistent, no matter what the track. Don't be afraid to talk to people. In fact, Charlie, Ronnie McDougal has a son who's right around your age. Be sure to introduce yourself to Stuart. I think you two probably share a lot of the same interests."

"I'll be sure to say hello," Charlie told Cynthia.

"Good, because Hart and Ronnie are friends," Cynthia said as she turned off the engine.

"Even after Richmond?" Charlie asked. "Hart knocked Ronnie right out of that race."

"Those things happen," Cynthia said. "The drivers know who they respect and who they don't. Both were running clean races. There's no ill will."

She then took them inside the motor home that would serve as their home for the next two nights.

"Wow," was the first word out of Charlie's mouth.

Kellie, who had seen the inside of Hart's motor home, still had to agree. While it was set up similar to Hart's, it was obvious the place had a feminine touch applied. The colors were neutral, the accents a light teal. Pictures hung in strategic places, and Kellie went to study a few of them as Cynthia showed Charlie how to operate the satellite entertainment system.

One photo was of a younger Hart sitting in a midget race car. Another had five people in it; Hart's family, Kellie surmised, for, although she only recognized Hart and Cynthia, she figured one of the older men in the shot had to be his father since the resemblance was so uncanny.

"Those are my parents," a voice said nearby, and Kellie jumped as Hart came up the stairs and into the motor home.

"Hart!" Despite an earlier resolution to be "cool," Charlie bounded over and gave Hart a high five.

"Hey Charlie," Hart said. He tapped Charlie's Marlins' baseball cap. "We'll need to change this one for a Hampton Racing one."

"Cool," Charlie answered.

"So did you have a good flight?" Hart asked, and even though his attention was fully on her son, Kellie could tell Hart was exceedingly aware of exactly where she was in the living area of the motor home. She knew from the little prickle that ran up her arms, the tingle in her toes. Maybe it was from the way her heart beat just a little bit faster despite her resolve to remain unaffected.

"The flight was awesome," Charlie said. "I can't believe that's how you travel."

"The novelty wears off quickly. I'm flying back and forth a minimum of two times a week," Hart said. "Testing weeks are really long when I also have to do PR events."

"Yeah, but you sure do travel in style," Charlie replied. He gestured to the room. "Thanks for inviting me."

Pride had Kellie smiling as her son remembered his manners.

"You're welcome. I'm glad you're here." He turned completely toward her. "Kellie," he began. "Thank you for allowing this."

His green eyes held hers for a minute before she glanced away. No doubt about it, Hart knew how to charm—and she wasn't immune. "You're welcome," Kellie said her voice catching a little. "And thank you, Hart for making this possible."

Cynthia coughed, drawing everyone's attention back her way. "Hart, I haven't shown them the sleeping quarters and or how to operate anything aside from the entertainment system." She glanced at her watch. "I'll let you take care of that as I have to run. Although, I have a feeling Russ will be coming to grab you soon. You've got to get ready for practice. Remember, tonight is the party at the condo for our truck sponsors." She smiled at Kellie. "You and Charlie are more than welcome to attend, and I'd love to have you both there."

Party? Kellie hadn't brought any party clothes. She'd brought a sundress, but that was not anything exceedingly fancy. She'd found it on the clearance rack of the local discount store last fall.

"As I might be wiped out from qualifying, we may just watch the truck race from here," Hart told his aunt before turning to Charlie and Kellie. "My parents own a condo in one of the buildings you see on the other side of the track, right at Turn One. Since six NASCAR events are held here throughout the year, it makes for easy entertaining and a place to be out of the elements during race time."

"Like watching a baseball game from a private box," Kellie suggested. Not that she'd ever done that, either.

"Exactly," Hart said.

"Well, in case I don't see you again, call me on my cell if you change your minds and decide to attend," Cynthia added.

Kellie said goodbye to Cynthia and watched as Hart began indoctrinating her son into motor home living. The refrigerator was stocked with everything from fresh fruit to soft drinks. "I won't eat dinner until after qualifying," Hart told Charlie as Charlie retrieved a soda pop. "We'll all eat lunch at the hauler in a little while. I think Elementals is catering food in. If not, someone will be barbecuing. If you want anything else, there are tons of concessions in the infield. I'll show you when we walk over. Here, take this."

Hart handed Charlie a fifty-dollar bill for whatever he might want to purchase. Kellie had opened her mouth to protest, but fell silent. From her son's nonstop grin, Kellie could see that Charlie had adapted to Hart Hampton and his lifestyle like a fish takes to water.

The two simply *got* each other, an understanding and camaraderie already evident between the two men. As her son stood beside Hart, Kellie could see that's what Charlie had become. A man. No longer just her little boy, but rather a teenager who wanted nothing more than to get his driver's license and experience all life had to offer. She trembled slightly at the realization. This weekend was going to be like opening Pandora's box. Nothing was ever going to be the same again.

"So are you hungry?" Hart asked.

"Not really. We ate a big breakfast before we drove to the airport." Kellie glanced at her watch. They'd left early in the morning, and it was almost eleven. Outside, she could hear the roar of engines as the truck series was taking its final practice.

The door opened and footsteps sounded. "Hey, Hart," a voice called. "You're due at eleven to draw for qualifying order. We gotta move."

"A lot of teams send reps to the drawing," Hart told Kellie and Charlie. "I actually like doing it myself if I'm available. That way, I only have myself to blame."

A giant of a man came fully into the living area. His Hampton Racing polo contrasted with his dark black skin. "Hey, you must be Kellie and Charlie. I'm Russ." He reached his hand forward and Kellie returned his firm grip. "We're gonna go pick up your hot passes, and then get Hart where he needs to be." He gazed at Charlie. "You get him a hat yet, Hart?"

"Nope," Hart said.

"I've got one in the hauler. Come on."

So this was Russ, Kellie thought as they filed outside, climbed into a custom golf cart, quickly got their credentials and made their way to the garage area. Russ and Hart wore their hard card passes on clips attached to their shirts, and every so often the group had to pass through a security checkpoint.

Their first stop was at Hart's hauler, a fifty-three-foot semi-trailer. The hauler was parked in between two others, almost like being lined up at a truck stop. The car lift remained pulled out, and the shaded area underneath was filled with director's chairs and a large barbecue pit at which a man in Hampton Racing uniform grilled.

"I thought Elementals was catering," Hart said.

"That's next week," Russ answered.

The outside roll door had been retracted, and the back doors to the hauler were mirrored. As Russ opened them up, a blast of air-conditioning escaped. Each side of the hauler was filled with cabinets, some floor to ceiling and others with countertop space.

The corridor between was a little wider than two people standing shoulder to shoulder, and the group walked single file all the way toward the front, then up some steps into a room with a table and booth-type seating. The flat-panel television was tuned to a country music video channel and an open box of donuts sat on the countertop underneath the recessed screen.

"You guys wait here for a few minutes and let me get Hart situated," Russ said. Kellie sat down and slid behind the table as Russ reached into a cabinet opposite her and tossed Charlie a Hampton Racing hat. He grinned at them. "Say hi to anyone who comes in. They'll be team members. And feel free to watch just about anything. The remote's right there."

With that, Hart and Russ disappeared back out the way they'd come in.

"Wow," Kellie finally said. She reached forward and pulled the sheet of paper sitting on the table toward her.

Charlie sat and scooted next to her. He gestured. "What's that?"

"I think it's the track schedule," Kellie said, pushing the sheet halfway between them. "I assume the NCTS represents the truck series and the NNCS is the Cup series but I have no idea what these events are."

"Let me see," Charlie said, pulling the paper closer. He pointed. "Hart's not in the open. That race is for those who didn't win during the season. They're trying to race their way into this one. Hart's already in the All-Star Challenge." Charlie pointed. "He still has to qualify to see where he starts. That's right here."

"Where he starts?" Kellie asked.

"Yeah, how they line up behind the pace car to begin the race," Charlie said. "The car with the fastest qualifying lap wins the pole or inside first position."

"Maybe I should have paid better attention when you and your grandmother were watching TV. I'm a little out of my league here," Kellie said. She reached for the remote.

"Qualifying is this evening and Hart's practice is at one-fifty," Charlie said, setting the sheet down. "He'll hang out in pit road with his car once it's pushed out."

"You really love this, don't you?" Kellie said.

"You would, too, if you gave it a chance," Charlie replied. "Seriously, Mom. Life's an adventure. Grab it."

"I'll try," Kellie said, surprised that her son was giving her such sound advice. "For this weekend, I'll attempt to be more open-minded."

"That sounds like a good idea, especially since I've seen how he looks at you."

"We said we weren't going to discuss that," Kellie whispered. She twisted her hands together. Experiencing Hart up close in his element was already a bit overwhelming. Thinking of him as something more than a friend was simply too much.

"Okay, fine. Just be open to anything. Deal?"

"Okay, deal," Kellie said, for it was easier to play along. It was natural for Charlie to want to be a whole family again, and he did worship Hart. He'd learn soon enough what Kellie knew—that once the weekend was over, their lives would go back to normal.

They watched TV for a few minutes and then Russ was retrieving them from the hauler, and acclimating them to the track's extensive garage area. They met up with Hart as his team gathered at the back end of the hauler for a lunch break.

"I always eat inside," Hart said as Kellie looked around for an open director's chair. He saw her expression. "I know. It's a nice day. But if I'm sitting out here, I'm media fodder. The unwritten rule is you can't bother a guy when he's inside the hauler."

"Especially when the media has to be invited into the hauler," Russ added as he took a seat outside.

Hart, Kellie and Charlie took their plates inside and made small talk until it was time for Hart to get ready for practice. A few of the team filtered in and out, and Hart introduced Kellie and Charlie to everyone.

"You can see practice better from on top of the hauler," Hart said as he got up, disposed of his plate and prepared to get ready for practice. "You'll have to climb up the ladder but the view's worth it. If not, you can take the tunnel and go hang out in the stands. Your passes will allow you to go just about everywhere. At this time, it's open seating."

"I'm going on top," Charlie said, his decision instantaneous. He pointed to his glasses. "My lenses darken."

"Whatever Charlie wants is fine." Kellie glanced at her jeans and tennis shoes. She'd forgotten her own sunglasses.

Hart grinned, reached into a cabinet and pulled out a spare pair of aviator Ray-Bans. "Here," he said, his fingers lightly touching Kellie's as he passed them over. "You'll need these."

"Thanks," she said. Something flickered in his green eyes, and then Russ was moving Charlie and her along so that Hart could go change.

From what Charlie told her the garage area was always busy as teams worked on their cars, but once practice started, the garage really came to life. Now those silent cars roared when their engines fired and drivers raced out onto the track to test their cars. They'd run until they needed gas, then come in and fill up. Russ explained that was to test the car's fuel economy, for often races could be won or lost in the final laps if the driver didn't have enough gas.

Aside from tracking mileage, Charlie told her, practice was also for drivers to get a feel for the track and to check on their car's performance. Kellie watched as cars needing adjusting would exit the track and roar into the garage area as fast as they were allowed, somehow missing all the people bustling to and fro who knew when to get out of the way. The car would pull into its assigned garage stall, and then the team would adjust this and that. Then the driver would race back out to run more laps.

Sitting atop the hauler, Kellie had an excellent view of all this action and the entire oval. She could see when Hart came in, see him and his team at work—as their hauler was directly across from their garage stall—and see him as he exited and drove back out on the track. Practice was an hour and fifteen minutes, but time simply flew by until Russ said, "He'll be getting out soon," and Kellie and Charlie climbed down.

Throughout the garage, race engines began being turned off, creating a strange silence and subsequent letdown as the constant roar subsided and the decibel level returned to something more normal. The whir of air-powered tools hadn't ceased. Kellie and Charlie stood at the end of Hart's garage as he handed his steering wheel and helmet out of the car, pulled himself out the window and sat on the doorframe.

Charlie took a step forward, but before Kellie could do anything to stop her son, Russ put a hand out and Charlie froze. "Give him a minute. He'll want to talk with his crew chief first about a few things, and then he'll be done," Russ said. "He's got nothing else until a little after six, so he'll be all yours."

"What about inspections?" Charlie asked.

"He doesn't have to be at those," Russ said. "Those are Wally's job."

Kellie and Charlie had briefly met Wally Warren, Hart's crew chief, at lunch. He'd said hello, welcomed them to the race and moved on. While he'd been friendly, his actions had made Kellie wonder how many other girlfriends Hart had introduced to the man.

But she wasn't a girlfriend, she reminded herself. Nor would she be. Still, Kellie watched as Wally and Hart moved toward the front of the race car, Hart unzipping and stepping out of his uniform while he talked.

"Uh-oh," Russ said under his breath. Hearing him, Kellie glanced around just in time to see a television crew headed their direction, shepherded by a woman wearing blue jeans and a blue polo shirt.

"Russ! Is Hart available?" the twenty-something woman called.

"He's still talking with Wally," Russ replied as she drew near to them. "He'll be a while."

"Oh, I've got some time," the brunette said. "I want to hear how he's recovered from sitting out last week's race. He lost a lot of points. I've heard rumors that his sponsors are edgy."

"Hart's fine and so are his sponsors," Russ said. "He spent the weekend volunteering. It gave Hampton Racing a chance to give Ricky Senate some experience in a Cup race."

"Is Hampton Racing thinking of moving Ricky to Cup level next year?" she asked.

"It's too early in the season to make that decision, especially as he's still a rookie in the Busch Series," Russ said.

Kellie glanced into the garage. As if sensing a reporter was waiting, Hart continued conversation with Wally, his back turned toward them.

"So Hart's not incapacitated in any way?" the reporter persisted.

"None," Russ said with a laugh. "Eileen, whatever gave you that idea?"

"So even though this race isn't for points, where does he think he'll place?"

"We're expecting a solid top five finish," Russ said. "If you'd excuse me. Kellie?"

Russ took her elbow and led her back over toward the hauler. Charlie immediately followed. "Who was that?" Kellie asked as they stepped in between the director's chairs.

"That's Eileen Swikle. She has a live call-in show on one of the sports cable stations. It's pretty popular. She also does pit reporting for the network broadcasting the races. Why don't you both wait inside? I'll go retrieve Hart."

"So do you do the interviews for him?" Kellie asked, hovering in the doorway, the cold air seeping out.

Russ shook his head and laughed a little. "No. But I'm allowed to speak for him, especially when Hampton Racing would prefer him not be interviewed."

Sensing Kellie's confusion, Russ added, "I know interviews are important, but because Hart went to the hospital after the accident at Richmond, and since he was AWOL at Darlington, right now a lot of reporters want to ask him all sorts of questions."

"Oh, like digging for gossip," she said.

Russ chuckled. "You've hit the nail right on the head. I'll go get Hart. He's going to be ready to head back to his motor home for a while."

Russ slid the hauler doors closed, and she and Charlie watched as Russ crossed the traffic lane and ducked into the garage.

"This is rather surreal," Kellie said as they made their way to the lounge area.

"It's great. It's so involved. The schedule's packed. I can't believe we watched practice from the top of the hauler."

"I have to admit, that was fun."

"I'm just glad that you got up there," Charlie told her. "I didn't think you would."

"Well, you told me to be open to anything," Kellie said. "I'm trying."

"Yeah," Charlie nodded and Kellie felt that parental glow one gets from making a child happy. "This weekend's going to be great," Kellie said.

"I agree. In fact, I think Hart's going to surprise you."

He had already amazed her by simply being different from the man she'd thought he was. She'd definitely prejudged him unfairly. But Kellie wasn't ready to share that with her son. No sense tempting him to play Cupid. Thus, "Uh-huh," was all she said.

"I SAW YOU get rid of Eileen Swikle," Hart said as Russ approached. "Thanks. I'm just not up to being interviewed by anyone right now."

"Figured that," Russ said. "She wanted to know how you were feeling. Told her all was well. How was it out there?"

"We're fast. The car's handling really well. I've got really a good feeling."

"Great," Russ stated. "I stashed Kellie and Charlie inside the hauler so I could get Eileen moving. They're waiting for you."

Hart nodded. "Thanks. It's a bummer she showed up. I wanted to show Charlie the car, but I don't want Eileen sniffing around. The last thing Kellie wants is for the media to think Charlie's a PR stunt. We'll have to bring him over later. Do we have some time tonight before the garage closes?"

"We should. Tomorrow you have an autograph session, but unless you're going to the condo you have tonight free and we can work whatever you want into the schedule. Your schedule's pretty clear since Cynthia did away with all but one of your sponsorship events. That's tomorrow at lunch."

"Make the time for this," Hart said. "It's important to me."

"So you're really interested in her?" Russ asked casually. He'd known Hart for about ten years now, having been assigned to the up-and-coming driver long ago. While technically an employee of Hampton Racing who reported to Cynthia, Russ considered Hart both his boss and his friend.

"Maybe," Hart admitted. "Just make sure Charlie can see the car up close."

"I will," Russ said, finding it interesting that Hart, who was used to everyone accommodating him and dancing to his tune, wanted to modify his weekend for the people waiting in the hauler.

Russ had watched Hart somewhat ignore his guests weekend after weekend, not because of rudeness, but basically because a driver's professional engagements always ranked first. Everything else was secondary. Sure, Hart would spend time with his guests, but only when he could slot them in.

Yet this weekend Hart had told both Russ and Cynthia that Charlie and Kellie were not to be left out or overlooked at any time.

Trouble was, Russ knew Hart was going to have to really sell himself to Kellie. Russ grinned as Hart entered the hauler. Had Hart ever had to woo a woman before? Ever since he'd started driving a stock car, women had thrown themselves at him. Hart had found most women to be too easy and too fast.

Maybe it was a good thing Kellie couldn't care less about Hart's fame. She was a woman who'd walk away, who wasn't with Hart for his celebrity. *If* she wanted Hart, it would be for himself, not who he was. And *if* she wanted him—well, that was one big *if*, Russ grinned to himself as he said hello to a crew member—Kellie would be a challenge, and the change just might do Hart a world of good.

CHAPTER SEVEN

"SORRY ABOUT that," Hart said to Kellie and Charlie as he entered the lounge. "Saw you standing there, but had to do the media thing first."

"It's fine." It was Charlie who answered.

Kellie, Hart noticed, was watching a commercial on the plasma screen and pretending to be immune to his presence. Hart grinned. He could tell she was aware of him as much as he was of her. "Well, I'm free until…" Hart glanced at Russ.

"Six-thirty," Russ filled in. He'd followed them to the front of the hauler.

"I thought qualifying was at seven-ten," Charlie said. He pointed to the schedule resting on the table.

"Russ always makes me leave ten minutes early, and in this case I still have to get into my uniform and out to the track. I'm going out seventh and I don't want to be late, which is a bad thing. Let's get out of here, shall we? I've only got a little under three hours and I don't want to spend them in here. Kellie?"

She rose, graceful in her jeans and short-sleeve sweater. Hart twitched slightly, as if the air conditioner had just emitted a large blast of air and given him a chill. Funny thing, no one else noticed. He had, though.

As he'd experienced the first time he'd seen her, he'd felt

something almost supernatural between them. For some reason, he found himself wanting to please her, and her son. He wanted to get to know her in all ways, and not just physically, which had been the full extent of most of Hart's previous relationships. With Kellie, he'd felt a deeper connection. It was as if fate had dictated that she was the one and hit Hart upside the head to let him know it.

"I've arranged for you both to get right up next to my car tonight before the garage closes. Immediately after qualifying. I want you to get to know my crew chief."

They stepped out into the warm May air, and Russ used his large frame like a bodyguard, parting the crowd to allow Hart, Charlie and Kellie to walk to where the golf cart was parked. Charlie coughed once, and Kellie stopped. So fast was her motion that Hart, who had been next to her, was almost three strides beyond before he realized she was gone. He immediately turned around and went back.

"Are you okay?" she was asking Charlie as he returned to her side.

"I'm fine, Mom," Charlie said. "I just lost my breath there for a moment. I caught some dust. It was nothing."

"Hart, you need to keep moving," Russ said.

Kellie glanced around, noticing that fans with garage passes were circling as they discovered they had Hart Hampton in their midst. Hart needed to get out of here, or he'd be signing autographs forever as the gate to the motor home lot was still some distance away. Already people had cameras out, snapping pictures.

"You're about to be ambushed. Go on," Kellie said. "Charlie and I will meet you there."

"No." The force of Hart's one uttered word surprised even him. "We're a group." He gazed down at Charlie. The boy looked maybe one hundred pounds, he was that small and thin. "Remember what it was like to do chicken races?"

Charlie smiled wistfully, his eyes hidden by the darkened lenses of his glasses. "Never did that."

"How about piggyback rides?" Hart said.

"Not since I was four." Charlie shook his head and something inside Hart snapped. This kid hadn't had a normal childhood. Hart's friends had given each other piggyback rides into their teens and often had hoisted each other onto their shoulders and wrestled in the family pool until someone fell off and splashed into the deep end.

"Well, cowboy up," Hart said. And that was how they proceeded to the motor home lot, with Charlie riding Hart's back, his legs around Hart's waist and his thin arms tightly wrapped around Hart's neck. All around people could be heard calling Hart's name and cheering. His hands full holding Charlie's legs, Hart ignored them and strode quickly to the gate, Charlie's bony frame bouncing into the small of Hart's back as if it were the most natural movement in the world.

As the security guard allowed them through the chain-link fencing, Kellie felt a mixture of both relief and agitation. In the garage area, fans had been thick, searching for their favorite driver. She hadn't realized that a trek from the hauler to the motor home lot could be so involved. She was totally over her head here, especially as her son's laughter reached her ears. Hart had ignored the golf cart she and Russ were in and was almost running as he trotted the last thirty feet before reaching the motor home, Charlie laughing with the thrill of it all.

"You've got it from here," Russ said. He touched the bill of his cap with his forefinger, parked the cart and walked back to the garage.

"That was great!" Charlie said as Hart set him down next to the motor home door. Charlie doubled over slightly, catching his breath.

"I don't believe you haven't had one of those in a while. My friends and I used to race that way before they'd let us into cars," Hart said. He was in excellent shape, Kellie noted. He was barely winded, even after running with her son on his back.

The door on the motor home next to them opened, and a young boy stepped out. Ronnie McDougal's son?

"Hey, Stuart," Hart called.

"Hi, Hart," Stuart said. His brown eyes flickered over Charlie with avid interest.

"Come on over here. Got someone for you to meet. Stuart, this is Charlie Thompson. I think he's about your age. You're what? Fifteen?"

"Fourteen," Stuart said. "Won't be fifteen until July."

"Then you're about a year apart. Charlie's birthday is the end of June and he's pretty good at video games, from what I hear. Didn't you just get the latest…" Hart named the third installment of a popular video game series and Stuart's eyes lit up.

"Yeah, it's cool. You should play it. Even my dad likes it."

"I will sometime soon, but not now," Hart said. "But you could show it to Charlie."

"I'm actually headed over to Taylor's for a bit." Stuart shifted his weight and studied Charlie for a minute before he asked, "Want to come? We're going to be playing basketball but he's got four controllers so there's plenty to go around. We'll just play three-on-three."

"Yeah, thanks. I'd like that," Charlie said as he moved away with Stuart.

Kellie turned to Hart. She had no idea who Taylor was and

she prayed he did, especially as he was just letting her son wander off with a boy she'd just met. "When are they coming back?"

"Hey, Stu?"

"Yeah, Hart?" Stuart paused and turned back, Charlie at his side.

"Estimated time of return?" Hart asked.

Stuart grinned. "My mom's insisting on some family time tonight, so I'm to be back by six-fifteen. It's Betsy's birthday so after qualifying we're actually going home tonight."

"Sounds fine. Have Charlie back by then." Hart reached behind him and opened the door to his parents' motor home as the boys disappeared from sight. "Come on. You can yell at me inside," Hart said.

"I'm not going to yell at you," Kellie replied as she climbed the stairs, Hart right behind her.

But she was miffed. This man had totally taken over her life, making decisions without consulting her first. He wasn't Charlie's father, yet he'd made the decision of when to have Charlie return. That had always been her job. She opened her mouth and then closed it. No sense in arguing with Hart about this. Come Sunday, he'd be out of their lives. "So who are these people?" she asked.

"Betsy is Ronnie's youngest daughter. She'd about six, I think. Taylor is sixteen; I know that because he just got his license before Richmond and was showing everyone. He's one of the outreach minister's sons. He's a good kid."

Hart moved directly into the kitchen area, retrieving a diet soda and uncapping it. He handed her the plastic bottle before getting another for himself. He was as comfortable here as he was in his own motor home.

"So is everyone going home tonight?" Kellie asked, taking a seat on a stool. Her position put the breakfast bar between her and Hart.

"The teams are. Most everyone lives within an hour's drive, and when we're in Charlotte a lot of drivers like to spend the night in their own bed. Really, it comes down to whether a driver wants to commute or not. Some are just happier in their motor homes and don't want to break their routine. Me, it just depends on my mood."

"I can't keep up with all this," Kellie admitted. "It's very overwhelming."

"Sometimes I can't, either," Hart disclosed with a grin. "That's why I have Russ. I guess the only way to understand our lifestyle is to compare it a rock or country music star who's out on tour. We're on tour each weekend and home during the week. This race is different as we're back at this venue next weekend, so we're not hauling things back and forth and flying from one end of the country to the other. Families who don't travel to faraway places like California will be here in force. The chapel services will be packed next Sunday morning."

Kellie took a moment to absorb everything Hart was telling her. She knew next Sunday's six-hundred-mile race would start in the afternoon daylight and end under the raceway lights.

"You know, you should consider bringing Charlie back next weekend. I can make arrangements," Hart said casually.

"I noticed that there are some RVs out there that have seen better days," Kellie said in return, deliberately avoiding the subject.

"Not everyone is at the high-end motor home level, especially if you're a rookie just starting out. We've all been there," Hart said. "We're not what you think of us."

"I know," Kellie said. He was, well, wonderful. "I'm realizing that. You aren't at all like I expected."

"That's good, I hope," Hart said.

"Yes," Kellie admitted, smiling. "You're kind and generous. And carrying Charlie like that shows you care. I admit to having perhaps misjudged you. You're not so bad."

Hart laughed. "So you like me a little?" he teased.

"Maybe," she said. Then she sighed. "But even if I did, this weekend isn't easy for me. I don't want Charlie worn out. You heard him coughing out there. He could suffer a relapse. His fever could spike."

"What-ifs," Hart said. "You have to let those go, Kellie."

"What-ifs?" She tapped the side of the soda bottle with her forefinger.

"Yeah. What-ifs are like *because*." He alluded to their conversation the previous weekend. "What-ifs paralyze you. What if this happens? What if I crash? What if I lose my sponsors? What if I don't make the Chase this year? Think of those enough and you'll never get anything done."

"I have to be concerned. Charlie's delicate."

"And what's worse? Being so afraid to die that you don't live, or living whatever time you have to the fullest so that when your maker does come calling you've done all you wanted to do? You can't protect him forever. You have to let him make his own choices. He's almost sixteen."

She sputtered slightly on her cola. "Is that what this weekend is about, you trying to assuage some guilt somewhere?"

"No," Hart said. "I like your son. I like you. A great deal." He reached forward and stroked her cheek. Just a featherlight movement from her cheekbone to her chin, but the touch had her trembling. She turned away as embarrassment flared. She would not let Hart's touch or his philosophy affect her.

"See, you are unhappy with me," Hart said.

"No, I'm not," she said, focusing on her attention on the twenty-ounce plastic bottle in front of her. One little touch, probably irrelevant to the man who'd just made it, had shaken her to her core. That tiny movement had exposed a truth Kellie had buried deep. She'd turned off a part of herself—the woman inside who loved. While she didn't need a man, there was still a part of her that desired male companionship. She wanted someone in her life who understood. Someone who would share her burdens and act as a foil to when she was being overprotective. Her other half.

She'd shut away a part of her heart, like locking a room and never allowing the door to be opened. Fate had to be laughing at her. Who would have thought that the person to chink her armor would be Hart Hampton, perennial ladies' man, a man with all the staying power of dish soap? A man she'd joked about for years. Yet Hart was a man who had reawakened her with a simple touch. He might just be everything she'd always wanted. Minus the fact that he was a race car driver. The thought was downright mind-boggling and scary.

"What are you thinking if you aren't mad at me?" Hart asked.

Kellie grasped onto the first thing she could think of. "Charlie's sick, Hart. He has tons left he wants to do, and this is a disease that can move like lightning. I'm not being overprotective for no reason."

"I didn't say you were," Hart said. "You're probably one of the most devoted mothers I've ever met. I admire you for that. My mom, she hated my foray into racing. Remember, it wasn't as safe as it is now. When my dad started, there were no HANS devices or SAFER Barriers. She lived with fear every weekend and never could get past it. She's a lot happier now that my dad retired. Me, I learned that you can't let fear consume you. You worry, yes, but you don't allow fear to grip you like a vise."

Why did Hart make so much sense? Kellie sighed and tried to make him understand. "As the years went on, it's become more evident that Charlie is one of the ones who isn't going to be cured," she said simply. "Half of the people with his condition go into remission and live normal lives. He's not in the lucky half."

"Half the guys out there on the track won't win a race this season. They won't even finish in the top ten, either," Hart said. "They don't let it diminish their love for the sport, or for their life."

"Are you always a glass half-full person?" Kellie asked, turning to fully face him.

"If it means balancing out your glass half-empty, then absolutely," Hart said, letting loose that trademark grin just for her.

Irritated with her reaction to his smile, she snapped, "I don't need anyone to balance me out."

Hart came around the high countertop so that he was a foot away from her. She'd sat in the farthest barstool from the wall, so nothing impeded him from totally entering her space, which he did.

"Kellie, you need so much balance it isn't funny," Hart said. "I have a suspicion that you've been off-kilter for quite a while now."

"I'm only off-kilter because you're crowding me," she shot back, struggling for the last fragments of control. He made her want to throw open that door to the hidden room in her heart. "My life was fine until I met you. Charlie and I were fine."

"You were merely existing," Hart observed. "As I think I was." He seemed genuinely surprised by that, as if he'd had a revelation. For a moment, he appeared a tad unsure of himself. He leaned closer. "This isn't a game, Kellie Thompson."

"I'm not playing one," she replied. "If anyone is, it's you. You've brought me and my son here just because...oh, I don't know why."

"You know why, which is the reason you're keeping me at arm's length."

"How can that be? You're six inches away," she said, her heart racing from his proximity.

"You know what I mean," Hart replied. "I'm not a joke. Stop holding out when I'm here."

Kellie's breath caught in her throat. No. Charlie couldn't have told Hart. He'd promised he wouldn't expose her like this.

"Charlie didn't tell me," Hart said quickly, reading her mind. "Brad Muldoon did. At camp."

Kellie felt embarrassed tears threaten to rain down. He knew about the family joke. Since camp. He'd known when he'd asked her here. Oh, dear God. She bit her lip as mortification washed over her. "You weren't supposed to find out. It's nothing serious. Is that why I'm here? Are you're paying me back?"

"No. That's not the reason. Not at all. I don't have time for silliness. I want to get to know you. The real you. If you like me, even a little, it's for the real me. For myself. Not for my image."

She didn't believe him. "You can't be serious about wanting me..."

Her next words were swallowed when Hart's lips came down on hers. The kiss was gentle and sweet, designed more to reassure and value than prove any type of domination. He slid his hand behind her head and into her hair, tilting her face up so that he could deepen the kiss, one that Kellie lost herself in.

Until she found her senses.

Hart recognized that moment, for he drew back and pulled

away as if she'd voiced her rejection. "Despite what you may think of me, I do not kiss every girl I meet," he said defensively.

"I know," she said. There had been something in that kiss that had simply been so pure and magical. Not mass-produced. Not forced. Almost as if two souls had found each other after a long absence.

The sensation scared the life out of her. Hart Hampton might have just told her he wasn't a joke, but that's what he'd always been. Yet he'd just kissed her. No way could this fantasy become real. She wasn't Cinderella. These days Cinderella saved herself and didn't have illusions about princes. This had to simply be some dream, some aberration of the moment that would all become nothing after a little time and perspective. Sunday, she'd fly home and...

Hart put both of his hands on hers. He gazed at her, those green eyes flickering in the light as he assessed her. "You are a paradox, Kellie. When I see something I want, I don't let fear stop me."

"I…" She stopped and shook her head. He couldn't want her, and even if he did, Hart traded women every few months. No matter what he said about fear, smart women didn't walk through minefields just to prove they weren't afraid. "This is too fast. Too sudden. I'm not one of those weekend women."

He shook his head and laughed, his tone incredulous. "Heck, no. You wouldn't be here if I thought that." He tenderly stroked her cheek. "As for moving too fast, we'll slow down. How about we get out of here tonight? Go to a little hole-in-the-wall I know of that has authentic Italian food. Get to know each other."

"Charlie," she said, reminding him of her son.

"Is coming, too," Hart said, without missing a beat. "This weekend is not just about you and me. You and Charlie are a package. While I want some time alone with you, I'm not asking for that at his expense."

"I don't know if being alone with you is wise," Kellie said, weakening. She'd been impressed with what Hart had just said. He'd wanted Charlie, too.

"We'll cross each bridge as we come to it. No hurries. No pressures," Hart said. He brushed a loose strand of hair off her face, the motion caring and intimate. Kellie's skin heated. Why had she said yes? She couldn't resist this man. Maybe she'd been off the dating scene too long. Maybe…

His lips lowered, and the trill of her cell phone sounding from the front of her jeans pocket was the only thing that stopped him from kissing her again. Hart stepped away and Kellie stood, digging out her phone. "It's Charlie," she said, recognizing the ring tone. "Hello?"

"Hi, Mom. Taylor's mom said he had some chores to do, so I'm on my way back with Stuart. I brought some anime in my suitcase, so we're coming in to get those. You know, just wanted to warn you."

In case you were busy with Hart. He didn't have to say it, but Kellie knew that's why he was calling. Her son had a maturity to him that was frightening, and a strong wish that his mother was doing something with Hart—which she wasn't. Only a kiss. That didn't count, she lied to herself. "Hart and I are talking in the kitchen. We're thinking of going out to dinner after he qualifies. How about that?"

"Sounds good," Charlie said. "See you in a few." He hung up and Kellie pressed the button ending the call. She set the phone on the counter.

"That's pretty ancient," Hart said, indicating her cell.

"Yeah. It's like a lot of things. I refuse to pay for a phone, so I'll upgrade when I'm eligible in another two months. I don't do any of that multimedia stuff, so we just have the cheapest family plan. My mom got it for us."

"So what was Charlie calling about?" Hart asked.

"He and Stuart are on their way back here. Charlie's got some anime magazines that he wants to share. They're in his suitcase."

Hart glanced at his watch. The motor home was pretty insulated, but every now and then the roar of engines could be heard as a truck sped by on one of its two qualifying laps. "How much time do you have?" Kellie asked.

"About an hour," Hart said.

The door opened and Charlie and Stuart bounded in, followed by a woman carrying a baby. "Hey, Alyssa," Hart said.

"Hart, these guys aren't going to bother you, are they? I've just got a busload of people over there. Since it's Betsy's birthday, everyone's here." She stood on the steps, the baby waving her fists and sucking on a pacifier as she took everything in.

"They're fine," Kellie said, moving forward before Hart could speak. "I'm Kellie, Charlie's mother."

"Nice to meet you. Alyssa McDougal, temporarily insane wife of Ronnie. And this is my ten-month-old daughter. What was I thinking doing a birthday party right after qualifying? And Ronnie's over there trying to take a quick nap. It's a good thing he can sleep through just about anything."

Kellie shook Alyssa's hand. Alyssa appeared to be in her late thirties. Her curly hair was cropped short and she appeared stressed. "Stuart's welcome to stay as long as you like," Kellie said. The boys were already out of sight, having gone into the back bedroom to dig into Charlie's suitcase.

"That'd be a lifesaver," Alyssa said. "You'd be amazed how one less kid in the mix makes the craziness lessen. This way, he and Betsy won't fight. Five TVs over there, and they fight over one. Just send him back sometime before six-thirty."

"Will do," Kellie said. With that, Alyssa left.

"That's going to win you tons of brownie points," Hart said.

"I didn't do it for points," Kellie said, frowning.

"She knows that," Hart said. "You're a mother and you understood. That'll go a long way with Alyssa. Don't be surprised if she takes you under her wing."

"I'm not going to be around long enough for that," Kellie said skeptically.

Hart simply arched an eyebrow at her, reached for a remote control and flipped the television on. "What do you want to watch?"

The satellite station was tuned to an old Julia Roberts and Richard Gere movie. "That's fine," she said, as Hart settled himself onto the couch. "An oldie but a goodie."

"Just so you know, you won't scare me off with a chick flick," Hart said.

"Wasn't trying," Kellie replied.

"Uh-huh," Hart said as he settled in. While quality time really wasn't watching a classic movie, the fact that Hart would rather be with her than in his own motor home spoke volumes. Kellie curled up her legs, safe on her own cushion a foot away from his. He smiled at her movements, but didn't comment.

As for Kellie, like the character in the movie, she'd entered a totally different world. Of course, she wasn't being paid anything, but Kellie still felt slightly like Alice dropping into Wonderland. She had no idea what would happen next. She had butterflies in her stomach. But she couldn't let herself go.

Whatever these feelings were, surely they would fade. Charlie had tests scheduled next week, and she'd worry about those the minute they returned to Myrtle Beach.

But for now, she forced herself to relax and enjoy Hart's company. As the movie played, a rare sense of comfort and normalcy settled over Kellie. This weekend, if only for a short time, she would let herself loose in the fantasy of Hart. Then she'd go home, savoring the memories. She took a sip of the diet cola she'd carried over with her. He'd kissed her. Sweetly. Maybe...

Kellie pushed those dreams from her head. This was a vacation. An aberration. No matter how much she was suddenly wishing otherwise, the clock was ticking. Come Sunday, reality time.

CHAPTER EIGHT

SHE'D NEVER SEEN anything like qualifying. Since Hart already had a spot in the Challenge, his qualifying would involve three laps—instead of the regular two—with a four-tire-change pit stop. She and Charlie followed Hart's team as they pushed the car to pit road, leaving Hart behind to change into his race gear. The entire event was scheduled to last approximately forty-five minutes, and Hart would go out seventh. Ronnie McDougal was up first.

"How are you liking it so far?" Russ asked as he came up behind them. He sat down on the pit road wall and gestured. "Take a load off. It'll be a while."

Kellie glanced around. The cars were lined up, and people walked up and down in between. She recognized other drivers because they were already in their uniforms, most of them unzipped and folded down at the waist.

"Mom, that's Kyle Doolittle," Charlie said, pointing. "And next to him is Dusty Burke."

Kellie glanced over. Indeed, the front-runner for rookie of the year and the former NASCAR NEXTEL Cup champion were standing just about ten feet over, deep in their own conversation. When reporters approached, the drivers paused, answered questions, and then resumed their conversation once the reporters moved on. "I don't know how they can get used to that. I can't imagine being in that situation," Kellie said.

"If you hang around, I'll give you some PR training," Russ said.

"That's sweet of you for offering, but we're leaving Sunday." Kellie reached into her pocket and drew out two pairs of earplugs. She handed a set to Charlie before putting in her own. Qualifying went quickly. Charlie and Kellie stood at the entrance to pit road as Hart pulled out, then they moved to get a better view of his pit stop. By the end of his qualifying run, they'd walked to the entrance of pit road, where Hart came back in after posting the second-fastest time. He parked the car, took off his helmet, detached his steering wheel and climbed out. Only the NASCAR officials stood on the track by his car. Charlie used his digital camera and snapped a few pictures.

"Hey Hart! Pretty good!" Charlie said, reaching up to give Hart a high five once he'd climbed over the pit road wall.

"Thanks," Hart said. "Walk with me. I want to get out of this uniform and I can't strip it off out here."

"What about the car?" Charlie asked as they left it on the pit road.

"The team will retrieve it and roll it back to the garage," Hart said easily. He'd donned a baseball cap of his sponsor. Since pit road was closed to only those with proper hot passes, no fans impeded their way.

They'd almost reached the garage when a woman holding a microphone stepped in front of Hart. Kellie recognized her from earlier. "Hart, how are you feeling?" Eileen Swikle asked.

"Great. I just had a fantastic run. I'm sitting in second position so far," Hart answered. He'd slowed his pace, but hadn't stopped.

"So your weekend at camp was refreshing?" she persisted, moving with him. Kellie and Charlie wisely fell a step behind.

"Absolutely refreshing. Did you see I'm holding the second-fastest time?"

"Yes, I did," she said, a little frustrated that Hart wasn't giving her the information she fished for. As they made a turn toward the hauler, Eileen Swikle caught a glimpse of Charlie and Kellie. She eyed Charlie's Hampton Racing hat. "Are these the friends you met at camp? Are you two the ones Russ and Cynthia were talking about earlier?" she asked, approaching Kellie and Charlie. "Hi. I'm Eileen Swikle. Besides working for the network, I also host a show called *Inside Groove*. So you met Hart at camp?"

Kellie glanced at Hart for help, and saw him glance down pit road for Russ. Russ saw them and began to jog their direction.

"Hart was kind enough to invite me to watch him race. I'm extremely grateful that he's provided me and my mother with this amazing opportunity," Charlie said.

Kellie blinked and stared at Charlie. Hart had stopped a few feet away, and Kellie exchanged a glance with him.

"So Hart invited you here?" Eileen asked.

"Yes," Charlie said. His glasses hid his eyes, as the lenses had once again darkened. "When we met during a session at camp, he asked me if I wanted to come to a race."

"That is so sweet," Eileen said.

"It is. I have acute myelogenous leukemia, and Hart has been very generous in extending this offer. He and all of Hampton Racing have been fantastic. Now if you don't mind, I need to stop by the medical center for a quick blood pressure test."

"Oh, of course. Thank you," Eileen said, looking delighted with her scoop.

"Hey, Eileen. Can I help you?" Russ asked as he came up to the group.

"I'm good."

"Let's go," Kellie said. She dropped her arm on her son's shoulders and drew him away as Eileen moved on to the next qualifier. Russ shielded them the rest of the way. Hart, seeing Russ had them, had gone into the garage.

"Great answer, Charlie," Hart complimented him as Kellie and Charlie caught up with him at the garage. "I heard most of it."

"Thought a version of the truth might work best," Charlie said with a grin.

Hart laughed. "Not only would you make a good journalist, but you could maybe give Russ a run for his money. Who knows how Eileen will spin all this on Monday? You'll have to tune in. Or better yet, we'll make Russ do it and send you a tape."

"Will do," Russ said.

Cynthia was waiting at the hauler. "Nice run. You're still holding second."

Automatically they all glanced at the scoring pylon, where Hart's Number 413 remained second from the top. "Thanks," Hart said. "Now, if you don't mind, we're all going out to dinner just as soon as I get a shower. Cynthia, can I take the Suburban?"

"That's fine. Liam and I aren't leaving, and we brought our car should we change our minds," his aunt said.

"Good." Hart glanced at Kellie and Charlie. "How about I meet you at your motor home in a half hour? Pick you up then? What you're wearing is fine. This place has the best food, but it's nothing fancy."

"Giancarlo's?" Cynthia asked.

"Yep," Hart confirmed.

"Oh, their bread is heavenly. Made on-site," Cynthia told Kellie. "I love that place. We found it when we all first moved here. You'll be eating better than I will tonight. They beat any catered food hands down."

Russ and Charlie were talking about Eileen Swikle, and Kellie nodded at Hart. "A half hour's fine. I figured you might need to talk to Wally." The time would also let her change into fresh clothes. She was starting to feel a little grimy from being out in the pit.

Hart winced suddenly.

"What?" she asked.

"I wanted Charlie to see the car tonight and have Wally explain how we set it up. If we go to dinner…"

Kellie reached out and touched Hart's arm. All she could feel was the texture of Hart's uniform, but her touch seemed to calm his agitation. "You've already done so much. We can do that tomorrow," she said simply.

"Once the garage opens, that can be arranged," Cynthia said.

"Then we'll see you in a half hour," Kellie told Hart. "Charlie, let's go." She and her son began walking toward the motor home lot, leaving Hart with his aunt as Russ disappeared inside the hauler.

"WHAT?" Hart asked, sensing Cynthia's scrutiny.

"She must be special if you're taking her to Giancarlo's. You never take anyone there."

"If I took Kellie to some of those upscale places the other women expect, she'd demand to leave. She's already thinking this is going too fast."

His uniform was starting to itch, and he wanted it off. The conversation was also a bit uncomfortable.

"So there's a *this?*" Cynthia prodded.

"I don't know," Hart said in exasperation. "I'm certainly not planning on a weekend fling, and neither is she."

"She's not the type," Cynthia observed.

"No, she's not," Hart said. "Which is just one of the things

I like about her. I asked her here next weekend and she turned me down."

"Smart woman," Cynthia teased. Seeing Hart's expression, she sobered. "Sorry."

"I don't know how I'm to get to know her if she won't come to the track. I have to be here. It's my job."

"So you do want to get to know her," Cynthia said, slightly surprised.

Hart exhaled. "Yes. Like beyond the preliminaries that lead to other things. Make what you want of it, but I told you last weekend that she's different. I want more."

If nothing else, the kiss had confirmed his determination to pursue a relationship with Kellie, but he refused to tell Cynthia. The kiss had seemed to make time stop, if that were possible. Whatever had happened when he'd kissed Kellie, the connection he'd experienced had blown him away. He didn't want one night. He wanted multiple. Long term. That kind of thing. The revelation should be scary, but Hart wasn't a man who feared much.

"Well, don't let me keep you," Cynthia said. "I've got to get back to the condo and to Liam. He's holding down the fort until I return. I just came over for the driver introductions."

The truck race would be starting soon, and Hart wanted to get out of the complex before that happened. He had other priorities.

SATURDAY WOULD BE a late day. Access to the haulers wasn't until one o'clock and the garage didn't open until two. The morning before a race Hart would sleep in as late as possible, and he didn't think that tomorrow would be an exception. Thus, after dinner, he took the risk of asking Kellie and Charlie if they'd like to see where he lived. He'd planned on showing them on Sunday, but found himself not wanting to wait.

Maybe it had been the cannelloni and the warm bread she'd eaten, but Kellie hadn't protested when Charlie had shouted his yes. Hart had been prepared with comeback arguments if she'd disagreed: if she'd said it was too late, he'd remind her she could sleep in. If she'd said Charlie was tired, he'd tell her that they were already more than halfway there, and her son could snooze on the way back to the track. But she hadn't said a word, only nodded her consent.

So here they were, beginning down the narrow, half-mile asphalt road that served as Hart's driveway. The road was almost impossible to find, and about halfway down it widened into a turnaround. Hart drove up to the gate, keyed in his code and soon was through. A little less than a quarter of a mile through the trees, the road made a sharp turn, and Hart's home was visible at the top of the clearing.

He'd called ahead to have all the lights turned on both inside and out, so the house sat like a welcome beacon against the night sky.

"Wow," Kellie said.

"Like it?" Hart was proud of the house. He'd designed it himself. When he'd found the property, the house his caretaker now lived in had been the only one already standing. Hart had added the office near that building and then, out of sight of both, he'd built his dream home. Unlike the often ostentatious, new construction that screamed money, Hart had worked with the architect so that the building gave off the feel of a large, centuries-old, rambling farmhouse. A wraparound porch framed three sides. A porch swing overlooked a large front lawn and an expansive wildflower garden.

The driveway curved around to the back of the house, and Hart parked in front of a four-car garage. The asphalt parking area was large enough for a number of parked cars side by side or his motor home. Once country star Beau Akers had visited for a few days during his tour.

Although Hart exited quickly, both Charlie and Kellie had climbed out before he could assist either of them, and he led them through a gate and onto an expansive back deck.

"This is nothing like I'd expected you to have," Kellie said. "Well, perhaps this part." She gestured to the in-ground pool just below the deck, and beyond that, a go-cart track.

"So can we go carting?" Charlie asked as Hart used his key and let them into the mudroom. He keyed in some numbers, turning off the beeping alarm system.

"Go-carting's up to your mom," Hart said, figuring he'd already pushed Kellie enough by bringing her here. She appeared a little shell-shocked as they walked past the laundry room and into the kitchen.

"If it were daylight, you could see the view," he told them, as they walked into the room. "I had all the windows specially tinted. I hate curtains, except in the bedrooms. I mean, why have windows if you cover them up?"

He took them on the guided tour, starting on the first floor, going up the front staircase to the second, and then down the back staircase two levels to the finished walkout basement. There a recreation room with gaming systems, a foosball table, a billiard table and a huge media area.

"It's a beautiful house," Kellie said. Although dozens of people had said the same thing, coming from Kellie the words were special. Hart knew her compliment was genuine. She wasn't trying to impress him or curry his favor.

"Hey, I've racked the balls. Who's up for a game?" Charlie asked. He stood by the billiard table, holding a pool cue he'd taken from the rack on the wall.

"I'm sitting this one out," Kellie said.

"I gotta warn you, Charlie, I'm pretty good," Hart announced.

Charlie laughed, his eyes twinkling behind his plastic frames. "I'll take my chances," he said. "You can break."

Hart grabbed his favorite cue and chalked it. "Okay. Kellie, there's some colas and things in the bar fridge. Help yourself."

"I'd like one, Mom," Charlie said. "Please."

Hart leaned down, broke and sank a ball. "Stripes." He sank one more before he missed and Charlie stepped up. And proceeded to clear the table.

"Okay, I've been hustled," Hart stated, reaching over to tap Charlie on the bill of his ball cap.

"This is one of the few things my mom lets me do," Charlie said with a wide grin. "She went to high school with the owners of the local billiard club and I can go in there during the day when it's not busy. I also like to bowl. My highest game was a two-eighty."

"I don't think I've ever gotten higher than one-eighty," Hart said, impressed. "Rack them up and we'll go again. I'm not going to go easy on you this time."

"Yeah, right," Charlie replied, laughing. "Bring it on."

They began to play, and as they'd tuned the TV to the truck race, Hart occasionally glanced across the room at the giant screen. However, racing didn't provide much of a distraction. Instead, Hart focused on stepping up his billiard game, refusing to allow Charlie another blowout. As Hart leaned over to take a shot, he was fully aware that he was giving Kellie a view of his backside. He grinned, and sank the solid he'd been aiming for before straightening and asking her, "Sure you don't want to play?"

"No," she said simply and Hart could see that she didn't feel left out at all. Rather, she was comfortable in her role as an observer. He found himself slightly irritated. Kellie watched life from the sidelines. He wanted her in the action. While go-carting wasn't an area to push, this was. He decided to shake her out of her shell.

"Nah," Hart stated. "Not acceptable. Come on, I'll teach you."

"She needs it," Charlie said. "I'll sit this one out. I want to call Grandma and see if she's watching the race." He pulled his cell out of his pocket, wandered over to the television and sat down on the sofa. All that was visible was the top of his head.

"Come on, scaredy-cat," Hart teased. He racked the balls again, removing the triangle and hanging it on a peg. "Break." He reached on the wall, selected a cue stick for her, and approached where she was sitting on the barstool. "Time's up."

To her credit, she grabbed the stick. "I'll have you know I'm terrible at this. It's all geometry, and unlike Charlie, I'm not good at math."

"Of course not, you're an English teacher." Hart snickered when she shot him the "look." She then bent down, aimed, and hit the cue ball on the side, sending it awkwardly down the table. The hit dislodged two balls maybe an inch.

"Told you."

"Let's try it again," Hart said, unperturbed at her inadequate billiard skills. Most women tried to impress him or used the opportunity to be coy and flirt. But not Kellie. He took the triangle back down and set the balls back up. Then he came around to the end of the table. "First, you need to stand like this."

He stepped behind her, putting his hands lightly on her and moving her into proper position. "That's better. Now bend over like this."

He leaned with her, his right arm wrapped almost across her body. His left hand moved her fingers, placing them up so that the cue stick could easily glide across her thumb. His right hand rested on her forearm, and he drew her arm back and forth, showing her how to slide the stick. "Now you'll need to put some force behind it. That's right. Like this." He guided her arm, giving her the example.

Then he stepped away. Touching her had done something to his equilibrium, and he needed some space to get his body back under control. She drew back and fired off her shot. The balls cracked, and she sunk one.

"I got one!" She seemed quite incredulous and happy, and at that moment Hart wanted nothing more than to kiss her again. Charlie, just the top of his head visible, wouldn't see anything; heck, he'd probably approve. Still, Hart refrained. If he kissed Kellie, he wouldn't want to stop. In fact, here he was on a Friday night, at home, enjoying himself more than he had in years or when this place had been filled with tons of partying people. He had a sudden vision of many nights like this: Kellie and Charlie in his house, him flirting with her before Charlie went off to bed and they…well…they…

"Great job," he told her, giving her a high five as he tried to tamp down his steamrolling emotions. She already thought they were moving too fast, and he'd just pictured her moving in.

Now he understood the other part of what his dad had always said—while you might know exactly what you wanted right away, sometimes you didn't get it immediately. Patience wasn't a virtue, but torture. "Let's make another shot."

He walked her through how to pick out the next shot. Then, fate help him, he wrapped her body around his and showed her how to make the next one before he stopped, his body needing the distance. She sank the shot, and he swore her eyes flashed triumphantly as she straightened. She'd come alive, and he reveled in it, continuing to teach her until he'd brought her to the point where he only had to point to where to hit the cue ball for her to sink one.

"I need to check on Charlie," Kellie said. He'd finished his phone call a while ago. Hart followed Kellie over to the sofa, where they found Charlie sound asleep.

"We need to get back," she said.

"Do you want to just stay here?" Hart asked. "I've slept on that sofa many times. I can get him some blankets."

"He has nightly medicine he needs to take when we get back to the track. I didn't bring it with me, since I didn't think we'd be out this late. He usually takes it at bedtime."

Hart could see her withdrawing into herself, as if inwardly blaming herself for failing in Charlie's care. He refused to let her do that. "It's fine. We can go back. Do you want to wake him up or just have me carry him?"

Kellie chewed on her lip for a moment. "You could probably just carry him."

"Then let me go and turn off the lights. We'll go out from down here. I can set the alarm via remote."

Within minutes, they were on their way back to the track, Charlie asleep in the back captain's seat.

"Stop berating yourself," Hart said.

"I can't help it. He wears out so easily," Kellie replied. "He didn't feel warm, so that's a very good sign."

"What do the fevers mean?" Hart asked.

"They mean he's caught some infection. His cells don't function like normal cells. Germs you and I don't even notice can turn into something major for him. We fight anemia. He bruises and bleeds easy because of a shortage of platelets. His white cells don't fight infections, and there aren't enough of them, either."

"How is all this treated?" Hart asked.

"Blood and platelet transfusions. Chemo. This next treatment hopes to take his few healthy white cells and multiply them."

"I don't quite get it," Hart said honestly.

"It's so complicated. In the simplest terms, most of his white blood cells are immature. They don't work. So not only does he not have enough cells, but the ones he has are useless."

"Oh," Hart said. Traffic was light heading to the race track and heavy going away from it as fans left after the truck race finished. He reached over and touched Kellie's hand. "You've been through a lot. Thanks for letting me give him this weekend."

She sighed. "We both needed it. Sometimes everything looks so positive. The tests come back with no malignant cells and then, boom! Two weeks later, we're worse off than where we started. I don't want to lose him. He's all I've got."

"No," Hart said, tightening his grip. "From here on out, you have me, too."

CHAPTER NINE

FROM HERE ON OUT, you have me, too.

The words echoed in Kellie's head as she finally tucked herself into bed that night. Once they'd arrived back at the track, Charlie had woken up enough to take his medicine and change into sweats and a T-shirt. Then he'd crawled into the side bunk, pulled the curtain closed and drifted back to sleep.

Kellie had walked back out into the living area and stared out the window. While she had a clear view, she could only see the faint glow coming from inside Hart's motor home since his windows were tinted. On the other side of her, the McDougals' motor home sat empty and dark. Even the track was quiet, the security lights providing a halo effect. A hush had fallen over the motor home lot and the infield fan camping areas, the only sounds coming from generators and the occasional insect.

Kellie went to the back of the motor home and turned down the queen-size comforter. Even though the race didn't start until seven-thirty, the next day promised to have some busy moments. She climbed into the comfortable bed and pulled the covers up to her chin. Then she clicked off the light, her eyes trying to adjust to the darkness.

Hart Hampton had said she had him. He'd kissed her. Touched her. Made her want things she didn't have time to think about. She'd found herself laughing tonight, a sound often missing in her repertoire. She'd enjoyed playing pool, reveled in Hart's flirtation as he'd assisted her with her shots. Hart had made her feel alive—and she'd let go and enjoyed herself. She rolled onto her side, long accustomed to having a big bed all to herself.

She'd cling to the memories of this weekend forever.

Her husband had once laughed and called Kellie meticulous to a fault. "You always plan life," he'd said. "You can't plan anything. Take what you can get, that's my attitude."

His lackadaisical attitude had gotten him killed.

Now she'd become involved with Hart, a man who also lived his life without fear, even if he did have a healthy respect for it. Tonight she'd lost herself in the fantasy he'd created. His house was a perfect example. She'd expected something huge and overdone; instead, it had been subtle, the racing memorabilia kept to a minimum as he'd told her most of that was at his office.

He had a lovely house, one so homey she could picture herself living there. His words hadn't helped dissuade her. "When I'm here, I don't want reminders of who I am. I just want to be me," he'd said.

So had she misjudged him? Could Hart Hampton, celebrity, coexist with Hart Hampton, the man who had tenderly carried her son? Could they inhabit the same body, and if so, could he set his love of racing aside to love a family? In her gut, Kellie knew Hart was trustworthy. However, her heart wasn't ready to believe he was serious. And she had no time for anything else.

THE MCDOUGALS arrived back at the track a little before noon, and Stuart immediately came over and grabbed Charlie. He also arrived carrying an apple pie, something his mother sent over as a thank-you.

"She's planning on coming over a little later," Stuart told Kellie before he and Charlie left for Taylor's. "She wants to know where you're watching the race tonight. Dad's pit is right next to Hart's."

Kellie had no idea why that mattered, but nodded. While it had taken her a little while to fall asleep, once she had she'd slept until almost nine, getting in a good ten hours of shut eye. She'd checked Charlie's temperature, and he'd been fine. His skin color had been good, and he'd insisted he didn't want to visit the infield care center. She'd seen Hart briefly around eleven and he'd told her if she was concerned, he could call his personal physician and have the doctor at the track within an hour. That had reassured her. Then Russ had arrived to take Hart to a sponsorship luncheon. She'd declined going, and now that Charlie was off at a friend's house, she suddenly had the afternoon free.

She took a moment to call her mother, leaving Anita a voice mail that all was fine and that everyone was having a good time. Then Kellie simply sat down and turned on the television, finding a great movie that she'd never seen on one of the satellite channels. Just to treat herself, she even microwaved some popcorn, having found some in a pantry. She hadn't eaten any apple pie yet, deciding to wait for Hart.

"Knock knock," a female voice called. The movie had ended twenty minutes ago, and Kellie had been watching previews as she waited for the next one to start. She called back, "Come in," and Alyssa McDougal came up the stairs and into the motor home.

"Hey, I came to make sure Stu gave you the pie and to personally thank you again for letting him hang out here last night," Alyssa said, taking a seat.

"Not a problem," Kellie said. "You didn't really have to send a pie."

"Oh, yes I did. I love to bake, especially when I'm stressed. I made that, one apple upside-down cake and Betsy's birthday cake." Alyssa patted her hips before taking a seat. "I certainly don't need to eat what I make."

"You aren't fat," Kellie told her. Alyssa had a few extra pounds on her, but she certainly wasn't obese by any means. Far from it.

"No, but I'm not skinny, either," Alyssa said with a regretful smile. "I'll never compete again with some of those young rookie girlfriends who would blow away in a harsh wind. I was that way, long ago in another lifetime."

"Me, too," Kellie said with a laugh. "Besides, you just had a baby."

"Yeah, ten months ago. The last one, I told Ronnie. We seem to keep spacing them five to seven years apart. Stuart's actually my second. I have one in college, as well. She's doing an internship in L.A. this summer."

"How long have you two been married?"

"Twenty-three years. He walked into my daddy's car dealership looking for a sponsorship and that was that. I knew I was getting a race car driver, but love's like that. When the heart leads, you take them no matter what they do for a living," Alyssa said.

"He's doing well, though, isn't he? Your husband? My son follows NASCAR avidly."

"Oh, Ronnie should make the Chase. He's pretty consistent. The pressure's off, in a sense, in that he's won one NASCAR NEXTEL Cup Championship. While he'd love another, some guys go their whole careers without, and Ronnie's one of those who are grateful for what they have and not despondent over what they don't. He's in his forties and probably will start cutting back soon. He's been at this forever, and he's going to be a co-owner of his own Busch Series team next year."

"That's a good attitude," Kellie said.

"Hart's like that, too, which is why Ronnie's been a mentor to him. They're actually pretty close friends, despite the thirteen-year age difference. The only disagreement they have is my husband's a Ford man and Hart's a Chevy."

"I never did understand that," Kellie said with a shake of her head. "To me, it's just a car."

"Or truck. I guess it's a guy thing." Alyssa laughed and checked her watch. "My mother-in-law's over there with the baby, but I don't want to leave her too long. What are you doing tonight?"

"Watching the race?" Kellie said, wondering for a second if this was a trick question. Not that Alyssa seemed like the type.

"No, I meant, from where? Will you be up on the pit box with Charlie?"

Now Kellie understood, and she had no idea. "I'm not really sure. Hart hasn't mentioned how this is going to work. But I don't think so. He hasn't mentioned anything about it. Why, should I?"

"Some wives and girlfriends are always in the pit. They like to be a member of the team, doing things like monitoring fuel use. Others wait in the motor home and watch the race on television. You know who they are because they're impeccably dressed at the end of the race."

"What do you do?" Kellie asked.

"When I first met Ronnie, I used to be on the pit box, but that seems like a lifetime ago. While there's infield babysitting, I'm usually at home in Charlotte with the little ones, especially the night races when I want bedtimes to stay somewhat normal. I don't go to as many races as I used to. But when I do, I'm watching in the motor home and I wanted to invite you over to join me. Dress code business casual. Nice pants, nice shirt, just in case they win. Nothing fancy. No dressing to the nines allowed. You can meet a few other wives. And my mother-in-law."

"Let me check with Hart," Kellie said, touched by the offer. "Although, I mean, we're not dating," she added quickly. "I'm just here because of my son. He's the real guest. This will probably be the only race I attend this year, and I'd hate to intrude."

"You won't be. I'd love to have you. It's a fun time, and you'll meet some good people. If Hart or Cynthia don't have anything better for you, come on over."

"Thanks. I can't tell you how much this means to me," Kellie said. The offer was sweet and generous, especially when made to someone who wouldn't be around again.

"Well, I hope to see you tonight," Alyssa said, her expression welcoming. "I'd better get going. My door is always open. Just come on over anytime after driver introductions. I'll be back by then. You know, you should ask Hart if you need to be there for those. Oh, and don't worry about bringing anything. I have everything covered."

With that, Alyssa rose to her feet and left. Kellie leaned back against the sofa, letting contented lethargy steal over her. She hadn't been this relaxed since, well, she couldn't remember when. She closed her eyes, allowing her body to sink further into the soft leather.

"You look comfortable," a voice said. Kellie felt a rustle next to her and opened her eyes as Hart sat down next to her.

"Was comfortable," she said, a bit disoriented from being jolted out of her nap. He'd crept up on her.

"Ah, she missed me," Hart teased. "And here I was thinking of you and even bringing you back some food."

Kellie's stomach growled as if on cue. She'd only had the popcorn, hours ago. On the coffee table in front of her were two plates covered with aluminum foil. Curiosity won. "What's in there?"

"One's a piece of chocolate cake, which my aunt said was fantastic. The other's some fresh fruit, assorted cheeses, and some veggies and dip. Oh, and some roast beef sandwiches on dollar rolls." Kellie's stomach rumbled again. "Didn't eat, did you?" Hart teased.

"I had some popcorn," she said in her defense. "Charlie went off somewhere with Stuart and I've been relaxing all day. That is, until you came in."

And disturbed her equilibrium. Not only was she hungry, but she was also highly aware of Hart Hampton. He wore a kelly-green polo shirt with Elementals Racing embroidered above his heart. This close up, she could tell that he smelled good, too, all freshly shaved, with a hint of crisp musk. His lips were close to hers, those green eyes of his hypnotic. Bringing her food was grand and spoke volumes.

He leaned over slightly, bending his lips to take hers in a gentle kiss. His touch was soft and supple, and Kellie allowed herself to be swept away as he deepened the kiss. Their second kiss, Kellie thought hazily as the thoughts in her head began to scatter. A second kiss meant that the first one wasn't a fluke. Maybe he really was interested in her as a woman beyond Sunday's deadline. For the moment, Kellie believed, and she allowed herself to touch Hart's face, feeling his jawbone with her thumb and his cheeks with her fingertips.

Then her stomach whined, louder than before, and Hart drew back, laughing as he pushed a plate of food toward her. "I know a woman's priorities. Eat."

But even though he'd made light of the moment, Kellie had sensed something different in his expression, hidden there in the darkening of his green eyes and hinted at in the flicker of his eyelashes.

She uncovered the plates, reaching for a carrot stick. While she'd love to indulge in the cake, habit and good nutrition had her eating the veggies and fruit first and saving the sweets until last. Hart, however, wasn't so patient and picked up a fork, dipped it in the cake and waved the bite at her. "This is the good stuff," he said.

No, he was the good stuff, Kellie thought as her mouth closed on the cake he'd pushed toward her. Hart reached over and brushed a crumb off her lips, the gesture intimate and familiar. "So was I right?"

He'd been right about a lot, and the armor Kellie shielded herself with cracked. If nothing else, she'd leave this weekend with a new sense of self, that maybe she needed to get back out there in the world of dating, at least take a baby step or two. "You were right," Kellie said. "Thank you. I…"

"So you like me a little more?"

"Just a bit," Kellie teased to make the moment light, holding her thumb and forefinger about an inch apart.

"Really?" Hart stepped closer, into kissing range.

"Hart, you in there?" Kellie recognized Russ's voice.

"Yeah, I'm here," Hart said, standing and moving toward the door, the tender moment ending.

"You're late for the autographing session for the season ticket holders," Russ called.

Hart rolled his eyes. "Come with?" he asked, holding his hand out.

"Charlie?"

"Will be fine if you're not here. I'll call Alyssa's cell on the way, and she'll keep him over there. If you've never seen one of these, it's an experience. You can bring your food."

Kellie glanced down. She wore jeans and a seafoam green scooped T-shirt. She and Hart were almost twins in their choice of top/bottom colors. "Okay," she said, covering the plates of food and stacking the cake on top of the veggies. She slid into her tennis shoes. "I guess I'm ready."

The day was unusually hot for a North Carolina May, and Russ was waiting outside the door with Hart's four-seater golf cart. Kellie slid in the back seat, balancing her food on her plate and grateful the cart had a hard plastic roof as she'd forgotten to bring Hart's spare sunglasses. Seated in front next to Russ, Hart took out his cell phone and dialed Alyssa. As Russ whipped through the infield, through a tunnel and outside toward the vendor row, Kellie simply balanced the plates in one hand and held on for life with the other.

A large white tent had been set up, and fans began to cheer as soon they saw Hart Hampton had arrived. Russ parked the cart, and he and Hart jumped out. A row of tables waited with one spot empty, and Kellie could see that other drivers had already started autographing. The popular drivers had longer lines, and Kellie, behind the scenes, watched as Russ seated Hart. Another Hampton Racing employee was already present and holding Hart's autograph cards, which were full-color, eight-and-a-half-by-eleven card-stock photos of Hart and his car. Kellie had seen one the day before in a holder outside the hauler. The other side of the card showcased Hart's racing statistics. Hart took a seat, and the line began to move. Most people had brought things for Hart to autograph, but for those who didn't, an autograph card quickly appeared on the table in front of Hart.

"Crazy, isn't it?"

"Very much so," Kellie said, grateful to see Cynthia. She slid into the front seat of the cart.

"I was on my way back to the infield from the sponsor lunch and decided to pop by. Is that the food Hart brought you?"

"He told me it was okay to bring it along," she said.

"Eat. This will take a while. They gave out two hundred tickets, and I can guarantee you all two hundred fans are out there waiting to meet him."

"Alyssa McDougal asked me to watch the race from her motor home," Kellie said.

For a second, Cynthia looked surprised. "That's a great idea. I'm going to be up in the condo with the sponsors, like always."

"I don't think I want to be in the pit."

Cynthia laughed. "Wise woman. You get more information on TV anyway, unless you have a race scanner. We actually have a monitor on the pit cart tuned to the television broadcast. So last night went well?"

Kellie felt a tad bit awkward discussing the night, so she said simply, "We went to dinner, and then Charlie and I played pool at Hart's house. We were back before midnight because Charlie needed his medication. Charlie's with Stuart right now. Hart called Alyssa."

"So my nephew's been treating you well?" Cynthia prodded.

"He's been a perfect gentleman," Kellie said, her face flushing slightly.

Cynthia smiled. "I'm glad. You know, you're going to have to come around more often."

Kellie removed the aluminum foil. "I have a feeling this

weekend is just a one-off," she said. She waved the baby carrot in the direction of the autographing. "Oh my goodness, that person is carrying a car hood."

"They bring in all kinds of stuff," Cynthia said. "It's worth more if Hart signs it."

Kellie shuddered. "This is so not me."

Alyssa's words suddenly popped into Kellie's head. *I knew I was getting a race car driver, but love's like that. When the heart leads, you take them no matter what they do for a living.*

Despite the heat, Kellie shuddered again. No way. She wanted someone nine-to-five. Stable. Someone home on the weekends. Definitely not someone famous, not someone on whom the spotlight shined constantly.

Flattery, that's all this was. She'd been without a man so long that a little attention had her losing her senses. She was not risking her heart for Hart Hampton. She was simply intrigued by his interest. It was nice to feel desired once in a while.

After a few more social pleasantries, Cynthia said goodbye and drove off in her own golf cart. Kellie sat there, munching on food, watching Hart. From her angle, she could see he smiled at every person, told them it was great meeting them, and signed his name over and over, holding his marker like a paintbrush—to avoid tiring out his wrist.

Never once did he turn around to look at her, but she still had the odd sensation that he was highly aware of her presence, just as she was of him. Kellie used her fork, cutting a piece of cake. Around her other people sat in golf carts, watching their drivers. She had no idea who anyone was. She'd discovered yesterday in the garage that while people glanced at your credentials, few made eye contact. Oh sure, some smiled, but most walked as if they had blinders on—

work being their main focus. Only fans had studied her, as if trying to ascertain if she was someone important.

She touched the credentials that were around her neck. Before she'd taken a leave of absence from her teaching job in December, she'd worn an ID badge, but that had been a magnetic nameplate she'd attached to her clothing. The lanyard itched, and she scratched her neck as she thought about Cynthia's words. *You'll have to come around more often.*

Kellie finished her cake. One thing her husband had done was to leave her and Charlie well provided for. Kellie sighed. Maybe it was time for her to leave the past totally behind and venture out again. But could Hart be her future?

She briefly closed her eyes. When she opened them, the scene hadn't changed. An endless line of people waited for a piece of Hart Hampton. And in a sense, here she was waiting, as well.

Waiting was something she'd sworn long ago she wouldn't do, especially after she'd waited by the phone for her husband to call. Waited for word from the Middle East that he was fine. He'd brush off her concern when he'd call late. He'd laughed and said not to worry.

But even though they'd had some problems, Kellie hadn't been able to help herself. She'd cared. She'd loved John, made a commitment for better or worse.

Now here she was, waiting for Hart Hampton, proving he had the power to make her compromise her principles, lower the bands of protection she'd placed around her heart. This was just an one-off, she reminded herself as she watched Hart sign a photo for a little girl. Kellie'd be back to her normal self come tomorrow. The man had kissed her twice and rattled her brain. He made her think of what might be beyond the horizon.

She couldn't keep opening Pandora's box. The risks were far too great.

CHAPTER TEN

"HI, RACE FANS. *Welcome back after that commercial break. I'm Gus Edwards along with Malcolm French at the NASCAR NEXTEL All-Star Challenge. We're in the final twenty laps and tonight's surprise contender is Hart Hampton. He's led several laps and been a constant in the top five.*"

"*You're right, Gus. This is a major change for Hart, taking him back to the driver everyone knows he can be.*"

"*Exactly. He hasn't had much luck lately, between crashes and taking last weekend off to do charity work, but now his performance has definitely changed. Not only did he start from the outside pole position, but he's had fantastic pit stops all night. As we continue under caution for debris, we've sent Eileen Swikle down to Hart's pit to find out his secret weapon.*"

OH NO. Kellie watched the events unfolding on the screen, her body tense with trepidation. She winced as her fears were confirmed. There, on the supersized plasma screen in the McDougal's motor home, was her son, Charlie.

He sat up top on the pit box, clad in an Elementals green jacket. He wore headphones over his ball cap, and his glasses seemed almost too big for his face as he watched the monitors.

The camera panned back to Eileen. "Thanks, Malcolm. I met Charlie Thompson yesterday after qualifying. He met

Hart last weekend, and Hart invited him here to make his wish of watching live racing come true. And he's getting quite a race. Even though this race isn't for points and is more about money and prestige, Hart's out there giving it all he has. Wally, what's making it so special for Hart tonight?"

Hart's crew chief had removed one earphone so he could hear Eileen. "Hart's just on fire. The Elementals Chevy is performing perfectly and he's having a great time."

"Would you consider Charlie Hart's good luck charm?" Eileen asked.

"Whatever it is, we'll take it," Wally said, putting his headphone back on and ending the interview.

Eileen faced the camera. "So there you have it, Gus and Malcolm. Hart's lucky charm, a boy named Charlie who, from what I also understand, has a pretty single mother to boot."

The screen shifted back to the press box. "Thanks Eileen. The next lap the caution will lift and we'll go back to green flag racing." With that, the television cut to another commercial, one of Hart Hampton in Elementals boxers and a T-shirt. Kellie wanted to bury her head.

"Don't despair, Kellie, that was a great clip," Alyssa said.

"Very positive and followed by a commercial. How fortunate. His sponsors will love that," another driver's wife said.

About six other women sat in the motor home aside from Kellie, Alyssa, and Ronnie's mother. Kellie shook her head. "I didn't want any attention drawn to us," she said.

"Oh, that's impossible. You'll get it no matter what if you hang around with Hart. The media loves him. Some drivers they sort of ignore, but Hart's one of the golden ones who gets constant attention," another wife said.

"That's because Hart's one of the good guys," the elder Mrs. McDougal said.

"He is," Alyssa agreed. "And speaking of Hart, Kellie, you and I need to get to pit road as this thing is about to be over and we have a bit of a walk."

"Really, I…" Kellie began. But the race was winding down, everyone was getting up and leaving, so she stood as well. She hadn't planned on going to the pit, but rather back to her motor home. But she allowed Alyssa to sweep her along.

"Watch the scoring pylon," Alyssa told her as they stepped out into the night and made their way toward pit road. "You'll know who wins as it reflects the track position. The race leader is at the top."

The pits were crazy by the time they got there. As the race was tight between Dusty Burke, Kyle Doolittle and Hart, media had congregated near those pits, positioning themselves so they could film footage of the top five finishers.

Kellie found Cynthia already at Hart's pit box, and she showed Kellie where to stand as the race became a three-way sprint for the finish. The checkered flag flew, and the pylon changed numbers, putting the Number 413 car in the third spot.

"Third!" Cynthia screamed as she hugged Wally and then Kellie. "Yes! He's back!"

The excitement was infectious, and Kellie found herself smiling as all around her people were giving each other high fives and congratulatory hugs. She put her hand up and people slapped it even if they didn't know who she was.

One by one, the cars that didn't win roared down pit road, and soon Hart's green machine purred to a stop and ceased. He lowered the net, detached the steering wheel, and took off his helmet before he crawled out of his car. The enthusiastic cheers of his team greeted him.

Charlie had climbed down and found his mom, and he grabbed her hand and drew her closer to the pit wall. "Don't you get it, Mom? Hart's third. Best finish he's had since Daytona. He'll carry this momentum for weeks to come. He's out of his slump."

Kellie just smiled, watching as Hart swallowed half a bottle of cola in one gulp. The area around her was chaos as the media invaded and Hart, Wally and Cynthia all began to answer questions. Hart saw Charlie and Kellie and walked toward them, giving Charlie a high five. Only Kellie was aware of the television crews filming the event. "Let's get out of here. I've got a little bit of time before I'll have to be in the media center," he told her, striding past his team who were already beginning to break down the pit area so that they could all go home.

Kellie followed Hart back to the hauler where only a handful of media personnel waited, most having headed off to Victory Lane for the interviews with the winner and then NASCAR's presentation of the prize money. The press knew they could catch Hart in the media center.

"Hart, congratulations on your third-place finish. Does this confirm that you're out of your doldrums?" Eileen shoved the microphone forward.

"Absolutely," Hart told Eileen.

"Some fans had said you were all washed up. What do you say to that?"

"I have years before I'm washed up," Hart said, charming smile in place.

"So were Charlie and his mother your lucky charms?" Eileen wanted to know.

"I wanted to show both of them a great race. I think I achieved that." With that, Hart opened the doors to the hauler, gesturing Kellie and Charlie to step inside. Once all were in, he shut out the mayhem behind them.

"Whew! You stink," Charlie said to Hart.

"Charlie!"

But Hart only laughed. "Yeah, I do. I'm covered in sweat and the stench of burning rubber and some other things. The only good part about not winning is that I'm not hosed down in cola and beer as well. You guys up for eating after this? While we're at dinner, my parents' motor home will be brought out to my house so that you'll have your stuff."

"We're not staying at the track tonight?" Hart hadn't explained this part, and Kellie frowned.

"Everyone's going to haul out of here as fast as they can. You'll start hearing the choppers taking off from the infield any second."

"Cool," Charlie said. "Will we be in one of those?"

"Yes," Hart said.

Russ entered the hauler. "Media center," he called.

"Excuse me," Hart said. "Cynthia should be on her way. She'll get you guys out of here and I'll meet up with you my house."

"So how was the pit?" Kellie asked her son after Hart left.

"Awesome." Charlie regained full animation. "The race feed was also on the monitors in front of me and…" Charlie began to relate the events and Kellie listened until Cynthia came and found them.

"Chopper time," she said, and within minutes Kellie and Charlie found themselves airlifted up and over Charlotte, zooming along with four other people for the trip back to Hampton Racing headquarters.

There Cynthia said goodbye, putting Kellie and Charlie in Hart's caretaker's car. The driver chauffeured them back to Hart's house.

"Imagine how this would be if we did this every weekend," Charlie said, his enthusiasm bubbling over.

"Not going to happen," Kellie responded, glad the man up front was focused on the winding country roads and thus oblivious to her son's excitement.

"Mom," Charlie protested.

"Charlie," she replied, mimicking his tone. "We are guests. That's all. Don't let what you hear in the media fool you. Just chalk tonight up as one of those magical moments and let it be."

They arrived at the house, and the caretaker let them in. "When I saw Hart was in the top five, I took the liberty of putting some of my wife's stew in the slow cooker," he told them. "I didn't want you to have to wait to eat if you were hungry. It's in the kitchen. Make yourself at home."

"Thank you. Stew sounds wonderful." Kellie said. She and Charlie found the housekeeper's wife had left fresh biscuits on the counter to go with the stew. They ate in the kitchen, the television tuned to a local cable show. "Hey Mom, there's Hart," Charlie said. Hart sat at a table with another two men and all were fielding questions from the media. "Hey listen, he's talking about us," Charlie said.

So Kellie focused, and as the media centered on her and Charlie, Kellie soon discovered that her temper was about as hot as the stew.

HART WAS LATE. Really late. And not very happy about his tardiness, either. So much for eating dinner, he thought wryly as the chopper touched down on his backyard helipad. Hart opened the door, climbed out and made a run for the house as the helicopter again took off to the sky.

Seeing lights on in the basement, he headed there first and wondered how Kellie was going to react to his arrival. He'd been cornered in the media center for what had seemed forever. Normally he relished the attention, not caring about how long anyone waited for him. But this was Kellie and Charlie. Kellie wasn't going to tolerate nonsense, and frankly, Hart had found himself rather wanting to be with her. His impatience had grown as the press conferences had dragged on.

"Sorry I'm late," he said, finding Kellie downstairs in the game room watching television. "Where's Charlie?"

"Out in the motor home asleep. He's worn out from all the excitement. I sent him out there about an hour ago. Your caretaker left us stew, so we've eaten," Kellie said stiffly. "We caught you on television."

"Yeah, we have a local cable program that covers everything at the area speedways live," Hart said, realizing he was treading on dangerous ground here. While he'd showered and changed, Kellie still wore the clothes she'd been wearing at the race track and she didn't look very happy. He'd been asked dozens of questions about his guests, and he had the idea that that was what was bothering Kellie.

"Charlie and I are not your lucky charms, Hart," she said.

Hart sighed. He'd been right.

"That's just Eileen talking," Hart replied, shrugging his shoulders in an attempt to lighten the situation.

"You certainly didn't put her off any," Kellie said, her forehead creasing. "I mean, the national sports magazines asked you questions about us. I saw the press conference. Charlie's thinking he's going to be in print. I don't want either of us exposed that way."

"You won't be," Hart said, hiding his wince. At least he hoped not. He couldn't give Kellie any guarantees, although he'd call Cynthia and put her on stopping any story. Maybe she'd be able to do something.

"Don't use me to boost your career, Hart," Kellie stated, and Hart could hear the tiredness in her voice. "This is a special weekend for us. Charlie chatted everyone's ear off on the helicopter ride. Hopefully they all turned their headphones off or something."

"I guessed he'd never been in a helicopter before."

"And neither have I. Where I come from, they're used for severe life-threatening emergencies that require immediate trauma care. They are not daily transportation."

"But it was exciting," Hart stated. He knew she was angry, could see the conflicting emotions in her eyes. She was mad. Tired. Probably feeling a little abandoned, as well. What was common to him was foreign to her, and Hart wished he hadn't simply sent her to wait for him. "I'm sorry for just leaving you like that. I can understand your frustration."

She stared at him. "Thank you." A small smile formed. "And yes, it was exciting," Kellie said, caving slightly. "But…"

"No *buts*," Hart said. "They're like *because* or *what-ifs*. Useless words that allow you to give yourself excuses. I would have won the race, but. I love you, but. I'd have been there, but. I hate buts. I don't believe in qualifications, Kellie. It either is or it's not. You didn't hear me come in here and say I would have been on time but the interviews took forever. I was simply late and I'm sorry for that. I erred in my judgment. Next time I'll plan better."

Hart stood there, willing her to understand. This was his life, his job. He doubted it would help to tell her he'd been chomping at the bit to go home, wanting to see her. And lest she think anything, he didn't plan to seduce her. Oh, he'd love to have Kellie in his bed, but she wasn't a one-weekend or a one-month kind of woman. She was the forever kind, and frankly, that scared him.

"It's been a long night. We're probably all very tired and

coming down off an adrenaline rush," Kellie announced, rising to her feet. "We're leaving tomorrow afternoon. Sleep in, and I promise you'll see us before we go. I know Charlie's excited to talk to you about the race. He loved being up on your pit box. He thought listening to the radio chatter between you and your team was fantastic. This has really been a dream weekend for him."

"I'm glad," Hart said, humbled that something he'd taken for granted all his life could bring someone else so much joy.

"I'm glad, too," Kellie said, her temper gone. "You've been wonderful. This has all been just perfect. Never think I'm not grateful. I am. You just rattle me. I'd like some time to figure it out."

She stood at the basement stairs. Once she went up them, she'd be out the kitchen door and to the motor home in a minute. He didn't want her to go. He'd be up for another few hours until the rush wore off. He'd like to talk with her, spend the time with her.

"Let me walk you out," he said.

Kellie shook her head. "That's not necessary. Not tonight." She was cutting off his attempt to be close to her.

"What if I insist?" he asked.

"No," she said simply.

He nodded, respecting her decision. Maybe it was for the best anyway. Outside, seeing her standing by the motor home door, knowing she was going to walk away from him, would be pure torture. Fate might have given Hart back his luck tonight on the track, but she'd dealt him a major blow to the solar plexus of his love life. This woman striding up the basement stairs mattered to him, and she was leaving.

From a kitchen window, he watched as Kellie entered the motor home that was parked on the expansive driveway behind the house. He couldn't see in the windows, so instead he helped himself to the remaining biscuits and stew. He sat down and ate the food, barely tasting the meal as he mulled over the current situation. Then he took out his cell phone and dialed.

"Do you know what time it is?" his aunt asked.

"I know perfectly well the hour, especially since I got back here too late," Hart said, glumly.

"For what?" Cynthia asked.

Hart rolled his eyes. "To talk with Kellie. She's not like any of the others. They'd be thrilled to see me. Instead, she gave me a lecture on how I shouldn't have discussed her and Charlie in the media center. Now she's out in the motor home."

"So?" Cynthia asked, stifling a yawn. "You didn't intend on seducing this one anyway."

"No, but I don't want her walking out of my life, either," Hart said stubbornly. "You've got to help me. This is unfamiliar territory."

"Hart, you'll be bored with her in a few months. She's already making demands. What happened to that 'I'm in charge and if she can't handle it, there's always someone else to take her place' attitude you always display? You've only known the woman a weekend. She sounds like trouble to me."

"Stop the reverse psychology. I've known her *two* weekends and she's not trouble. At least not like that," Hart said. He inhaled. "When my dad saw my mom, he knew. You said you were that way with Liam. Well, I know."

Silence.

"Are you still there?" Hart demanded after a few seconds passed.

"I'm here," Cynthia said. "You just took me by surprise, that's all."

"Well, get unsurprised and help me figure this out. This is new territory for me."

"If I promise to help, will you at least let me sleep on this? It'll probably do you a world of good, too."

"Fine," Hart said. He shut the phone, and then quickly called his aunt right back.

"What?" she asked, as if she had been expecting him.

"Kellie doesn't want to be in a national sports magazine. Can you make sure she and Charlie aren't tomorrow's news?"

"Hart, you know I don't have control over the press, but I'll see what I can do. As for the magazine, they're going to be out Tuesday for an insider look at Hart Hampton. Maybe I can hold that over their head."

"Threaten to cancel it if they won't cooperate," Hart said. He added a hasty good-night and ended the call. He finished the stew, rinsing the plate and putting it in the dishwasher. A cleaning service came once a week, but Hart had been raised not to be a slob. He surveyed the kitchen, took one last look out at the motor home, and turned out the light.

"He won't call back," Liam said. He'd rolled over, shielding his eyes from the wall sconce on Cynthia's side of the bed.

"He might," Cynthia said, turning the page on the latest legal thriller she was reading. Besides, waiting for Hart gave her an excuse not to set the book down. She was riveted.

"So he really said he knew what he wanted?" Liam asked.

"He said it." Now at the end of the chapter, Cynthia forced herself to put the book on the nightstand so that she wouldn't keep reading. Thankfully the race had been on Saturday night. That meant Sunday was a free day, unlike when the races occurred Sunday afternoon. Then it was right back into the office Monday morning by nine-thirty, with no time off. The seven-day schedule could be brutal.

"I told Hart I was going to sleep on it," Cynthia said. "But if this really is the woman he wants…"

"I've never seen him like this. Lusting, yes, but enamored and committed, no."

"I agree," Cynthia said. She sighed and clicked off the light, sending the room into darkness minus the glow from the lights in the street. Unlike Hart and his acreage, Liam and Cynthia lived in an upscale townhome community and had one of the end units.

"So what are you going to do?" Liam asked.

"I don't know. Having disliked just about everyone Hart's ever brought around, I didn't expect to like her. But she impressed me. She's not hanging around Hart because he's a celebrity. In fact, I think she could care less. So I'll see what I can do. Starting with getting her to the track."

"I CAN'T COME to the track next weekend," Kellie told Hart on Monday afternoon. She shifted the phone, cradling the hard plastic device next to her ear. He'd asked her twice yesterday, before they'd left for the airport. The image of Hart, standing in the driveway and waving goodbye as the car pulled away, was burned into her mind. Sunday had been surreal.

Once everyone had gotten up, Kellie had allowed Charlie to race one of Hart's go-carts around the track. She and Hart had even gotten along famously, almost as if they were an old married couple. The day had been so much fun that Kellie had embedded it in her memory as one of the best of her life.

But before she'd known it, the hired car had pulled up the driveway to take them to the airport where Hart's private plane had waited to take them home.

The moment she'd walked back into her small three-bedroom house, the letdown had come. Square-footage-wise, her one-story ranch was only slightly larger than Hart's basement. She comforted herself with the fact that this place was hers, paid in full with insurance money. She could mortgage it again if she needed money for Charlie's treatments.

She clenched her fist and opened it slowly to defuse her body's tension. Like being at a tropical beach and eventually having to wash off the sand and go back to the concrete jungle of suburbia, she'd needed to close the door on the weekend. Even if she really didn't want to, Kellie just couldn't fathom how anything between her and Hart could ever work. Best to nip it in the bud than suffer greater disappointment later.

"Hart, Charlie has tests later this afternoon to check his cell counts. His teeth bled more than normal today and I'm worried," she told him.

"Kellie—" Hart began, but she interrupted him although it pained her greatly to do so. She knew people might call her foolish, but Hart's priority was racing. Hers was her son.

"Hart, we had a really great weekend. But we need to leave it at that. I know Charlie would really like to be there this weekend, but he's lying around today, not feeling well. Too much excitement can wear him out."

"Mom?"

Kellie turned, seeing Charlie standing in the doorway to the kitchen. She covered the mouthpiece. "Yes, honey?"

"Don't say no. If nothing else, you go to the track. He likes you. I can stay home with Grandma. Don't miss this chance."

"I'm not going to leave you," Kellie said stubbornly, her hand still on the mouthpiece. As for a chance with Hart Hampton…all she'd done was kiss him.

"Mom," Charlie protested. He began to twitch and Kellie's

hand shook as she realized the implications. Although body tremors could be common, they were not a good sign, especially when he hadn't had them for a while. Suddenly a slight drop of red formed underneath Charlie's left nostril. Kellie's hand flew to her mouth and she gripped the telephone even tighter as Charlie reached on the counter and grabbed a napkin. She uncovered the phone. "Hart, Charlie's nose is bleeding. I have to go."

"Kellie..."

"I'll call you later and let you know what's going on. I'm promise." She hung up on him and went to her son. "Let's head into the clinic early," she told him, fear gripping her tightly. She could already predict what the doctor would tell her. Charlie's counts would be low. He'd probably need an infusion. She touched her son; his skin was on fire. "You're feverish."

This time, he didn't argue.

"Mom?" Kellie called out. "Mom!"

Anita came out of the laundry room where she'd been ironing. "Yes?"

"We need to go," Kellie said.

Anita reached for her purse. "I'll get the car."

HOURS LATER, Charlie's pediatric cancer specialist stood outside the hospital room. Dr. Murphy had been with Charlie for several years now, and Kellie had always been impressed with him. "It's returned full force, hasn't it?" she asked, referring to the leukemia.

"It's not as bad as you think," the doctor said before proceeding to give Kellie the exact medical details, including Charlie's cell counts. "We're not seeing the resistance to chemo, and that's encouraging. His body is trying to make cells. However, he's got an infection and we're administering antibiotics."

"The weekend took it out of him," Kellie said, blaming herself.

The doctor shook his head. "Not necessarily. Physically it might have exhausted him. He told me he did a lot of walking."

Kellie bit the inside of her cheek. No matter what the doctor said, she knew the weekend had simply been too much.

"However," Dr. Murphy continued, "mentally and emotionally, this is the best I've seen Charlie in a few years. It's like he's had a new lease on life. He loved being at the track and he told me he wants to go back to watch a few more races. He said that if he can get better, Hart will let him come to a few more."

"I don't think we'll be doing that."

The doctor assessed her quietly. "You might want to reconsider. Charlie needs something to fight for."

"You can't just wish cancer away," Kellie said.

Dr. Murphy shook his head. "No, you can't. But the power of positive thinking is a very mysterious thing. People told they'd never walk again are out running marathons. We see miracles every day in this business. Maybe not as many as we'd like, but we see them. Charlie's a very positive boy and he wants this. We're on schedule for another round of chemo later in the summer. I'm very optimistic about that."

"I hope so," Kellie said. She'd had her hopes dashed before. The bone marrow transplant that had worked—for a while. The first round of chemo and the subsequent drugs that had gotten a short remission—before the cancer had come back full force again.

"As soon as we get the infection under control, we'll be able to send him home," the doctor said. "A couple of days, barring anything else."

Kellie nodded. She'd been through this so many times it

was rote. Tests. X rays. MRIs. Red cell transfusions. Platelet transfusions. Pain medication. Her son had no resistance to infections of any sort. His body ached just because. He had frequent headaches. An occasional batch of shingles. It was as if he was allergic to everything, although allergic wasn't the right word. But that gave people the general idea, an analogy that helped them make sense of the incomprehensible.

She pushed open the door to Charlie's hospital room. He was awake, watching television. "Hey," she said.

"Hi."

"Dr. Murphy says he's optimistic about the next round of chemo," Kellie told her son. She sat down in the chair next to him. "What are you watching?"

"Reruns," Charlie said as he used his fingertip to change the channel. "I wish the hospital would get more channels. They need pay-TV. I'm bored. I'm out of here by Sunday so I can watch the race at home and have pizza."

"You know, speaking of racing, Dr. Murphy says that he's never seen you so excited about something."

Charlie kept his gaze on the TV. "I told him about my visit to the track. He's not a race fan, but he told me his wife buys him Elementals undershirts."

"That Hampton magic at work," Kellie said, with a smile.

Charlie yawned. He moved his arm, the intravenous tube moving with him. "I'm tired. It's been a long day."

"I saw Jane just come in."

"My favorite nurse," Charlie said with a sleepy nod. He'd been in and out of the hospital so often, he knew everyone in the cancer treatment center. "Did they give me something to make me sleep? My eyes feel like they have weights on them... And I don't ache as much... I want to see Hart again."

"They did give you something. It's kicking in now," Kellie said. "We'll talk about visiting Hart when you wake up."

His pale blue eyes opened and gazed at her intensely. "So I get to go?"

"You aren't going to be up for it this weekend, sport," Kellie said. "After that, we'll see. But I won't outright say no."

"That's enough for now," Charlie replied, closing his eyes again. A small smile formed on his lips. "Thanks, Mom. I love you."

"I know." Kellie brushed his hair away from his eyes and leaned over and pressed her lips to forehead. He was much cooler now. "I love you, too."

"Don't forget to call Hart… You hung up on him…said you'd call him back. He should know…what's going on. He cares, Mom."

"It's too late to call him now. I'll phone first thing tomorrow morning," she said. "Promise."

"I'm holding you to that," Charlie said as he drifted off to sleep.

Tears formed and Kellie brushed them away. "I know."

HART PACED the small conference room like a caged animal. Every Tuesday morning at ten, he and Wally had a meeting with Liam to go over the previous race weekend. The fact that he'd placed third and not made any mistakes should work in his favor and keep the meeting short.

"You're going to wear out the carpet," Wally said. "Relax. No questionable pit stops. No poor driving. No wrecks to explain this time."

"Yeah," Hart replied, his agitation not ebbing. He'd been trying to reach Kellie since she'd hung up on him yesterday.

He'd gotten an answering machine and her cell phone voice mail. No news was not necessarily good news.

The door opened and Liam walked in, a file folder in his hand. Often he might also have a DVD containing footage of the weekend's race. Today, though, the folder contained very few sheets and the meeting went quickly once everyone was seated.

"Hart, stay behind a second," Liam said as he dismissed Wally. Hart had been halfway up out of the leather chair, and he sank back down. "Few things. One, your sponsors were thrilled with your performance. You ran a good, clean race and calmed everyone's jitters."

He'd indicated as much to Wally, so Hart wasn't sure why Liam was repeating this. "Cynthia spoke with Eileen Swikle's network, and there's not much we can do. The story had so much of a feel-good quality that Eileen launched it on her news show yesterday afternoon."

Hart winced. He'd been at the shop, working with the guys getting the following weekend's car ready.

"I'm sure Kellie didn't see the show," Hart told Liam. In fact, Hart was pretty positive she hadn't, or she'd have called. Then at least he'd know what was going on.

"Maybe Kellie didn't see it," Liam said, "but your interviewer today did. He sent over a list of questions for you to look at. They want to use the same angle."

Hart exhaled sharply.

"You have to admit that it's an area you've never been strong in before," Liam said. "You've been known as a playboy, not a hands-on, do-gooder family man."

"Just because I don't have my own foundation or run my own charity events…"

"Yes, I know," Liam interrupted the spiel. "You give tons of money and show up at just about any event any of your friends organize for their charities. That's all well and good. But you touched the heart of a child. That's big, newsworthy stuff."

"I promised Kellie she wouldn't come into this. She's not planning on returning to the track any time soon."

"I'm sorry to hear that," Liam said. "I know you like her."

"I do. I don't want to risk alienating her. If I can't handle this interview, it could seal my fate and ruin any chance I have." Hart tapped his fingers on the table as he contemplated a strategy. "I want Russ there. He's always good interference. I know I granted this magazine an exclusive interview so they're not going to want to lose that. Just having my photo on their cover will sell tons of copies."

"True," Liam acknowledged. "Any magazine featuring you always sells well."

"I'm not happy about this angle." Hart saw Liam's expression. "Don't tell me it'll help my sponsors. You and I both know that I've reached the level where I can afford to be picky."

"Yes, except they've been nervous lately," Liam said.

Hart pulled his cell phone out of his pocket. He'd had it on silent during the meeting, and he had a missed call. He hit the button and the display read Kellie. He'd programmed in her number, and she'd called. "Hold on. I have to take this," Hart told Liam. Ignoring his uncle's curiosity, Hart hit the button that connected to his voice mail.

"Hi, Hart, it's Kellie. I'm sorry I hung up on you but I needed to get Charlie to the hospital. He has an infection and will be there a few days. We won't make it this weekend, but…" Hart heard her take a deep breath. "If you're still willing to have us visit a track some other time, Charlie would really like that. His doctor thinks it's a good idea and I agree. I'll call you when he's better."

Hart closed his phone, saving the voice mail. "Charlie's in the hospital," he told Liam. "If we're done here?"

Normally Liam wouldn't tolerate Hart's insubordination. Although Hart did own part of the company, he was technically an employee and Liam his boss. But Liam simply appeared shocked. "Sure."

"Thanks." Hart rose, and hit a number on his phone as he strode from the conference room. "Hey, Russ. Cancel everything for the next two days. Yeah, even today's interview. Tell them Charlie's in the hospital and we need to reschedule." Hart listened to Russ for a moment. "No, I don't care. Some things are more important than press and racing. Russ, this is one of those times."

CHAPTER ELEVEN

BY LATE TUESDAY afternoon, Charlie's condition had greatly improved. Kellie had been thrilled that her son had been eating, for oftentimes an infection meant dramatic weight loss. She sat in the chair, a novel open in her hands. Outside the sun was bright, a gorgeous spring day. Soon school would be out, the beaches would be full seven days a week, and summer would be here full force.

She glanced over at her son. Aside from talk shows, one of his secret vices was watching afternoon soap operas, those silly and dramatic shows that hooked people with their story lines. Since he loved everything to do with ghosts, the paranormal story line of the current show had totally caught his attention.

A light knock sounded at the door, and both Kellie and Charlie turned their heads. It was too early for the doctor, and too soon for blood work. "Come in," Kellie called.

They heard the door swing open. "Hey, anyone home?"

Kellie stilled, her fingers dropping the book into her lap.

She knew that voice, as did Charlie, who said, "Hart! What are you doing here?" when Hart came into the room.

"I heard you couldn't come visit this weekend, so I came to see you instead."

Kellie stared, tilting her head so that she could see around him. No entourage. No cameras. Just Hart, holding by the ear a large overstuffed bear at least two feet tall. He offered the present to Charlie, who reached for it eagerly.

"Are those for me, too?" Charlie asked, teasingly, seeing that Hart held in his other hand a bouquet of mixed flowers wrapped in clear cellophane.

"Nope, these are for your mom. Figured she probably needed a present, too, if she's had to hang out in this place with you," Hart joked.

"Good idea," Charlie said, propping the bear beside him. Kellie knew that even though he was just about sixteen, her son had instantly fallen in love with the bear.

"So you came all this way to see me?" Charlie asked.

"I did," Hart said. "You met my pilot. He flew me here as soon as I heard your mom's message."

"That's awesome," Charlie said, giving Kellie a pointed glance. Charlie had said Hart cared. Her son had been right. Again, Kellie had misjudged, and she softened her further opinion of him.

"Oh, by the way," Hart said. "That bear has a zipper on his right side. Take a look."

Charlie's fingers found the zipper and pulled it down. He shoved his hand inside and removed a brand-new handheld gaming system, several games and a few movies that could also be played on the system. "Thought you might need something to keep you busy," Hart said, glancing up at the soap opera.

"Thanks! The system I have is way too old, and they don't make any games for it anymore. This is perfect!" Charlie said.

"Then I guessed right," Hart said with a smile. He handed Kellie the flowers, and the clear plastic wrap crinkled. "I guess I forgot to buy a vase."

"I'm sure I can scrounge one up," Kellie said, touched by the fact that he'd brought her anything at all. "If not, the gift shop downstairs will have something."

"Not very decorative in here, is it?" Hart asked, glancing around. While the room was cheerily decorated in a hot air balloon motif, the room lacked homey touches.

"I don't want to personalize the room," Charlie answered with a shake of his head. "That means you're settling in. I'm ready to get out of here and go home. The food's a lot better."

Hart laughed and took a seat in the room's second chair. "You made quite a splash last weekend. Everyone at Hampton Racing sends best wishes. In fact, Cynthia's overnighting a huge care package. It'll arrive at your house tomorrow. She raided the gift shop. I think you could probably outfit all your nurses and doctors with Hampton Racing gear with the amount she told me she sent."

"You didn't have to do that," Kellie said.

"Yeah, I did," Hart said, his gaze holding hers across Charlie's bed.

The soap opera having ended, Charlie had turned on the game system and installed a game. "This is too cool," he said as the device made dings and beeps. Kellie could see the program reflected in his glasses. Charlie suddenly gave an unhappy protest. "Hey, I already died."

"You know what they say about practice," Hart said.

"Yeah, it makes perfect," Charlie answered. He set the handheld aside. "I'll play later, after you leave. So what car are you driving this weekend?"

"Wally and I talked about that yesterday, and we're going to run the same setup as on Saturday. We'll need to work fast to get the car we're bringing ready, but my team's great with stuff like that."

"I've never seen a car built," Charlie said. "I mean, you guys do it all, right?"

"We do."

"All your cars?"

"In the past, Hampton Racing has built about seven hundred engines a year and maybe forty to fifty new chassis. Even the Car of Tomorrow can take six weeks to build, and we use around thirty-eight different templates to build a car. Those help make sure all the parts match up."

"Wow, I'd like to see that," Charlie told Hart, his eyes wide.

"Well, the fabrication shop's pretty noisy. Mine's a little quieter. You get better, and I'll take you on a personal tour." Hart looked at Kellie. "Do they have wireless Internet here?"

She shrugged. "I have no idea."

"Because if Charlie's got a laptop, he could go online. Some race shops have cameras on the floor, and you can watch what's going on. Hampton Racing's got one in Billy Easton's area."

"I'll ask," Kellie said.

"Do," Hart insisted. "And I'm serious about the tour, Charlie. You pick the day and I'll fly you out. Mondays through Wednesdays work best. Depending on where and when the race is, we leave for the track either Thursday or Friday."

Charlie glanced over at his mother, seeking her approval. Kellie looked down at the flowers she still clutched in her hands. This was her son's dream. His hero had taken a personal interest in him. She'd left a message only this morning, and Hart had hopped on his plane and flown here to be with Charlie. He'd brought cool gifts. Who was she to deny her son that?

And, as much as it pained her to admit it, she'd taken just a tiny interest in Hart herself. Oh, who was she trying to kid? She'd taken a huge interest. The flattery was awesome. Mind-blowing, actually. To think a man of his stature could be interested in her was beyond comprehension. Still, she refused to let herself get too carried away. She rose to her feet, deciding that escape might be a good thing as she tried to sort out all these sensations flowing through her.

"I'm going to find a vase," she said.

"Okay," Charlie replied.

Hart rose to his feet as she passed by.

"I'll be back soon," she said, ducking her head and exiting.

She carried the flowers out to the nurses' station. Since Charlie was such a frequent visitor, Kellie knew everyone pretty well. "You don't have a vase back there, do you?" she asked.

"We might. Let me go check." Suzanne said. She came back in a few minutes with a large white vase, the mass-produced kind that were sold with thirty-dollar arrangements down in the gift shop. "You can use this one."

"Thanks," Kellie said. Suzanne lent her some scissors and Kellie began to remove the flowers from their packaging.

"So is that really Hart Hampton in with Charlie?" Suzanne asked, grabbing a few fallen leaves and tossing them into the trash.

"Yes."

"I thought I recognized him from his Elementals ads. He's cuter in person."

Not sure how to answer that, Kellie kept arranging the flowers.

"So do you think he might be willing to meet with a few of the other kids? Charlie's got a bunch of them hooked on NASCAR."

"I don't know. I'd have to ask him. He dropped in unannounced, so I don't know what his schedule is," Kellie said. Suzanne removed the trash and Kellie lifted the vase. She'd fill it with water back in Charlie's room.

"Let me know," Suzanne said. "Charlie will know exactly who I'm talking about."

"Okay," Kellie replied, feeling a bit uncomfortable. While she wanted to have Hart meet everyone and make their day, part of her felt awkward and on the spot. Just because she knew him didn't mean she felt comfortable requesting favors.

"Those look great, Mom," Charlie said as she returned. Kellie glanced from Hart to Charlie. They'd been talking but she had no idea about what. Somehow, though, she sensed at least part of the conversation had been about her. She set the flowers on the windowsill and emptied the water pitcher into the vase.

"Hart, I feel awkward asking this, but Suzanne, she's one of the nurses, wanted to know if you'd be willing to pop in on some of the other kids. Charlie's got them all hooked on NASCAR."

"Oh, Quan's here!" Charlie said excitedly before his face fell. "Quan's not doing very well. He's pretty resistant to the chemo. They're trying a new drug but if that fails…"

"I'd be happy to meet him," Hart said, and Kellie could tell his response was genuine. "And anyone else. All your friends. I just don't have any of my autograph cards with me."

"They won't care," Charlie answered. "They'd be honored just to meet you." Charlie hit the call button and Suzanne appeared within seconds. "Am I able to leave the room?" he asked.

"You're still pretty weak, but…"

"Can I have a wheelchair?" Charlie asked. "Hart and I are going to start by visiting Quan."

"I think he'd like that," Suzanne said. "But why don't you let me check with his mother and get the official go-ahead? Better yet, write me a list of people you want Hart to visit and I'll make the arrangements."

"Okay," Charlie said. He gestured to his mom for a pen and paper, then he grabbed the cup full of Cheerios in front of him. He popped a few into his mouth. "Want some?" he asked Hart.

Hart shook his head. "Thanks, but they're all yours."

Kellie was ready with a piece of paper and a pen. She wrote down Quan's name. "Okay, who's next?"

The rest of the afternoon passed in a blur. Someone found a digital camera, and Hart visited no fewer than fifteen rooms. He posed for pictures, chatted with each child, signed autographs—real ones, using his wrist—and throughout it all always had a genuine smile.

Only Kellie had seen how shocked and touched he was, especially when he'd gone into Melissa's room. She was seven, but looked years younger as cancer had stunted her growth. Hart had made the little girl's day.

After seeing him in action, Kellie knew she owed him a big apology the next time they were alone.

What she'd seen in the media and what she'd read in the magazines didn't come close to capturing his true personality. Hart was actually a deep person who truly cared and gave completely of himself. After promising each child a special care package to follow, Hart left each room with an address.

"I don't know how you do it," he admitted to Kellie as they walked back toward Charlie's room. "I can't imagine facing that day after day."

"But you just did," Kellie said. "You flew here to be with Charlie." She reached out and touched Hart's arm. "Thank you. You were awesome, and I appreciate what you did."

His half smile lifted his right cheekbone. "I still couldn't do enough."

"None of us can," she said. "I—" She paused until Charlie

and Suzanne disappeared into Charlie's room. "I really owe you an apology. You're nothing like I thought you were."

With that, she didn't wait for an answer but darted into the hospital room.

"I wondered where you'd gotten to," Anita said. "I was starting to… Oh my God!"

"Hey, Grandma. Glad you got here before he left. This is Hart Hampton," Charlie said easily.

Tears came to Anita's eyes, and she quickly brushed them away. "Anita Wertz. Nice to meet you." She held out her hand, and Hart shook it. "Thanks so much for everything you've done for Charlie."

"It's been my pleasure," he said.

"You look a little tired, sport," Anita said, turning her attention to her grandson. "How about you eat the dinner that just arrived?"

"I am hungry," Charlie said. "But what about you, Mom?"

"I'll get something later, after Hart leaves," Kellie said. She usually got something in the cafeteria and often ate dinner with her son.

"I bet Hart's hungry, too. How about you take my mom out to dinner? Like La Cantina." Charlie named a Mexican restaurant.

"Charlie, that's way too fancy. And I'm sure Hart has other things to do," Kellie protested.

"Nope," Hart said. "I think it's a great idea. If that's too fancy, you pick the place. Anything but the hospital cafeteria."

"They actually have great food here," Kellie said. "People from around the community come in just to eat."

"That sounds fine, but I'd rather skip it this visit, if you don't mind. I want somewhere you don't carry your own food on a tray. Name the place."

"Fred's Pub is pretty good. Great burgers and steaks," Anita suggested.

"Perfect," Hart said, settling the matter. He pulled out his cell phone. "Shall we go? I've got a car service on call."

"I can drive," Kellie said simply, and soon she and Hart were seated across from each other in a booth at Fred's. The room had photographs and memorabilia posters everywhere—the authentic, antique kind, not the ones reproduced and sold mass market through restaurant supply stores. The wooden bar was octagonal and ornate, and it filled the center of the high-ceiling room.

The happy hour crowd was moderate for a Tuesday evening. Many were in work attire, while others were dressed like Kellie and Hart, who were wearing jeans and casual T-shirts.

"Can I take your order?" their waiter asked, and Hart requested a bottle of his microbrew, a cola and water.

"I'll just have iced tea," Kellie said.

"I'll be right back with those," the waiter said.

Their waiter moved away and Kellie arched an eyebrow at him.

"What?" he asked.

"It seems like an odd combination," she remarked.

"Flying makes me dehydrated," he told Kellie. "I go through at least three bottles of water when traveling. As for the beer, my contract stipulates that it's the only alcohol I can drink. It's mostly on the table for show."

"Yeah, I guess that would look bad if you were imbibing something else. Like being sponsored by one store and seen shopping at the other."

"Exactly," Hart said. He opened the menu. "What's good here besides burgers and steaks?"

"Everything," Kellie replied, beginning to relax. The waiter hadn't even given Hart a second glance, except to take his drink order. No one in the place was staring at them. Hart's presence in her life was also becoming more comfortable. "I'm going to have the southwestern chicken. My mom swears by the rib eye."

"This bison burger with mushrooms sounds pretty good."

"It is," Kellie said. And, as soon they'd ordered, they found themselves deep in conversation, probably the first real conversation they'd had that hadn't related to Charlie or racing.

"So, even after this weekend, you still weren't impressed with me," Hart said.

"I apologized," Kellie said as she polished off her chicken. "I let myself believe in the stereotype. You don't fit the bill at all."

"Really? I never would have noticed," Hart's sarcasm was meant in jest.

"Ha ha," Kellie said, accepting his jest as a way to keep the conversation from getting too deep. "Today you showed a lot of courage and generosity. There was nothing for you to gain today."

"I don't do things just for what I can get out of it," Hart said.

"I've realized that now," Kellie acknowledged. "I guess not being one of those who wants fifteen minutes of fame, it's discomforting to have it. My mom's friend caught Eileen's show. She told me we were plastered everywhere. I wasn't very happy yesterday, and then you called and Charlie was burning up and I was just rude. I shouldn't have been."

"You're a mother. You were worried." He waited a second. "Did that make it better?"

"A little," she said with a smile. "I still feel rather silly for overreacting. You aren't doing this for nefarious reasons." She pointed to the table. "I mean, you're here with me because…"

"Because I want to be," Hart finished for her.

"It's a little overwhelming," Kellie said. "To think you're with me just because…" Her voice drifted off again.

"I'm very serious about you," Hart said. Silence descended for a moment. "This is one of those times that I'd love not to be a celebrity. Sort of. I hate some of it. But other parts are fantastic. I'm living my dream. I can do things like drop everything and fly here to see you and Charlie. But being a driver means other dreams I have are often put on the back burner or given up. Few want to deal with someone who has something all-consuming in his life."

"I can understand that," she said, toying with her napkin before she pushed it away. "I've quit teaching for now. Charlie's much more important than my having a career. But with all the changes in education, I'm afraid that when I do want to go back, I'll have been left behind and my training will be obsolete."

"Isn't teaching mainly about caring and loving kids? Maybe learning new stuff is like riding a bike. You'll just pick it right back up."

"That's kind, and I hope so. I guess I just want normalcy for a while. Life in and out of the hospital is not normal."

"Life can't be put on hold," Hart said.

"No, but I can't put my needs above my son's, either," she said. "He's had it rough. His father was never around. So busy trying to grasp that brass ring, John took a job as an overseas contractor. It paid well because of the dangers. Sometimes I think I drove him to it. Charlie had been sick for a while, and he couldn't handle it. Providing for us from afar was a safe way to avoid facing what he saw as our failure."

"Failure? I don't understand. You are a fantastic mother. How could you be a failure?" Hart asked.

"We failed Charlie. Whatever genes he got from us, they weren't good enough."

Kellie choked up slightly, and she took a sip of her iced tea to hide the emotions that threatened to come back. Hart reached his hand out and covered hers.

"When you find out your child has a life threatening illness, you blame yourself," Kelly continued. "I gave him life. I should have done a better job. I should have protected him better."

Hart sat there thinking for a moment. "Maybe *should haves* ought to be added to that list. I should have gone low instead of high. I should have pitted a lap earlier. I should have made better decisions."

"You might be right," Kellie said, glad he hadn't been condescending as others had by offering patronizing comments such as, "It's not like that," or "Don't be so hard on yourself."

"It's hard not being able to fix anything," Kellie said.

"I know," Hart replied. "You have no control. However, it's like racing. You have to toss off the blame. Blame is like fear. While some amounts may be healthy, too much becomes all-consuming and eats up your sanity. You can second-guess yourself to death. You want to overcompensate, which, trust me, makes things a lot worse in the long run."

Maybe Hart did understand. The weight of his hand on hers was a welcome comfort, and it was sending delightful little signals to her brain.

"Hindsight's always twenty-twenty, Kellie. You just have to make the best decisions as you go forward and try not to kick yourself too much if you make a mistake. I'm sure you've heard doctors tell you that Charlie's disease is not your fault, so I'm not going to venture down that path. I'm not going to offer you any advice. I'm just going to say that I've been in similar situations. I took a guy out of the race last year. My car got loose and I caught him on the rebound as I bounced off the wall. Knocked him right out of the Chase and ended his championship dreams. I had to let go of the guilt. Once it was done, it was done. Fluke. Fact of nature. Whatever. We were simply two objects occupying the same space at the same time. I didn't do it on purpose, and everyone knows that in this business accidents happen, but the media still dogged me for weeks asking about how I felt about it. At some point, you have to let it go and simply deal with the cards fate dealt you. All I could do was go on."

"I've been trying," she said, for it was important to her that he believed that.

He nodded. "I know. That's why I think it's important that I tell you that you impress me a great deal. Even when you seem like you are pushing me away, you still amaze me with how selfless you are. As cheesy as it sounds, I hold you in the highest regard. I also want to tell you that you're not going to get rid of me that easily."

"No?" Her word caught on her breath. His touch and declaration had short-circuited her.

"No," Hart said with such conviction that she tried to withdraw her hand, except that he gripped it tighter. "Don't be afraid of me."

"I'm not. I'm…" Kellie paused, her lie obvious. She was afraid. This was Hart Hampton, one of NASCAR's most popular drivers. Thousands screamed his name. Hundreds stood in line for hours just for five seconds of face time. She wasn't model-pretty. How could she compete? Better yet, how could she keep up?

Hart was stroking her hand, his fingertip soft on hers. His touch soothed, calmed her nerves. He made her want to

believe. The man could sell snow in the winter. He'd told her
he wasn't toying with her. He'd promised to be there for her.

"You're going to have to make time for us," Hart said.
"I'm already here. All you have to do is let me in."

The waiter appeared at that moment, saving Kellie from a
reply. "Would either of you like dessert?"

"Kellie?" Hart asked.

"No, I'll pass. I'm ready to get back," she said.

"Just the check," Hart told the man. "Please think about
what I said," he said to Kellie.

"I will. I don't think I'll be able not to," she replied
honestly. "I admit, there is something between us."

"Good." Hart leaned back. Kellie knew he was satisfied,
and so was she. He'd pushed her, yes, but he'd eased up at
exactly the right moment. John would have kept picking and
picking. That Hart knew when to fold his hand spoke volumes.

"Excuse me a moment," he said. She studied him as he
dialed the car service, directing them to pick him up at the
hospital in forty minutes. He then called his pilot and gave him
the itinerary.

"Is it safe flying this late?" Kellie asked, her worry evident.

"It'll be fine. We do it after every race most weekends,"
Hart reassured her. "I told you I'm not going anywhere, and
I'm not."

But he was, Kellie thought later, as she kissed Charlie
good-night and headed home. Hart had boarded his plane and
returned to Charlotte. She couldn't date the man long distance.
Everyone knew that didn't work. She had a marriage that
failed because of distance—out of sight meant out of mind.

As for Hart, as much as Kellie believed him, she also
worried that she could be just a novelty that would eventually
lose its luster.

After all, every man in her life eventually left. Her husband. The few men she'd dated. Even Charlie would leave the nest at some point. Why should Hart be different? Her heart had been hurt too many times to risk hurting it again. It had nothing to do with fear, just practicality.

CHAPTER TWELVE

PROOF THAT HART was serious about a relationship with Kellie arrived in the form of couriered Hampton Racing hard card credentials for Kellie. With it came a note, scrawled on notepaper in what Kellie assumed was Hart's real handwriting.

I know you can't be there with me this weekend, but this will get you and Charlie into whatever race you're coming to next. I'm going to expect you soon. If not, expect me on your doorstep. I'll call you when I get a break.

"That's cool, Mom," Charlie said. He'd been home for a few hours, resting on the couch. The longest race of the year was tomorrow, and he was ready. "Let's hop in the car and go."

"I don't think so," Kellie said with a slight smile, knowing her son wasn't *totally* serious. "The doctor says not yet. Your infection is pretty much gone, but we want to make sure that the infusion of platelets did the job. Everything looked great, and I want to keep it that way."

"Yeah, but I've still got chemo ahead."

"Which will work this time," Kellie replied, donning her positive hat. "Dr. Murphy did say he thought you could go to a race before that starts."

"Then let's go to Dover next weekend. That's in Delaware."

"I know my geography, and we'll wait and see how you feel," Kellie said. She refused to let Charlie push himself. Her son would go to everything, tire himself out, and then develop another infection, which would set his recovery back.

"Well, we aren't going to miss Pocono," Charlie said stubbornly. "I heard that track's wild. It's an intermediate track, and it only has three turns. I want to see it in person."

"Again, we'll see," Kellie repeated. "What you can do is start planning your birthday party. That's only a few weeks away."

"I want to go racing for my birthday."

Kellie folded her arms.

Charlie glared right back. "Fine. But I'm getting my driver's license. I'm already eligible for my permit and ready for the written test."

Kellie exhaled, trying to relieve her growing frustration. "You won't be able to drive without someone in the car."

"Yeah, I know," Charlie said, suddenly irritable. "State law. Don't you think I know that?"

"Sorry," Kellie responded. She raised her hand, willing to concede this one. Charlie was a boy trapped in a body that didn't work. His mind wanted to do things, but physically he couldn't. "I'll talk driving lessons over with the doctor. But I'm not a good teacher. Not with autos. Maybe Grandma can do it."

"I asked her. She'd rather not."

"Then let me look into some driving instruction. Maybe we can go that route." Kellie tried not to wince as her brain calculated the additional cost. That was another reason she'd been putting Charlie's driving test off. Car insurance was outrageous for teenage drivers, and she'd have to insure him immediately and with high medical payments.

Charlie turned his attention to the screen. The NASCAR Busch Series race was on tonight, and tomorrow afternoon they'd all sit down about four o'clock and watch the Cup race.

Kellie's phone rang and she went to answer it. "Hello?"

"Did you get my package?"

Hart. "I did. Thank you," Kellie said, her adrenaline spiking. She gripped the receiver tighter, delighted he'd called.

"I expect you to use those," Hart replied. Kellie could hear noise in the background, as if he were calling her from the hauler. "Will you make Dover?"

"I'm not sure. Charlie would like to, but I've told him that we may have to wait until he's a little better. He's insisted that you'll see us by Pocono."

"That's two weeks," Hart said, not sounding happy. "What if I place in the top five tomorrow?" Hart asked.

"Then we'll definitely come to Pocono," she said, her decision instantaneous. "Although if you don't, I think we could still probably make it. Charlie really wants to go."

"That's not much incentive to win tomorrow," Hart said.

"What do you want?" Kellie asked, playing along. "For me to tell you that I want you and that I'll reward you for a top five finish?"

"That sounds absolutely perfect," Hart said with a laugh. "Thanks for offering. Don't make any plans for Wednesday night. I'm coming to collect."

"Hart!" Kellie said, her heart jumping both with anticipation and nervousness. Was he serious?

"Tell Charlie I'll call him later. I have to go. See you Wednesday." And with those parting words the phone went dead in her hand. Dazed, she walked back into the living room. "Hart's coming in on Wednesday, and he said he'll call you later. I also told him we'd be at Pocono."

Charlie's face burst into the widest smile she'd seen in a long time. "That's super!" He leapt off the couch to give her a hug, wobbling on his feet as the blood rushed to his head.

"Careful now."

"I'm fine," Charlie said, wrapping his arms around his mother and holding her tight.

She let herself be warmed by the squeeze, feeling the love and adoration her son held for her before he let her go.

"This is the best news I've had. And Mom?"

"What?"

"I told you so," Charlie announced.

"Told me what?" Kellie asked, her forehead creasing as she tried to guess what he meant.

"That Hart was going to fall for you."

"Charlie, we are so far away from that," Kellie said quickly.

Charlie grinned, not daunted in the least. "Keep telling yourself that, Mom. Keep telling yourself."

HART PLACED SEVENTH, still a strong finish and one that moved him up in the points. The next weekend at Dover he placed sixth. Both times he fell short of the top five finish, so even though he'd visited, he hadn't tried to claim any "reward."

Although, after seeing him two Wednesdays in a row, Kellie was loosening the strings around her heart and letting him in, little by little. He hadn't tried to kiss her again and she'd found herself missing his touch.

She also found it odd that she hadn't minded as much as she thought she would when Eileen Swikle had interviewed Hart and asked if he were planning on having Kellie at the track again.

Elated with a top ten finish, Hart had smiled at the woman and said, "Definitely, she'll be back."

"So her presence at the challenge wasn't a one-time deal?" Eileen had asked. At that, Hart has simply smiled wider, his eyes hidden by sunglasses and walked away.

At the time, Kellie had groaned, knowing that everyone would be speculating on what was going on. But now that she and Charlie were in the hired car taking them to Pocono, she was more interested in seeing Hart.

It was early Friday evening, close to five, and the race was Sunday. Hart was already at the track. He'd wanted Charlie and Kellie to fly to Charlotte on Thursday so that they could travel together, but Charlie'd had a doctor's visit. After his treatment, the clinic had let him loose, telling him to have a good time.

"Hi, Kellie! Charlie!" Russ greeted her the minute she arrived, pulling up in a golf cart as the car dropped her off. "Hart's out on the track practicing but he should be back soon. It's great to see you both again."

"Thanks," Kellie said as Russ put their luggage in the cart.

"Are we by the McDougals again?" Charlie asked. "I've IM'd Stu a bunch and we've got a lot planned for this weekend. He said he's going to be here."

"You guys are all in a row like last time," Russ said as they started rolling toward the motor home lot. "Also, Charlie, you have your own golf cart at your disposal. It's outside the motor home. I'll go over the rules for it when we get there. Hart's orders that you are not to tire yourself out. Next weekend's Michigan, and that's one of Hart's favorite tracks. He'd love to have you there."

"Okay," Charlie said, his excitement bubbling as they drove into the lot.

Stuart McDougal must have been watching out the motor home window, for he raced outside the moment Russ parked. "Hey, Charlie! Taylor and I have been waiting for you!"

"I'll carry the suitcases in," Russ told Kellie as they exited the car.

"Thanks."

"Hey Stu, I brought some new anime," Charlie said.

"Excellent," Stuart said. "Mrs. Thompson, I want Charlie to come visit, maybe in the fall when the races are in Charlotte again." He glanced at Russ. "Can we arrange that?"

"That might work," Kellie said. She then stepped into the motor home to avoid more questions. Who knew what life would hold in mid-October? It was only early June. With Charlie's condition, she just couldn't plan that far ahead. Within moments, she saw both golf carts speed off.

Hart arrived about an hour later, having showered and changed out of his uniform. "Hey," he said as he entered. "I'm all yours. The evening is ours." He walked right up to her, invading her space. "I ran third fastest in practice today."

"And should I be impressed by that?" Kellie teased. His proximity had already melted her equilibrium. She hadn't seen him in several days, and now that he was in front of her, she realized she'd missed him. She struggled for some composure as she realized the profound implications.

"You should never be impressed with me," Hart said. He tilted up her chin and stared down into her eyes. "But you should be afraid of one thing. I'm going to be in the top five. I'm planning on collecting."

"Really? I wasn't aware I'd agreed to reward you for a top five. You were the one who put those words in my mouth."

He arched an eyebrow, trying to assess whether she was serious or just flirting. "You're already rewarding me. You're here, aren't you?" he countered.

"Yes but..." she faltered under his intense stare.

"No buts," Hart said, lowering his mouth to hers. "They're

against the rules." He kissed her gently, taking his time to make the moment tender. Finally he withdrew his lips from hers. "Now that's the right way to say hello."

They heard a knock on the door, and a voice call, "Hey, Hart, you in here?"

"Dusty, that you?" Hart called back.

"Yeah. We're going to start racing soon. You joining in?"

"Not tonight. Kellie and Charlie are here," Hart replied, and they heard Dusty leave. "That was Dusty Burke. A bunch of us race remote-controlled cars on nights we're free."

"Don't let me keep you," she said.

"I'd rather be here with you," Hart replied. He tapped the tip of her nose and grinned. "Besides, I won last week and don't feel like defending my title. They're all out to get me. Did you and Charlie eat? Don't know if you noticed the barbecue pit outside, but I've got steaks marinating in your fridge."

"You're cooking?"

He nodded. "I'm quite handy with a grill. And any fool like me can open a can of baked beans and microwave those special shrink-wrapped baked potatoes. My driver even stocked your fridge with chocolate cake from the best bakery in town."

Kellie sighed, her tone light. "And here I actually had such high hopes of you truly being domestic. Just opening some cans doesn't count."

"It proves I can delegate."

"Creative excuse."

"Yep. And I do wield a decent spatula." He leaned in and stole another long kiss before they finally broke apart and went to start dinner.

Kellie noted that this weekend seemed less stressful, or maybe it was because she'd relaxed around Hart and also knew what the schedule was like. The day of the race she was again invited to watch the race with Alyssa McDougal. Charlie was again atop the pit box.

"So how are you and Hart getting along?" Alyssa asked Kellie during a caution late in the race. The two were back in the small kitchen area, restocking the veggie tray. "I'm not wanting to pry, but this is the first time we've had a chance to chat since Charlotte."

"I'm just along for the ride," Kellie tried.

"Not the way he looks at you," Alyssa said. "I know Hart. There's more than that brewing."

"Caught me. I admit. I like him. But there are so many variables."

"Like you aren't sure if it's real."

Kellie popped a carrot in her mouth to keep from replying and Alyssa answered for her. "I can tell you Hart's very serious. I've seen enough of the, um, women…"

"Bimbos, Cynthia called them yesterday when I saw her briefly. She told me she was very glad I wasn't one and that she was delighted to see me again."

"She would call them that." Alyssa chuckled aloud. "She's originally from the Midwest. Being a Southerner, I always try to be more delicate. Anyway, Hart's different with you. He talks about you and Charlie. A few of the guys were giving him grief that you were too smart for him and would wise up and never see him again. He didn't think it funny, and normally that type of razzing wouldn't bother him at all. The guys had him really worried."

"I just have so much going on," Kellie said. "Charlie is going to start chemo again in a few weeks. I've told Hart that I can't give him any guarantees. I'm not able to travel with him and I don't think that it's fair for him to be waiting for something I might never be able to do."

Kellie glanced up at the monitor. Hart was still the race leader, having led the last twenty laps. The commentators had already mentioned that Hart's lucky charms were present and twice had shown Charlie sitting atop the war wagon. Oh, she knew Charlie was in heaven. But he was now sort of a public figure. His life, including his disease, was out there. Yesterday people with garage passes had pointed at him, recognizing him. She'd been unnerved and her mother's instinct to protect her child had kicked in full force. She wasn't finding tonight easy, either.

A half hour later, Hart was still leading the race. He'd slipped behind for a few laps after he'd pitted, but come right back and regained his lead, passing Kyle Doolittle on the inside of Turn Two. Doolittle had now slipped back to fifth place, and Hart was three car lengths ahead with ten laps to go. Unless a caution came out, he was uncatchable.

"You better get ready for your first Victory Lane," Alyssa said.

Kellie glanced at her outfit. She wore tan pants and a seafoam-green short-sleeve T-shirt, almost the same outfit she'd worn last time she'd been at the track. "What am I supposed to do? I'm not pretty enough. I've seen women dressed to the nines carrying their Chihuahuas in those little purses."

"That's not everyone. Not all of us are purposely glamorous. Besides, you don't have to be on camera, but if you do, you look great. Hart will climb out of the car and immediately have microphones shoved in his face. He's got to do those interviews before anything. All you do is smile a lot and follow his or Wally's lead. After a bit, you can fade into the background and leave. He's going to have tons of team photos to take, sponsors to greet and such. It takes forever."

"If I can fade into the background, why be there at all?"

"Because he'll know if you're not," Alyssa said, as if that explained everything.

"Move, girl," one of the other wives called from her spot. "You've only got five laps. You can meet him in Victory Lane or in the pit."

Kellie grabbed her hard card, putting the pass around her neck. She stepped out of the air-conditioned motor home and into the June heat. The noise of cars roaring around the race track surrounded her. She had just reached a checkpoint when Russ arrived. "I was coming to get you," he said.

"Thanks. I can't tell you how relieved I am to see you," she said.

Russ smiled widely, and Kellie's stomach churned. "Oh, don't relax yet. It's going to be chaos. Welcome to the fun house."

"WE SENT RUSS to get her." Wally said over the radio.

Hart pushed the gas pedal down, accelerating the car out of Turn Two. One more and his victoryless streak would be over. He hit the straightaway, the race clearly his. His body pumped with adrenaline and psyched itself for the celebration to come. He eased up on the gas and braked, taking Turn Three and heading for the finish line. Everyone else was at least five seconds back—he could practically coast in, but Hart hit the gas for one final push. He could see the checkered flag waving and then he was across the line, taking home his first win since Daytona back in February. Hart Hampton, driver of the Number 413 Elementals Chevrolet, was back.

He lowered his net and stuck his fist out the window, staying out and taking his victory lap.

"She's here," Wally's voice called in his ear. "Don't you dare destroy the engine this time."

Hart grinned to himself. He'd been listening to Wally and his spotter Matt all night. Matt was his eyes in the sky, and together he and Wally had led a team that had outdone themselves. "Boys," Hart called, "we're going to celebrate tonight."

Hart brought his car back to the finish line and stopped his front wheels, causing smoke to rise from the back pair. He winced once as he knew the stench from the burning rubber was going to permeate his hair and skin. He was going to really stink and hoped Kellie wouldn't care that much when he arrived at Victory Lane. He grinned, knowing that the moment he got out of the car he'd be hosed down with shaken bottles of microbrew. Yes, he was going to reek. She wasn't going to be too excited to see him, but the thing he liked most about Kellie was that he knew she'd handle any curve thrown her way. He knew she'd be in Victory Lane because of him, not because she wanted to be on television herself. He'd dated one model who'd been in every single frame she could get her face into. He'd been so annoyed he'd sent her straight home.

Hart turned the car into pit road, making his way to where his team waited. Giddiness consumed him. Yeah, the word was cheesy, but it described his emotions perfectly.

There she was, standing on the edge of his pit box, right next to Russ, Charlie at her side.

Hart tapped the steering wheel impatiently as the car was moved to Victory Lane and final preparations for the celebration began. Finally the officials gave him the signal and he climbed out of the car, standing on the door ledge for a moment while he raised both arms skyward, fists raised triumphantly. Around him his team erupted into ear-deafening cheers, and the first liquid drops rained upward, and, as Hart jumped to the checkered concrete, the spray increased, drenched him, and dripped off the bill of his Elementals ball cap.

"Hart, fantastic win! Tell us about your final thoughts when you knew the race was yours." The first question always came from the network providing live race coverage.

Hart craned his head, trying to see Kellie through the crowd. "The Elementals Chevy ran great all night. We were definitely the fastest race car out on the track. We knew we had something during happy hour when we ran second."

"So do you think your unlucky streak has braked to halt?" the reporter asked.

Hart took a sip of cola before answering. He was parched. "We were never unlucky. All teams have setbacks at one point or another, and my team's worked hard all year to bring us this second win. We'll be celebrating in the shop tomorrow."

"But do you think having your lucky charms here helped?"

"It certainly didn't hurt. I'm always glad when Charlie's here with me. I'm living my dream; it's great to see him living his," Hart said.

The radio interview came next, and Hart remained pinned next to the car as he answered a few questions. All around him mayhem ensued as people celebrated the win. Cynthia was there, hugging him. Wally came up and grabbed him. But no Kellie. She remained just out of reach.

Suddenly fed up, Hart strode across Victory Lane and headed to Kellie. Hart was aware of cameras following him but he didn't care. The interviews could take forever, and he wasn't waiting another minute. Charlie reached up and gave him a high five. "Congratulations."

"Yes, congrats," Kellie said.

"I'm here to collect." Hart told her. Her eyes widened as she realized the implications. He wasn't just top five. He'd won. He swooped down, planting one on her right there. The touch of his lips to hers was quick, but there was nothing brotherly or chaste in the kiss. The movement had been full of unspoken promise. "I'm going to be forever, but don't you dare take off without me," he said.

And with that, Hart allowed himself to be sucked back into the interviews.

Then he had to pose with his team for the winner photos, which lasted forever as each sponsor got a copy of the guys wearing the sponsor's hat. In all the hat changes, Hart lost track of Kellie and soon Russ swept him along to the next commitment.

Adrenaline flowed and Hart enjoyed himself, but, for the first time, he discovered that something about winning races had changed. He wanted to celebrate with Kellie. He wanted her to be a part of this. She wasn't just there to be an outlet later for his excitement and excess energy. He wanted her to be a part of his revelry.

Yet, tonight, after the race, she and Charlie would fly to Charlotte with him, and then later that night on to Myrtle Beach. He'd tried to convince her to stay, but she'd cited that Charlie might need to go to the clinic on Monday and that had been that.

"You seem pretty frustrated for a man who just won a race and moved himself up in the points standings," Cynthia said at the end of the picture session. Russ and a NASCAR P.R. manager were moving everyone around, giving her a private moment with Hart as they traveled to the next location.

"I'm just realizing that if I'd lost I'd be spending time with Kellie and Charlie. They're going back home tonight."

Cynthia simply laughed and patted him on the shoulder. "Maybe you can lose next weekend," she joked.

The absurdity of her suggestion caused Hart's mood to lighten somewhat. "I'm pretty gone, aren't I?"

"It's a nice change," Cynthia said, smiling. "Imagine, you having to work for Kellie as hard as you have to win a race."

"You don't think that's why I'm so interested in her, do you? Because she's a challenge?" Hart frowned as he considered that.

"No," Cynthia replied. "She challenges you, but only in the sense that you're changing for the better because of her. She's not playing games and neither are you. Just take things slow."

Slow was an understatement, Hart thought, as the sun had dipped below the horizon by the time he was finished with all his commitments. He finally made it to his hauler, one of the last ones in the near empty lot. Even the motor home lot had been vacated.

Russ waited outside the hauler, and the minute Hart saw him, he knew.

"They're gone, aren't they?"

Russ nodded, and, for first time since he'd been five, Hart swore.

BY MICHIGAN, Hart was out of sorts, taking nineteenth. He chalked it up to a slow car, but he wasn't much better the next weekend in California, taking twentieth on the road course. He'd always been decent on the road courses, but both driver and car had tanked. Worse, the media had commented on the lack of Kellie and Charlie's presence at both events, citing those as the reason for Hart's poor performance. Two weeks were enough to make a man extremely irritable.

Oh, he'd seen Kellie. He'd flown to Myrtle Beach twice since Pocono. However, he'd been unable to get close to Kellie in the way he'd wanted. Sure, he'd stolen kisses, but he hadn't gotten promises of a future. She'd pull him close and then push him away. He knew that kissing her in Victory Lane had freaked her out, sent her back into her shell.

He'd moved too fast.

For a man used to women tossing themselves at him, Kellie

was driving him absolutely crazy. "You've got a call," Russ said. They were on the tarmac, ready to board Hart's plane for the way home.

"Who would be calling me on your phone?" Hart asked, but he took the cell. "Hart Hampton."

"Hi," Kellie said.

His voice instantly softened. "Hi." Then he panicked. California was three hours earlier than the East Coast. "Nothing's wrong with Charlie, is there?"

"No," she said. "Nothing except that he's mad at me. He went to bed in a huff tonight. He's very disappointed we haven't been there for you." She sighed. "I'm sorry I've been distant."

"No, it's as much my fault," Hart said. "I thrust you into the limelight."

"I'm not good at handling this," Kellie said. "Perhaps we can talk this week? Could you come to a small birthday party for Charlie on Wednesday?"

"I'll make sure I'm there," Hart said, realizing he probably sounded quite desperate. Kellie had him wrapped around her finger and she had no idea. Maybe it was time to tell her exactly how much she meant to him, where this relationship needed to go. Hart wanted more—everything. He wasn't going to settle for anything less. "What time?"

"Five," she said.

"I'll see you and Charlie then." He quickly said goodbye and hung up before she could say anything more. He felt guilty afterward for being rather abrupt, but instinct told him not to call her back. It was better to talk face-to-face. They could work things out Wednesday.

BY THREE WEDNESDAY AFTERNOON, Kellie found herself nervous. By four-thirty, she understood the term walking on eggshells. Charlie, however, was as enthusiastic as one could be for turning sixteen. He had a spring to his step today, as if finally reaching this milestone had taken a load off his shoulders.

By five, the small house had started to fill up as Anita, Kellie and Charlie welcomed guests. The next-door neighbors dropped in, as did Charlie's homeschool teacher. A few of the nurses were friends, and they popped by. Hart didn't show until almost six, and while Kellie's blood pressure had skyrocketed by his late arrival and failure to call, Charlie simply took everything in stride and greeted him with a huge hug.

"You're getting quite a haul," Hart said, gesturing toward the table where a bunch of opened presents lay.

"Most people couldn't come so they mailed things," Charlie said. "The Muldoons—you remember Brad, don't you—sent me this cool new computer game. Hampton Racing sent me last year's NASCAR yearbook and look, this ride-along book you did."

"I didn't do it," Hart said. "They just sort of followed me around for a season."

"Do you think I'll be in the next one?" Charlie asked.

"I don't know. Russ or Cynthia approves those. I don't even see them before they go to press. Show me the book later and I'll give you the real story."

"Will do," Charlie said. He showed Hart a few more of his gifts, explaining each one. Kellie found herself proud of her son as he offered Hart pizza, cake and ice cream. Not once did her son ask Hart for anything, or act as if he'd expected him to bring him a gift. Hart had walked in the house empty-handed, and Kellie knew she'd asked for a lot when she'd requested he fly to see Charlie.

"So you haven't been doing well these past two races," Charlie said as Hart ate a bite of now room-temperature pizza.

"No. I think you've been making the difference," Hart said, honestly. "Maybe the press is on to something when they call you my lucky charm.

"The media might say that, but don't believe the hype. You were doing fine without us," Charlie said.

"I'd still rather have you there," Hart pointed out, his gaze finding Kellie. She flushed and turned away. Hart finished his pizza, ate a piece of cake, minus the ice cream, and stood up. "Hey, Charlie, want to take a walk? I need to stretch my legs and work off the cake."

Kellie blinked. It was the last week of June and hot outside, as sunset wouldn't be for another three hours. Even though both Hart and Charlie wore T-shirts and shorts, she didn't want the summer sun to tire Charlie out. But Hart was here and Kellie knew this was a time when she had to let go.

"We won't be long," Hart told her. He glanced at his watch. "Only a few minutes."

"Just put your hat on," Kellie said. Her son's hair was in desperate need of a trim, but she'd been unwilling to take him to the barbershop since, when he started chemo next week, the brown locks would all fall out again. Kellie hadn't yet told Hart that Charlie was going to celebrate the Fourth of July in the hospital. She also wanted to ask if he'd let her and Charlie attend one more race—New Hampshire, this coming weekend. Afterward, they'd immediately come home and start treatments Monday.

"So you ready?" Hart asked as Charlie put on his baseball cap. He adjusted the plastic frame of his glasses behind his ear. "I'm good," Charlie said.

"Then let's go." Hart stopped a moment. "You can come, too," he told Kellie.

"I'm..." Kellie paused and changed her mind. "Okay."

She walked outside with them and the heat instantly enveloped her. Even though they lived away from the beach, the smell of the ocean still reached their house, filling the air with a sweet tropical scent.

Charlie made it down the walk—then saw the car at the end. "Wow! Did you drive here? Sweet! Look at that car."

Kellie was looking. In fact, her mouth had dropped open slightly as she stared at the shiny new Corvette parked at the end of her walk. The dark green paint gleamed, the clear coat polished to a sheen so reflective that she could probably see herself in the hood. The chrome was buffed and shined. The convertible top matched the tan interior. "It's very impressive," she managed to say.

"Glad you like it," Hart told Charlie. He reached into his pocket and withdrew some keys.

"We're going for a ride?" Charlie asked, hope growing.

"Yes," Hart said, that famous grin widening.

"That's so awesome." Charlie's excitement was infectious. Kellie hadn't ever seen him this thrilled to be taking a car ride. Then again she didn't own a sports car.

"It gets even better. *You're* going to drive it. Although, first you need to climb in and fire her up." Hart tossed Charlie the keys, the remote control and silver keys arcing through the air. Charlie reached out with one hand, capturing everything firmly in his fist.

"Nice catch," Hart said. He reached over to the car and opened the driver's side door. "Happy birthday, Charlie. She's all yours."

CHAPTER THIRTEEN

SHE WAS GOING to kill him. Hart Hampton wouldn't be racing this weekend for he was going to be dead. She was going to tear him apart limb by limb for what he'd done.

"It's really not that bad," Anita said, spooning more chocolate ice cream into her mouth. "So the man bought the boy a car."

"A very expensive, next-year-model, new car! Loaded with every option." To say she was shaken by the gesture was an understatement.

"He paid the taxes, licensing and car insurance," Anita said, finishing the portion in her bowl. Whereas Kellie stopped eating when stressed, Anita dug in. She reached over and cut another slice of birthday cake.

"Him paying for everything doesn't make it okay." Right now Hart and Charlie were out tooling around Myrtle Beach, the top down. Since Charlie didn't have his permit, after letting her son start the car, Hart had switched places with Charlie and taken him for a ride. However, Kellie had no doubt they'd stop at a deserted parking lot somewhere and switch places, letting Charlie drive around the wide-open space at no more than twenty miles per hour. Admittedly, if she'd just turned sixteen and received a car—no, a Corvette, she amended—that's what she'd do.

Kellie sighed. Somehow her life had entered *The Twilight*

Zone. "I only wanted him to celebrate with Charlie, not buy him a gift that costs double what I used to make in a year. It's got a V-8 engine. How am I going to afford the fuel for that?"

"Sweetie, Hart didn't give that car to Charlie so he could go driving around all over town at your expense. I'm sure Hart realizes that the Corvette will sit covered under the carport most of the time. But giving it to Charlie made him happy. That's Hart's only motive. He cares."

"Charlie can't keep it," Kellie stated. "I don't make millions like Hart."

"Oh, honey." Anita reached across and covered her daughter's hand. "It's not a competition. It's not your world versus Hart's. Giving that car gave Charlie hope and incentive. Be happy for that. Charlie needs a father figure in his life. So what if that's Hart?"

"His actions undermine me as a mother. Now I have to let Charlie get his driver's license. Hart had no right give him a car without asking me first," Kellie insisted.

Anita chuckled. "Do you remember when you were little? Your dad used to bring you gifts when he returned from a business trip. He'd be gone for weeks, and the day he'd come home you'd go stand at the window and wait. Once you were there for almost an hour, just standing and staring down the street waiting for your dad."

"He was never home," Kellie said. She realized she'd married a man just like her father, constantly out seeking the adventure of being on the road. Her father had driven semis for a living until his sudden and fatal heart attack ten years ago.

"No, he wasn't," Anita said. "But that still doesn't change the fact that you'd run to your dad and throw your arms around him the minute he got home. And when you did, it always felt like a knife stabbed me right here."

With her free hand, Anita patted her chest. "Here I was, with you day in and day out, cooking, cleaning, taking you to school, and your father seemed to be the love of your life. It took me a long time to realize that you loved us differently and that your actions didn't mean you loved me less. It wasn't a competition for your affections."

"I always loved you. You've been my rock my entire life," Kellie said. "I'm sorry if you ever felt otherwise."

"Ever since JT's been gone, I think back on that time and realize how foolish I was. I know how much you cared and loved me. But I never got the running, throw-yourself-in-my-arms excitement. I got other things. What I want you to learn from my story is that you shouldn't compare yourself with Hart. Don't make my mistake. There's no competition between you two for Charlie's affections. He's not trying to take Charlie away. If anything, that man is trying to win *you*."

"No, he's not." As soon as the denial left her lips, Kellie sat there for a moment. Hart had always been a fantasy. Sure, she'd indulged, but not everything was good for you long-term.

"Okay, let's say he was," Kellie suggested. "But he's like Dad and John. Constantly traveling. On the road. He works seven days a week. My weekends would be spent at the track, hanging out in a motor home, my life dictated by a prearranged schedule I have no control over. What kind of a life would that be?"

"It would be a life," Anita said simply.

"What do you mean by that?" Kellie asked sharply, not liking her mother's response. "I have a good life."

"Oh, honey." Anita's sympathy was obvious. "Your life's on hold."

Hart and Charlie's return kept the conversation from continuing. "We need your keys so we can park," Hart said, standing in the back kitchen doorway. "I need to move your car."

"Hart's going to let me park the 'Vette," Charlie said.

Anita and Kellie both went out to the backyard, watching as Hart jockeyed cars. Then he let Charlie drive the Corvette underneath the single carport. Hart then pulled a box out of the trunk, and together he and Charlie worked to protect the car with the custom cover. Her son's grin covered his entire face as he pressed the remote, locking the car.

"I think this has been the best birthday ever," Charlie said as he settled into a kitchen chair a few minutes later. Anita cut him a second slice of cake—he'd had one earlier.

"Well, I have one more surprise," Hart said. "I contacted an old friend of mine from when I raced on the track here and we've found someone safe and reliable who will give you driving lessons. He's got a car built for driver's education— basically, two brake pedals—and he's ready for you to start anytime. I've already paid him for a full set of lessons, so he should be calling you tomorrow to set up your appointments."

"Too cool," Charlie said. "But what about the 'Vette?"

Hart had an answer for that. "He'll teach you on his car first, and when you're ready to learn how to handle yours, he'll teach you using it. He's also going to take you to get your permit. That way, your mom can have some free time."

Kellie sat there, stunned. Hart had thought of everything, including how to get around her procrastination. Her son's blue eyes shone with unbridled excitement. "Isn't this great, Mom?"

"It is," she agreed as a fist clenched her heart. Hart Hampton had made her son's dreams come true. It might not be a competition, but she still felt a profound loss. The pain was tangible. Maybe misguided, but real. Hart could give Charlie everything.

Charlie yawned suddenly and Kellie resisted the urge to touch his forehead and check for a fever. "Even though it's still early, I'm going to call it a night. I don't want to wear myself out before this weekend," he said.

"Are you coming to New Hampshire?" Hart asked, surprised.

Charlie gave his mother a pointed glance, as if he'd already expected her to have told Hart. "Mom?"

Kellie sighed. "Yes, we're planning on being there, if that's okay."

"Of course," Hart replied.

"Let me help you take some of this stuff into your room," Anita said, rising to her feet. She and Charlie grabbed the gifts and left the kitchen.

"Classy and tactful exit," Hart said.

"Yeah, they're real subtle," Kellie answered, her anxiety level rising now that she and Hart were alone.

"So you'll be there? I've had my parents' motor home there every weekend just in case you'd change your mind," he said. "I've missed you."

That admission shook her. *This wasn't real.* "You shouldn't have bought him a car," Kellie stated. "It's too much."

Hart shook his head. "Doesn't matter if I'd gotten him a Malibu or a Ferrari. You wouldn't have liked it. He's growing up, Kellie."

"Yes, but he's special." She slumped back in the chair. She and Hart had had this discussion before. There was no sense retreading old ground. "You've been more than generous. You made Charlie's day. Maybe I'm just nervous. Charlie starts chemo Monday. It's usually pretty hard on his body. Often he develops secondary infections because the chemo destroys all his cells, both the good and bad."

"Ah, so that's part of what's been bothering you."

"Yes. I always have a mixture of dread and hope. He'll be in the hospital for a few weeks because after that he has to get treatment to produce more cells, and hopefully they're not cancerous "

"I'll stop by as often as I can," Hart said.

Although she was scared of her own feelings growing even more for this man, Kellie would never deny Charlie access to his hero, especially in a time of need. "He'd like that very much."

Hart touched her fingers, weaving his through hers. "I want you to like that, as well." She said nothing and Hart exhaled his frustration. "I'm sorry I pushed you too fast. I was so excited about sharing the win with you that I kissed you on national television."

"Maybe some of your other women like that, but I…" Kellie sighed, trying to find the perfect words to say. "I'm a private person, Hart. I heard about our kiss at the hospital, from my neighbors, even the checkout girl at the market looked at me and exclaimed, 'Hey, didn't I see you kissing Hart Hampton?' I mean, the media used my name. There I was. I've had people ask me for tickets. They've asked me if I could get them autographs or free underwear. We let the home phone go to the answering machine first because of all the calls."

"I'll get you caller ID."

She shook her head. Stuff wasn't a solution. "No. You can't keep getting me things just because you can. I like you, Hart. I feel a connection between us. But I'm afraid. I don't want to become dependent on you."

And have you leave. She didn't say the words, but she heard them deep in her head. This man could let her be a queen for a day or maybe a week. But after his interest waned, she'd just be a scullery maid again, returned to her daily grind. Upon arriving home, her father had always hugged her, kissed her and given her gifts. Then he'd always been too tired to play and had wanted to watch television instead. John's interest in her had also faded quickly, so much that they'd been like two roommates in the same house long before Charlie developed his illness. There was no guarantee that any other man, even Hart, would be different. No certainty that the third time's a charm. She couldn't risk having her heart broken again, especially when she had to use all of her mental, physical and emotional energy to be there for her son.

Hart's phone rang, the call indicating that the car service had arrived to pick him up. "I understand you're conflicted and I think I can alleviate some of your fears. I want to talk about this more, but unfortunately, there's some bad weather headed this way. I have to go. "

Of course, he did. Hart didn't live nearby. Kellie's emotions tumbled inside her head. Didn't he understand that long distance never worked? He rose to his feet, and suddenly, without warning, pulled her to him. He wrapped his arms around her and brought his mouth to hers. Gone were the sweet kisses he'd bestowed earlier, and in their place was a thorough exploration of her mouth that left her ravaged and wanting more. He drew back, his face inches from hers so that his breath was hot on her cheek. He'd laced his fingers into her hair so that his hands framed her face.

"That's what I raced for at Pocono. I kept seeing you waiting for me at the end. I didn't kiss you to put you in the spotlight, but rather because that's something I'd wanted to do for miles. I've had girls in Victory Lane before and couldn't have cared less. I care about you, Kellie. God knows how I'm going to prove that and get you to believe that you're different, but I'm willing to pull out all the stops if that's what it takes. I'll see you in Loudon on Friday."

And with that he was gone, leaving her trembling.

THE TRACK at Loudon was a little over a mile long, with banking twelve degrees in the turns and two degrees on the straightaways. The race would be three hundred laps. Hart and his team lined up perpendicular to the car, facing the American flag off in the distance as the pop singer belted out the national anthem.

Hart stood closest to his car, which happened to be parked next to his pit. He'd won the pole and thus was starting in the first spot inside, right after the pace car. He'd chosen the first pit stall. While it would take him a while to get down pit road, he'd be right at the end to accelerate off. He'd managed to talk both Kellie and Charlie into doing the driver introductions with him. She stood next to him now, enduring the camera in her face as it panned down his team, showing them to both the live fans and television viewers. He hadn't found the perfect time to talk with her about everything else.

He had, however, had a moment to clear the air and tell her that he didn't see her as something temporary. "I want you with me," he'd said, and then she'd nodded.

He suddenly felt a small tug, and he realized Kellie had slid her hand into his. Hart smiled. Such a small gesture, but an important one that everyone nearby, including the press, could see.

"Thank you for everything," she mouthed. He smiled and focused, her hand in his a welcome weight.

Since Independence Day was on Wednesday, the track had planned several patriotic events, including the flyover of Air National Guard planes that was roaring into view. He'd never been one much for praying before the start of the race, but the last few races he'd been having the guys from the outreach ministry stop by. Today wouldn't be an exception. Before

Kellie released his hand, he pulled her toward him, giving her a hug before letting her go.

Charlie was already up on top of the war wagon, ready to watch the weather. NASCAR allowed seven guys over the wall and now that the anthem had ended, they were moving into place. Hart's teammate, Mitch Bengal, sat in the outside pole position. Cynthia had been ecstatic with Hampton Racing holding the top two fastest qualifying times. Hart had simply been thrilled to have legitimately qualified for the Shootout next year at Daytona. The only ones who could participate were pole winners or past shootout winners and, like the NASCAR NEXTEL All-Star Challenge, the event was all about prestige. Hart gave Mitch a salute before climbing into his car. Wally came over and patted the side of the green Number 413 car. "You gonna win this for us?"

"Gonna try. If nothing else, I want a top five finish," Hart said as he attached the steering wheel. He couldn't fire up the car until the official gentlemen-start-your-engines command. Hart scratched under his chin. His new helmet smelled fresh. No matter how many times he'd put on a helmet, the weight was always something that took a second or two to get used to. That was something that never changed.

"If you win you can kiss the girl in Victory Lane," Wally said for incentive.

"Planning on kissing her no matter what," Hart replied as Wally put up Hart's net and backed away.

Hart smiled to himself. He'd kissed Kellie quite a bit over the weekend, practically every chance he got. He'd actually gotten up early so he could spend the morning with her and Charlie, and that had been extremely successful. He'd never had to prove he'd be a good family man before, but he was determined to do just that. Kellie and Charlie had come to mean a great deal to him. And if she thought he was ready to let her go…

Hardly. He planned on winning her heart. They were going to have that talk tonight, once he won this race.

He focused on his job as the command was given, and, with a flip of some switches, all forty-three drivers fired up their engines.

The car rumbled to life underneath him, and now that the engine was going, the cockpit heated. NASCAR drivers raced in all types of weather, and Hart was grateful for the cooling unit that circulated cool air underneath his helmet to his face. The track had been hot during practice and qualifying, but a cold front had come through last night dropping the temperature by eight degrees. A big difference, and one he hoped worked in his favor.

"Okay, let's do this," his spotter Matt called through the speaker in Hart's helmet. Matt was perched high above the main grandstand.

Hart followed the pace car out onto the track. They'd do several warm up laps first before the pace car would move onto pit road. That was always an exhilarating moment—seeing the green flag waving and pressing the pedal to the floor. Hart shifted, adjusting his speed and weaving so he could warm up his tires. Sunk down in his custom seat he could see only what was in front of him and a peripheral side view.

Being the pole sitter, he saw the pace car duck over and head onto pit road at the same time Matt told him. "Green flag," Matt added.

Up ahead in the middle of the straightaway Hart could see the official waving it. Adrenaline punched through his veins. He wasn't staring at the back end of someone in front. Nothing but clean air ahead. He readied his hands and feet, prepared his body for the race ahead and accelerated.

KELLIE AND CHARLIE were waiting for him outside the hauler when he arrived after the end of the race, having placed eighth.

"Another top ten," Charlie said, giving Hart a high five.

"Congrats," Kellie added.

"Thanks," Hart said, somewhat glumly. "Let's get out of here."

Several hours—and a short plane ride—later, Hart and Kellie were sitting in her kitchen. "Thanks again," she said.

"No problem," Hart replied. He reached across the table and took her hand. Now that Charlie and Anita had retired, he had Kellie all to himself. "I told you I'd be here for you."

She nodded.

"Starting to believe me?"

She nodded again. "Yes. I shouldn't have doubted."

"I'll try not to push. I know with Charlie you have other priorities. But I'm not planning on going anywhere. You can trust me on that."

"I do." Her voice was quiet and sure.

"I'm glad." Hope soared inside him. He cared for her and wanted her in his life. She'd just taken another step closer to him.

"I have to be honest, though," Kellie said. "Charlie's treatment comes first."

"Of course," Hart said quickly. He understood that.

"No. I mean, I want this. Us. But I can't make any guarantees. It's not fair to you to wait for me. I don't know what weekends Charlie and I can come to the track. I…"

"Shh," Hart said. He got out of his chair and came to squat beside her. He balanced himself on his feet and placed his arms around her. "Kellie, you and I said no buts. I don't want guarantees. We can just take everything one day at a time."

"I'm scared. I don't want to fall in love with you and lose you," she whispered.

"You won't. Lose me, that is," he clarified, grinning at his near gaffe.

She smiled, her softened face reassuring him that he was still on course to win her. He gathered her into his arms and somehow she was in his lap, both sitting on the floor. He kissed her gently for a long while. Finally they drew apart.

"I've got to get going," he said, finding himself in no hurry to leave her side. While she might be afraid of falling in love with him, he'd already taken the tumble.

"I wish you didn't live so far away," she said, and his decision was instantaneous.

"Charlie's starting treatments tomorrow?"

"Yes," she confirmed.

"I'm going to get a hotel room so I can be here. I'll call my pilot and let him know I'm not going back tonight."

"Really you don't have to…"

"I want to," Hart said.

"No," she replied, shaking her head. "I mean, you don't need a hotel. You can stay here."

"I'd like that," Hart said. He stroked her hair gently, letting the silk strands wash over his fingers. "Just tell me your couch is soft. While I want nothing more than to take you in my arms and hold you all night, I'm a believer in propriety."

He kissed her again, his lips exploring the change in her their conversation had brought. She opened to him, giving of herself through kisses and caresses until both realized that it was time to go to bed—alone.

Hart closed his eyes and made himself comfortable on the sofa. Kellie wasn't ready to make love to him and he didn't want Kellie to lose herself, or to use him as a diversion from thinking about her son's treatment tomorrow. When they made love, he wanted both of them to only be focused on each other. As for tonight, well, they also needed their rest tomorrow.

Hart knew it was all about timing. Like fine-tuning a race car, a relationship took work and precise mechanics. Nothing ever worth winning came easy, but he wasn't worried. Like running in the NASCAR NEXTEL Cup Series, he was in this race for the long haul, and would do whatever it took.

CHAPTER FOURTEEN

"HI, EVERYONE, and welcome to Richmond. I'm Malcolm French and I'm here with Gus Edwards. What a wild summer it's been! This is it, the final race before the Chase. It's a great September day, but for the contenders, it's more than that."

"That's because today's race determines who's still in contention for the NASCAR NEXTEL Cup Championship. The ten-race Chase officially starts at New Hampshire next weekend. Everyone's been pushing hard, and today won't be an exception."

"We've seen Dusty Burke trying to nail down his rookie title and make the Chase. Ronnie McDougal sits firmly in the top twelve and unless he finishes forty-third today, he's guaranteed a spot."

"And Kyle Doolittle has cracked the top three and is closing on the leader. Those top spots aren't concrete yet."

"No, they aren't. But the surprising comeback story is Hart Hampton, who has moved back into contention since his eighth-place finish at Loudon in July. Hampton currently sits twelfth in points, an astonishing feat considering some had him washed up after the first Richmond race."

"But that was before he met his lucky charms. We've seen them at most races this summer, and the trend doesn't seem *to have stopped yet as Kellie Thompson and her son, Charlie, are at the track today."*

"While no official word has come from Hampton Racing, after that kiss we saw in Victory Lane a month ago in Indianapolis, one can only assume that Hart Hampton is off the market."

"Ah, that will disappoint a lot of women out there."

"Indeed."

KELLIE WOULD NOT bite her nails. She clasped her hands together and tucked them underneath her thighs. This had been where Hart had wrecked way back in May. As only one hundred points separated the top thirteen drivers, nothing was set in stone. That meant the drivers in contention were racing all out, fighting for every inch of pavement. The grandstands were crowded, and already three cars had packed up and gone home: two from collision and one from engine failure.

With fifty laps to go, the race was still anyone's. As the last caution had been long ago, all teams were looking at green flag pit stops. The commentators were saying that most teams didn't think they had enough fuel to stay out. Hart's car was fast, and so far had been performing well. He'd needed few adjustments during his earlier stops.

But like the rest of the leaders, he'd have to pit once more, and then the crew chiefs would make their decisions as to whether the drivers took fuel only or also took on fresh tires.

From her seat in the McDougals's motor home, Kellie was amazed at how much she'd learned over the past nine weeks she'd been officially dating Hart Hampton. While she hadn't made it to every race because of Charlie's health, when at the track their weekends had become routine but certainly not less exciting. Hart had spent his July week off by coming to stay with them in Myrtle Beach, and that had been wonderful. With the chemo looking as if it had been working, Anita had insisted that Kellie take an evening off, and Hart had surprised Kellie with a flight to Savannah where they'd had a romantic dinner at one of the city's best restaurants. They'd then spent the night in a historic hotel suite, making love for the first time. If she'd had any doubt of Hart's long-term intentions, he'd cleared them up that night when he'd told her he loved her. She couldn't yet say the words in return, but she'd taken him into her arms and shown him how much she'd grown to care.

"They're pitting," Alyssa said, interrupting Kellie's reverie, as the race leader veered to the left and headed down pit road. A long line of cars followed him, a few choosing to stay out in hopes of gaining track position.

There were less than thirty laps to go on the short track so Hart and many of the leaders took only two right side tires and fuel. Two laps went by with the drivers jockeying for position, some cars touching. The camera panned and Kellie frowned. "Did something just fall off that car?" Kellie asked.

"I'm not sure," someone answered.

But indeed something had dislodged from one of the cars, and seconds later before the caution flag came out, one of the lap-down cars caught the debris with his back right wheel, slicing his car's tire to shreds. His sudden reduction in speed and subsequent one-eighty spin had the fifteen drivers behind him scrambling into evasive action to avoid wrecking as the field careened into Turn Three with no room to spare.

"Hart's loose!" Alyssa cried out.

Kellie's whole body tensed. Having been in wrecks herself, she'd lived in dread of this moment, and here it was live on TV. She watched with horror as Hart's car began to turn and the back end of the Number 413 car hit the wall. The sheet metal crumpled like paper, and the car spun around again as another driver clipped it. She'd never been so afraid and she barely registered Alyssa's hand covering hers as the rest of the drivers tried to avoid the crashed cars. Both the driver with the cut tire and Hart were against the wall in Turn Three, and Kellie held her breath as the other drivers made it around safely. But suddenly, flames shot from the right front of Hart's car.

High up in the turn, Hart had lowered his window net and Kellie's heart relaxed for only a second while Hart climbed out of the car, helmet still on. Already emergency crews were there putting out the fire, and Hart removed his helmet and climbed unassisted into the ambulance for the mandatory trip to the infield care center.

Kellie tried to breathe. She'd seen news images from the Middle East but she'd never once seen John "at work." Hart had just survived a car wreck going 100-plus miles per hour. While that said volumes for NASCAR's safety, the event had still shaken her. What if he'd been hurt? At this moment Hart's what-if lecture seemed irrelevant. She couldn't let go. She tried to calm herself as she realized she'd fallen deeply in love with Hart Hampton.

"I'll walk you over there," Alyssa said. "Unless you'd rather wait for him in the hauler."

"No." Kellie shook her head, her loose blond hair swishing against her shoulders. She'd worn it down because Hart liked it that way. "I'll go."

The night was warm as the two women stepped out of the motor home and made their way to the care center. "You don't have to go in with me," Kellie said as they reached the building. "I've got it from here."

"Are you sure? You look a little pale."

"I'm fine," Kellie insisted.

"You call me if you need anything," Alyssa said, giving Kellie a quick hug. Kellie watched her friend for a second as she made her way toward her husband's pit. Then Kellie took a deep breath and entered the building.

"You know, Richmond just might not be your track," the doctor was saying as the nurse brought Kellie back to where Hart lay.

"Yeah, win one and crash twice," Hart said in a poor attempt at a joke. He heard Kellie approach and turned his head. She could tell he ached from the impact, but other than that he looked okay. "Hey," he said, managing a smile.

"Hi," she said, a lump forming in her throat. She wasn't one hundred percent certain she was going to keep her composure.

"You can come closer," Hart encouraged as the doctor moved away. "I promise not to bite if you do. Neither will the doctor. I'm just waiting for the okay to get out of here."

"When will that be?" she asked, suddenly overcome by the myriad of raw, conflicting emotions powering through her. Hart lay on the examination table, his uniform pulled down to his waist, exposing the T-shirt he wore underneath.

"Should be real soon." He propped himself up on an elbow so he could see her better.

She trembled. She'd walked into so many clinic rooms, only then it had been Charlie on the gurney. She'd waited for the doctor's news, her whole body fearful of the words he'd relate. Each time, a fist of worry clenched her heart and tore at her soul. Stress would build up, causing her to tremble and shake. She'd pray for the best and expect the worst. Now instead of Charlie, it was Hart.

"Hey, are you okay?" Hart said, his forehead creasing. He gave her a reassuring smile. "Don't cry, honey. I'm going to be fine."

He was going to be all right, but that didn't matter. Kellie fought to hold back the tears. Sometimes, when in this situation with Charlie, she'd cry tears of joy. Those were the happy, relieved tears, when she could take a deep breath and relax. However, most times she shed tears of frustration as yet another treatment didn't work. The push-pull of hope—sometimes rewarded like today, sometimes not—took a huge toll.

"Kellie?" Hart prodded. "Hey, sweetheart, it's okay."

She shook her head from left to right, her entire body shaking. How she wished she could tell him she was okay. As she'd walked over to the infield care unit, fear had clawed at her. Unlike her constant dread of bad news with Charlie, this time it had started slow, like a little trickle. She'd mentally chided herself she was being irrational. Hart had clearly been fine, as he'd climbed into the ambulance on his own. He'd waved to the crowd. But fear was like water. Once it worked its way through an opening, the hole became bigger and bigger, letting more and more through, until the emotion flooded everything in its path, washing away all rationality.

She stepped forward and Hart reached for her hand. His touch warmed. "You're like ice," he said.

"I'm fine," she replied, a tear escaping.

Hart worked himself to a sitting position. "You aren't fine," he chided gently. "You're trembling."

"I was worried," she admitted.

"That's because you care about me," he said. He rubbed her hands between his. "You love me."

"Way too much," Kellie said, admitting the truth of just how deeply she loved him. Hart swung his legs off the table and drew her toward him, his legs framing her. Kellie took a deep, steadying breath. Sometimes love just wasn't enough. Hadn't John proved that? Could she stand to risk losing another person? Could she willingly put herself in that situation? "I can't do this," she answered.

"You just did, and the first time is the hardest," Hart told her gently. He threaded two of his fingers into her hair, drawing a strand toward him. "I'm so glad you're here. Do you know how much your presence means to me? You've become one of the most important people in my life."

"I just don't want to lose you. John was difficult enough. This isn't easy for me."

"I know."

"I love you," Kellie said. "But I've learned that sometimes love isn't enough."

Hart's jaw tightened with raw determination. "In our case, it's going to be."

The doctor returned, intruding on the moment. "You're free to go," he told Hart. "I'm clearing you to race next weekend."

"Thanks." Hart slid off the table so that he stood next to Kellie, his taller frame shadowing hers. "Let's get out of here," he told her.

They'd barely made out of the care center door before Russ and Cynthia were there with a four-seater golf cart. "Sorry not to have been here sooner. I was up in the skybox," she said. "What did the doctor say?"

"I'm free to race next weekend," Hart said. He assisted Kellie into the cart. "Not that it really matters. I'm guess I'm out this year."

He meant the Chase, Kellie knew. Hart wouldn't have the points to compete for the NASCAR NEXTEL Cup championship.

"Yeah, but we can use the final races as testing for next year," Cynthia said. "You've had a lot go wrong this year. Let's look forward and fix that."

"I've also had a lot go right, on and off the track," Hart said, squeezing Kellie's hand. She averted her face, watching as they wove their way through the garage area to the haulers. Hart's team was already tearing down—loading the wrecked car and preparing to go home. Charlie was inside the hauler, and his face whitened slightly as he saw his mom. It was almost as if he knew she was freaking out, and his eyes pleaded with her not to make any hasty decisions.

"Hey, sport," Hart said. He tapped the bill of Charlie's cap. The Hampton Racing hat was a permanent fixture on Charlie's head as his hair had fallen out after the latest round of chemo.

"I called your pilot to let him know you're about to be on your way," Russ said.

"Thanks," Hart said. He smiled at Kellie and Charlie. "Let's get out of here."

Soon they were in the sky, headed to Myrtle Beach. From there, Hart would fly home to Charlotte. He accompanied them to Kellie's house, the hired car waiting outside. Inside, Charlie headed off to his room, leaving his mother alone with Hart.

"You've barely spoken to me since the race," he said, drawing her into his arms.

"I know," Kellie answered. She stepped back slightly.

"Hey, come here. Still rattled?"

"Very," Kellie said, deliberately putting space between them. "How about we talk later?"

She knew she was pushing him away, and Hart understood. "Okay," he said, agreeing although not looking very happy about it. "I'll come see you on Wednesday like always. We do have a lot to talk about. There are a few things I want to ask you. Next step things."

"Charlie has doctor appointments that day."

"I'll be here anyway," Hart said, closing the gap between them.

She opened her mouth to protest and then simply let go as Hart leaned in for a goodbye kiss. She lost herself in the feel of his mouth, kissing him with everything she wanted to tell him but knew she'd never say. Tonight had shaken her to the core. She didn't think she could take the next step. The risks were too great.

He drew back from her, his gaze intense. "You've never kissed me like that," he said.

Kellie shook her head, but remained mute. She let her fingers trail over his arm, memorizing the shape and texture as she stepped away and let him go.

"I'll see you Wednesday," Hart said. "Call you tomorrow."

She'd moved back into the shadows, turning away so that she couldn't see Hart leaving. The door clicked softly behind him as the lock caught.

"Mom?" Charlie called out.

Kellie turned. "I thought you'd gone to bed. It's really late."

"Don't break up, Mom," Charlie said. His blue eyes glistened, and Kellie's pain increased.

"Charlie…" Kellie began.

"He loves you. I can tell. Don't blow this. It was an accident. People have them all the time. NASCAR's safer than driving on the street."

"This is not a conversation to be having with my sixteen-year-old son," Kellie hedged. "You need to go to bed."

"Maybe, but know that I only want what's best for you. And that's Hart."

"I…" Kellie stopped, her heart heavy and her head throbbing as a headache took hold. "I don't want to talk about this.

You and I need to both get some rest. It's been a long weekend already."

"Don't push him away," Charlie said. "Please. For me."

"Sometimes adults do things that kids don't understand, but you will someday. Life isn't a fairy tale, Charlie. You of all people know that."

"It doesn't mean I still don't believe," he said. He turned and walked away, his anger with her evident.

Kellie stood for a moment, and then let herself collapse into the nearest chair. The silence of the room descended as the world around her settled down for the night.

Oh, she knew what people would think. This was Hart Hampton. NASCAR's most popular driver. And on Wednesday, she planned on breaking up with him. They'd say she was crazy. Foolish. How could she turn down such a gorgeous man who cared for her and her son? Who loved her.

But Kellie knew that independence was safer. She couldn't risk even the slightest chance of losing them both. Better to let go now then to suffer a greater loss later. Oh, they'd say she was irrational. Firefighters, military personnel, stuntmen, even police officers faced more danger than a NASCAR driver. But tonight's visit to the infield care center had shaken Kellie more than she'd realized. She visited the clinic enough for Charlie. She simply couldn't add another person to that mix.

CHAPTER FIFTEEN

ON TUESDAY, Hart's impending arrival and their conversation had dropped from Kellie's priority list.

"Mrs. Thompson. If you could come with me," Dr. Murphy said as he came to get her.

Kellie closed her eyes for a moment. Charlie had needed an emergency trip to the clinic and Kellie knew that *tone*. Oh, anyone else standing in the waiting room wouldn't recognize it for anything but a doctor asking her to come back to his office. But Kellie had been through this too many times to count.

She knew.

He didn't even have to tell her that Charlie's chemo had failed and that the leukemia was getting more aggressive. The doctor did so anyway, and she listened, her brain trying to absorb the overload of information as he discussed treatment options.

"So in a nutshell, Charlie's cancer is becoming resistant to the chemo and we have only a few more chances," Kellie summarized. She'd known something was wrong when Charlie hadn't wanted to get up Sunday morning. By Monday evening, his fever had spiked. They'd been able to get it down with acetaminophen, but by early this morning she'd known he had to go in.

"We're going to admit Charlie today," Dr. Murphy said,

confirming her fears. "The secondary infection bacteria are strep and the immature cells coming back in are leukemia blasts. We're going to start another round of chemo and head them off. We'll also give him morphine if the pain increases to an unbearable level."

Kellie bit her lip. "Have you told him all this yet?"

"I thought I'd tell you first and we could go in together."

Kellie nodded her approval. Charlie had some of the best doctors in the nation, but doctors plus modern science didn't necessarily equal miracles. "So we need to face that we might be at the end," she said.

The doctor's expression turned sympathetic. "I'm sorry. We have a few more things we can try, and I'm hopeful this next one will work."

"Thank you for being honest," Kellie said, as hope fled. They'd been fighting the disease for years. "I think I'd rather go in to talk to Charlie myself. If you don't mind."

"That's fine. I have to make my rounds. I'll stop by Charlie's room later and see if either of you have any questions."

A few minutes later, Kellie pushed the door open to her son's room. He lay quietly against the adjustable bed, watching television.

"Don't say it," he said as he saw her face. "No, don't you say it."

"Charlie," she said, trying to hold it together.

"I say *when*," he said stubbornly. "I did the research. There are a few more drugs they can try. I'm starting one today. Don't say it, Mom."

"Charlie." Tears of desperation came to her eyes. "We just have to be prepared. There are decisions we must make…"

"No!" His vehemence surprised her. "I'm not quitting. Not yet. I have things left I must do."

"This new drug they're going to try. It's brutal."

"I can handle it," he said. "You taught me to be a fighter. I'll handle it. I'm not going down until the very end, and if I do, I'll go down swinging."

The tears really began to flow and Kellie couldn't stop them. "Of course, you will," she said, grabbing for a tissue. "I'm not saying that. I'm not saying quit. Look at you, so much braver than me right now. You're together and I'm falling apart. But Charlie, how much more can you take?"

"All that I have to," he replied. She began to speak but he shook his head. "I'd like to be alone for a while. Please."

He looked so tiny and frail in that hospital bed. She wanted to stay but knew to respect his wishes. He had to face this himself, and her being teary-eyed and emotional wasn't helping.

"Okay. I'll go down to the cafeteria and read my book. Call me on my cell phone when you want me to come back up."

He didn't answer, only turned his face away to gaze out the window.

Kellie's hands shook as she pulled open the door to his hospital room. She trembled as she entered the elevator. In the cafeteria she almost spilled her coffee as she fought to get the lid on the cup. She finally sat down at a table and hit the speed-dial button. "Mom?" she said when Anita answered. "I think I need you."

HART HAMPTON'S CELL vibrated in the middle of a meeting with his sponsor's representative. Tomorrow was Charlie's visit at the clinic, and today some strange premonition had Hart refusing to turn the device off. As Liam discussed a contract point, Hart pulled the phone out of his jeans. Charlie had sent him a text message. He read it and frowned. "Call me ASAP" were the only words.

"So Hart, are you in agreement with that clause?" Liam asked.

Hart focused. They'd been discussing the amount of money Elementals was going to pay to sponsor Hart's car next year. They'd also get a limited number of commercials featuring Hart. "Yes, but I'm keeping my shirt on from here on out," he said simply.

Liam appeared surprised, as did Jackson Henry, the Elementals rep Hart had been working with for years.

"Hart?" Liam questioned. "You've never mentioned that before."

Hart tapped his fingers on the table. "I'm almost thirty-three. Enough with me partially in the buff. I don't want my children wondering why Daddy's half-naked in the magazine."

"You're getting married?" Jackson asked. Now Liam appeared stunned.

"No. Maybe. Eventually," Hart said. He picked up a pencil and rolled it between his fingers. "My point is that no other driver wanders around in just a pair of boxers unless they're a twenty-something model. Not even those other celebrities who work for your competitor do. I'm happy hawking Elementals products. I like wearing the stuff. But I want to present a more mature image from here on out."

Liam and Jackson exchanged glances. "I think that can be arranged," Jackson said.

"Good," Hart answered. He stretched. He'd been sitting in the conference chair for over an hour. While a driver's seat never bothered him, he hated long meetings.

"Is everything else agreeable?" Liam asked.

"Yeah," Hart said. He and his personal attorney had pored over the contract yesterday. "Change that clause and get it back to me."

Within fifteen minutes he was out of the meeting and calling Charlie.

"Hey, what's up?" Hart asked.

"I'm not good," Charlie said.

Hart listened as Charlie described the situation. "I'll call you back in a few minutes," Hart said. He strode back into the conference room. "Liam, I need to talk with you. Well, I guess you, too, Jackson. I need a substitute driver this weekend for New Hampshire."

"You're not racing?"

"No. Charlie's in the hospital. They've told him to prepare for the end if this round of chemo fails."

"Oh." A look of shock crossed Liam's face.

"I'm flying to Myrtle Beach now. I'm not even going to be stressed out by giving myself a timetable," Hart said.

"So Dover's iffy?" Liam asked.

"Let's not worry about that. I might be in the driver's seat for Dover," Hart said. He glanced at Jackson. "If this throws anything contractwise, then I'm sorry, but it's better for all of us if we know where I stand. I care for these people a great deal, and this is something that can't be rescheduled. I'll leave you and Liam to sort this out."

And with that, Hart strode from the room, leaving a stunned Liam and Jackson in his wake.

LIAM TURNED to Jackson. He sat there with a flabbergasted look on his face and Liam's gut clenched. While they could find another sponsor, life would be so much easier if they could get this deal done. Elementals had been very generous.

"I don't think I've ever seen Hart like that," Jackson said. "I'm shocked."

Liam shifted uncomfortably.

"I've been following Hart and Kellie via the media," Jackson said. "I've known Hart a long time, but never seen him fly off like this."

"Yes, well…" Liam began.

"No, it's okay. I like this new Hart. We're still going to sponsor him. Hart's matured, just like he said. He knows his priorities. I never thought I'd see the day."

Liam relaxed. Neither had he.

"So shall we go over a few more things?" Jackson asked.

"Absolutely," Liam said.

FIVE HOURS LATER, Hart entered Charlie's hospital room. "Hey, sport," he said.

"Hey, Hart," Charlie replied.

Hart immediately noticed the paleness of Charlie's skin and the sunkeness of his face. He was hooked up to IV and oxygen tubes. "You don't look that great," Hart said.

"I'm not." Charlie coughed a little, and Hart sat down and drew close.

"Take it easy there," Hart said. The whole situation had a surreal tinge to it. He'd been in plenty of hospital rooms but never like this. Charlie was simply too young to be in this spot. "Don't talk if it gives you fits."

"I need to talk," Charlie said. "I never told you what I wished for. Remember, from camp?"

"Wasn't that to attend a race?" Hart asked.

"No. That was just something I'd never done. You told me your wish was for a family. Remember, you said you'd need a wife first."

Hart laughed. "That seems so long ago, doesn't it?"

Charlie smiled a little. "Yeah. We just never got back to me."

Hart mentally cursed fate. He wished he could do so much

more, somehow relieve Charlie's physical pain. As for the wish, he recalled that Charlie was right. "So tell me, what do you wish for?"

"I want the joke to be real. I want you to marry my mom. Those are your intentions, aren't they? I want to know how serious you are."

Hart sat there, the machines giving the occasional beep. He'd spent all summer with Kellie. He'd known he'd wanted her from the moment he'd first seen her. He'd proved himself to be more than a joke. He'd never be tired of her. He kissed her and felt the world move. Every time they'd made love had been heavenly, proof that together they were magical. He wanted nothing more than to wake up every morning with her by his side. The stolen moments before she returned to her motor home and Charlie weren't enough.

"Those are my intentions," Hart said.

"Good." Charlie sunk into the pillow, as if the short conversation had exhausted him. A minute of silence passed before he was able to speak again. "I'm glad, you know. I need to know if anything ever happened to me that she wouldn't be alone. She'll have you."

"She'll have me," Hart said, although deep down he worried that she wouldn't have him. Kellie hadn't been the same since Hart's visit to the infield care center. She'd been distant, almost as if she were beginning to push him away. Hart wanted nothing more than to be with Kellie. All he could give, all the love he could show her might not be enough. Hart had the strangest sensation that he was driving a race he couldn't win. No matter how many times he went around, he wouldn't finish. He wouldn't win Kellie's heart.

He'd never known fear before. Never gave the emotion much credence beyond taking common-sense precautions.

He strapped himself into his car, hit the track and pushed the engine full out. He never worried or questioned, living each moment as they came.

Kellie and Charlie had changed that.

For the first time, Hart was afraid of losing. He couldn't lose Charlie, a boy he loved and wanted to see grow into adulthood. He couldn't lose Charlie's mother, the woman he wanted in his future.

"I'm not racing this weekend," Hart told Charlie. "I'm going to hang out with you, help out your mom and grandma."

"They'll like that," Charlie said. "I do, too." He coughed again and the machine beeped. They fell silent again, the images on the television screen muted. The door creaked open and Kellie walked in. She didn't appear too surprised or too happy to see him.

"Hi, Kellie," he said.

"Hart," she replied, her body posture closed and tight. He longed to go and take her into his arms, kiss her senseless and tell her everything was going to be okay. As the doctor arrived to check on Charlie, Hart did neither.

THE STRANGE DEPRESSION of that moment lingered in the air during the week. He and Kellie went through the motions, dancing around each other for days as they focused only on Charlie and his needs. Hart found himself wanting to somehow shake her, wake her from the doldrums she'd wrapped around herself. While physically she still gave herself to him, mentally she slipped away. She'd retreated, compartmentalized and shut him out.

"Kellie, you know we have to talk," he said as he followed her to the hospital cafeteria. Charlie and Anita were in his room watching the Sunday afternoon race.

"You should be racing today," she told him. "In New Hampshire."

"This was more important," Hart said. "You're more important."

"No, I'm not," Kellie replied. Seeing a few interested observers looking their direction, she led Hart outside into a quiet, deserted courtyard. She walked among the plants, the mid-September day warm and sunny.

"Kellie, you've been avoiding me all week."

She arched her eyebrow. "You've been here with me."

"Oh, you've been in the same room as me. You've given me your body and lost yourself in my arms. But you haven't been open. You're pushing me away and I want to know why."

"You shouldn't have given up a weekend of racing for us," she said.

He shrugged. "Why not? I'm out of the Chase. My sponsors can deal with it. I just negotiated another multiyear contract. Being here for you and Charlie was much more important. Kellie, don't you realize how much I care? How much I love you?"

She jutted her chin forward. "You care too much and for the wrong reasons. If something happens to Charlie, you won't need to come around anymore."

He drew up next to her and stared down. "Kellie, stop being afraid. You know that's not true. I love you. Those are words I've never said to any woman besides my mother. I want to marry you."

Her lip trembled slightly. "You're just saying that because of Charlie. I heard what he told you on Tuesday. I was standing in the doorway. I didn't know you'd arrived. He wants the joke to be real. He wants you to marry me."

"If you overheard our conversation, then you know those are my intentions, but not because Charlie asked me, either."

"This is unreal."

"Why? I love you. I don't say anything that I don't mean and I don't want to marry you simply to keep Charlie happy. Even I wouldn't go that far. But I love you. Those are my intentions. Long-term. Nothing less."

From her expression, Hart knew she didn't believe him. It was as if he were shooting darts but couldn't hit the target. Her husband had hurt her terribly, and Hart knew he was fighting an uphill battle. Kellie had told him about John. Hart simply hadn't realized the full implications until now.

"It doesn't matter," Kellie said. "Hart, I…I…"

No. He couldn't let her say the words that would allow her to slip away, allow her to retreat back into her comfort zone. "You can't lie to me and tell me you don't love me. I feel it. Here." He placed her hand on his heart. Her skin heated under his touch.

"No, I can't lie," Kellie admitted. "But sometimes love isn't enough. If it were, I would have loved Charlie's illness into oblivion and John wouldn't have left."

"Kellie…" Hart began.

"No. I can't risk it. I'm repeating the same patterns of my life over and over. I didn't choose this route, but I have to be here for Charlie. I want to be here for him, never think otherwise. While I might love you, I can't be at the track when you need me to be. I also can't add more worry to my life. What if you get hurt?"

"You don't have to worry about me," Hart said.

"I do. I can't help it. I worry about you wrecking or having a poor finish or about whether you'll still think I'm pretty years from now. Maybe other wives and girlfriends can handle it, but they don't walk into a clinic on a weekly basis. I do that enough with Charlie. I can't turn around and worry about whether I am going to have to do it with you, too. That's asking the impossible of me. I'm tired. I can't give any more. The well's dry. As much as I care about you, the risks that come with loving you are way too high."

"Kellie—" he started.

"No. Don't tell me how safe your job is. I know my argument is irrational, but to me it's not. You can't be anything but a race car driver. I can't be anything but a mother with a very sick son. In the end, our lives are too different to converge for long. We knew this before we started, but we chose to ignore the fact that you and I were destined only to be temporary. That's why I tried not to go to the first race. That's why I tried not to fall in love with you. Everyone I love dies. My father. My husband. If this chemo doesn't work, Charlie."

"Kellie, I'm not planning on dying, at least not until I'm a very old, old man. I'm not leaving you. I'm no more at risk than anyone else."

She stood silhouetted against the foliage. "I know you mean that. In the end, though, the only one I've ever relied on is me. I have suffered disappointment after disappointment. For both of our sakes, I have to do this. If you really love me, you'll understand."

She'd thrown out the ultimate female weapon. If he really loved her, he'd abide by her request. It was a terrible trump card, only to be used in the most serious or most desperate of situations. This was both, and Hart knew that battling with her would only make her dig in further. He was in a no-win situation.

"I see," Hart said. His jaw twitched as he held his emotions tightly in check. He'd have to think this through—later, when his heart wasn't shattering.

"You'll get over me," she said, as if those words could be some sort of consolation.

"No," Hart said. He shook his head. "No woman has ever broken my heart before."

"I'm sorry," she whispered. She couldn't hold back the tears, and he felt guilty for his harsh words. No matter what, he never wanted to hurt her.

"I know you're sorry," Hart said, gently. "I know you are, but that doesn't make me feel any better. Kellie, I love you. I know you're afraid, and for once in my life, I am, too. I'm afraid of losing you, and that's exactly what's happening. Maybe we shouldn't talk anymore. Give both of us time to think."

"I don't need any more time to think," she told him.

"Maybe you will anyway," Hart said. "If you don't mind, tell Charlie I'll be in touch later. I'm going to fly back home. I'd like to rest up for my meeting with Wally tomorrow. I have to be in Dover next weekend."

"I understand." She looked broken standing there, and Hart wanted to draw her into his arms and convince her that everything would be okay. But he knew that bulldozing would only be a temporary thing. Maybe that old cliché did hold true—if you loved something, you had to set it free; if it came back to you, it was yours. Hart had never experienced such pain or fear, but somehow he turned and walked away, leaving Kellie behind.

CHAPTER SIXTEEN

"HELLO, RACE FANS, and welcome to Atlanta on this warm, sunny weekend before Halloween. I'm Guy Edwards and I'm with Malcolm French and we'll be your guides today for all the prerace and race day activities that will start in a few hours. Thanks for joining us for our early show."

"Chasers aside, we have to take a minute to focus on Hart Hampton. He's been in a huge funk ever since Dover, not even reaching the top twenty the past two races."

"He was fifteenth at Talladega, but Hampton fans have to be wondering what has been going on with their driver. It's like he doesn't care anymore. Even his lucky charms have seemingly left him high and dry as we haven't seen them at the track."

CHARLIE MUTED the television set. He couldn't listen to the early morning cable show anymore. Hart did care. He cared way too much. That was the problem. Heck, Charlie didn't even want to watch the race today. He would, though, for he was actually feeling much better and his grandma had declared they could have pizza later.

Charlie surveyed the living room. This was the sixth weekend since Hart's departure. The last round of chemo had been harsh, but so far it had worked. He was on the upswing.

He just wished Hart were the same. He knew he wasn't, for he'd talked to him yesterday.

Charlie hated hiding the fact that he kept in touch with Hart from his mom, but Charlie knew his mother was stubborn. Usually that was one of the things he loved most about her. His mom's stubbornness in believing that he'd get well had paid off this time. Once she'd shed her tears, she'd become the fighter he knew her to be. If only she'd fight for Hart and her own chance for happiness. Charlie glanced up as his mom came into the living room about nine o'clock. "You got up late," he told her.

"I didn't sleep well," Kellie said. "Bad dreams."

"You sound like me a few months ago," Charlie said. He changed the channel to a show on ghost hunting. Since it was the weekend before Halloween, this particular cable station was having an all-day marathon, and there was nothing Charlie loved better than ghosts.

KELLIE WALKED INTO the kitchen, leaving her son behind with his show. She filled the coffeepot and pressed the Start button. Then she leaned back against the cabinet and yawned. She'd dreamt that two stock cars crashed and that Hart's car disappeared into the smoke. She'd jolted awake about four, the dream so vivid and real that she had no idea of the ending—what happened and whether Hart was okay. This is why I let Hart go, she thought, although not speaking with him had been the hardest thing she'd ever done in her life. She reached for a mug and set it on the counter.

Kellie had lost Hart, by her own choice. But he was still in her heart. Even now, a month and a half later, she still thought about him constantly. She told herself that surely he'd moved on. Certainly he'd forgotten her. She'd started doing her grocery shopping and errands during race times, leaving the house so she didn't hear the broadcasters calling his name. She avoided the sports section of the newspaper, didn't listen to any of the radio programs or watch the cable shows with her son.

Despite all her actions, Hart was still as real to her as ever, and she didn't have to see him on the screen. She still worried about him and fantasized about what could have been, if she'd had the guts.

"So what did you dream about?" Charlie asked, coming into the kitchen, his oatmeal bowl in hand.

"Nothing," she said.

"You know, Mom, I'm sixteen. I have a driver's permit and I'm getting my license next week. I'm not a child anymore and that means you can talk to me. If you're this grumpy, I'd say you had a pretty bad nightmare."

She smiled. "No, it's not like that."

"Hart, maybe?" Charlie asked.

"What makes you so perceptive?"

He shrugged and set the bowl in the sink. "Don't know. You've just seemed out of sorts lately. So did you dream about him marrying someone else?"

"No," she shot back, aghast that he would even think such a thing. "I dreamt that two cars crashed and Hart went into the smoke. Then I woke up."

"Ah," Charlie said.

"Ah, what?" Kellie asked suspiciously.

"You still care about him," Charlie said matter-of-factly.

Kellie blushed and looked away. "These aren't things you talk about with your mother."

"Mom, I'm grown up," Charlie said. "Or at least close enough. I mean, I've faced my own mortality. Don't you think

I'm adult enough for this? Besides, I know Hart still cares for you. I know he's still in love with you."

Kellie turned her head sharply so she could see him. "How would you know that?"

"Because I asked him. He said he still loves you."

Kellie inhaled quickly. "You shouldn't still be talking with Hart!"

Charlie wasn't in the least bit repentant. He shrugged. "Why not? I didn't break up with him. We're friends. Sorry, but you may not want him in your life, but I want him in mine. And I'm old enough to make my own decisions. I'm just not a 'fraidy cat like you are."

Kellie stood there, dumbfounded. Had Charlie just...

"Yeah, I just called you a name. You can punish me all you want, but I'm not afraid to call you that because it's the truth. You love Hart but you're afraid to let yourself. You're afraid of losing him. Well, Mom, you already have lost him, only you did it to yourself. Punish me if you want, but it's the truth."

"I..." Kellie blustered. "I'm not discussing this with you."

"Mom." Charlie came over and put his hand on her arm. "Mom, I may not have dated—okay, not at all. My only experience in male-female love might be from soap operas and talk show psychologists, but I think I can recognize that you two love each other a great deal."

"He's a race car driver," Kellie said.

"Yep. That doesn't make him bad husband material."

"I don't want to visit another hospital," she tried.

"You might have to anyway. You will someday with Grandma. You will with me. Are you going to block out all the people you care about you because eventually you'll have to face their mortality?"

"We shouldn't be having this conversation. I'm your mother. You shouldn't be psychoanalyzing me."

"Mom, Grandma and I have talked about this. I'm sick. I might get lucky this time. I made my peace with death a long time ago. I don't live in fear of what the future might bring, but I try to live each day to the fullest."

"You sound like Hart."

"Yeah, he's like me or vice versa. We respect fear but don't let it chain us. Where would the world be if the Wright Brothers had feared flying? What about those astronauts who risked it all so that man could explore space? Fear is healthy, but, Mom, you've let it take away the one thing that could make you happy."

"You make me happy," Kellie replied. She busied herself with washing the dishes as she waited for the coffee to finish brewing.

"But I can't make you happy like Hart can. You need both of us, Mom. Life is to be lived, one moment at a time as if each moment is a blessing."

She paused. "Okay, you got that line from your grandmother."

"Yep," Charlie answered with a grin. He gave his mom a big hug, his thin arms tightening and releasing. He stepped back. "Hart won the pole."

"That's great," she said, the moment bittersweet.

"You should be there for him," Charlie said. "Grandma and I will be fine. Atlanta's only six hours away. If you leave now, you can be there in plenty of time before the race ends."

"Really, that's rather far to drive. My car needs a tune-up and…."

"Take the Corvette. I'll go print you some directions off the Internet."

"I don't know," Kellie said. Her little boy was a man now,

and she recognized that he was right. He'd matured before her eyes, especially during this last round of treatments.

"Look, if I'm not afraid of the future, you shouldn't be. You still have your hard card. You'll get in. Or you could call Cynthia. I'm sure she'll send a plane."

"No, that's okay. I'm not sure how Cynthia will take my presence."

"It'll be fine. Get your coffee and get going. I'll go get you those directions."

"So, are you going?" A few seconds after Charlie went to his computer, Anita spoke up from where she'd been standing in the doorway.

"How long have you been there?"

"Long enough. So?" her mother asked.

"I don't know," Kellie replied.

"You probably should go," Anita said, coming in and helping herself to the freshly brewed coffee. "You've been pretty miserable to live with lately, and my favorite driver's lost his mojo. I'm sure quite a few Hampton fans would be thrilled if you helped him get it back. Besides, if you have doubts, six hours in a car will give you plenty of time to think. You've been avoiding that lately."

"You're taking Charlie's side," Kellie protested.

Anita took a sip. "Kellie, I'm taking your side. Your son is right. You've let fear control your life. You're afraid that loving Hart will make you vulnerable. You're strong, Kellie. Love makes you even stronger. Whatever fate hands you with Hart, you'll be able to handle it because love is like that. It helps you weather everything, just like I did with your father. We may not have had our golden years together, but the time I had with him was the best. I wouldn't have traded it for anything or another man who might have lived longer. Don't throw away a chance of being happy just because you're stubborn. Those who risk are the ones who are rewarded."

"You sound like a fortune cookie," Kellie said, grasping for a glib reply since she was so shocked and awed by her mom's admission.

"You're out of excuses, so stop trying to discredit my philosophical gems. Go to Atlanta. See Hart. If you realize that you've moved on and you don't love him, then turn around and come home. If not, Charlie and I will be fine here. Go."

"Okay, I'm going," Kellie said, leaving her untouched coffee cup on the counter and heading to the bathroom.

NOT MUCH LATER, she was on I-20, snug in the Corvette, tooling along a little over the posted speed limit. The car seemed happier that way, and she had to admit it was a pretty sweet ride.

The car had satellite radio, and Kellie found the NASCAR station. She listened to the announcers start the race. By the time Hart finished, he would have driven five hundred miles. She would have covered three hundred and fifty.

She reached for the bottle of water she'd picked up at the last gas station and took a drink. Charlie and Anita were right. She'd been an idiot. She'd always prided herself on being tough enough to handle anything, but when fate had given her Hart Hampton, Kellie had crumbled. She'd chickened out and run for cover, hurting him.

She paused. He loved her. She loved him. Hopefully this wasn't a fool's errand. What if he didn't want to marry her anymore? Could she deal with a relationship where they cohabitated if that was all he offered?

Stop! Kellie told herself. She focused. All she needed to do was talk with Hart. She needed to look him in the eye and tell him she loved him. If he rejected her, well, she'd deal with that. If he said he loved her but didn't want to marry her, well, she'd cross that bridge when she came to it.

She was going to live like Charlie and Hart. Risk everything. This trip was a gamble, but one for which she was ready. One day at a time. To the fullest. She tapped the steering wheel's Cruise Control button, easing the car up another notch. She'd risk the ticket. She had a race to attend.

THE ONE-AND-A-HALF-MILE TRACK at Atlanta wasn't really in Atlanta per say, but rather in Hampton, Georgia, a town just thirty miles to the south. Hart had always like racing here—the NASCAR NEXTEL Cup Series visited two times a year. The turns were banked twenty-four degrees; the straightaways five. Average speed was usually around 143 miles per hour, meaning the average race length ran about three and a half hours.

Since the first practice hadn't been until three Friday afternoon, Hart had flown in early that morning. Billed as the fastest track on the circuit, he'd won the pole Friday night with a speed of over 190 miles per hour. The elation had lifted him somewhat from his funk, and he'd used the final two practices to perfect his strategy, which he'd already changed several times now that he was actually out racing.

It felt good to be out on the track and in today's top ten. He could lose himself in the race, forgetting his troubles for a few hours.

Hart rounded Turn Four and accelerated. Back from their extended tour of Europe, his parents were in attendance, high up in one of the corporate suites he was speeding by. The track had come along way in since its inception, even surviving a tornado that had caused extensive damage.

"Outside! Go low," Matt's voice called into Hart's ear, and Hart took a lower groove, moving away from the wall as

Dusty Burke came up on Hart's back right quarter panel. They were almost double-wide entering Turn Two, Hart on the inside and Dusty on the out. Hart had the lane, but as he entered the turn he knew he'd need to drift up the banking else he lose speed and have to fall back, which would then let Dusty Burke move into the fourth spot.

Hart had been holding in the top ten all race. He was halfway through the miles and determined that today's finish would be in the single digits. As he was already out of the Chase, Hart knew he should give Dusty the spot; after all, Dusty was a lucky rookie who'd made the Chase and Dusty could use all the track position he could get.

Normally Hart would let him pass and fall back a spot. Instead, he drifted up the banking, forcing Dusty back. "Ronnie'll thank you," Matt said, for Ronnie was also in the Chase and fighting to move forward from the ninth spot. Hart hit the backstretch hard.

"Bengal's cut a tire on One," Matt said in his ear. "Caution's out."

"Pit stop," Wally said, and that meant he wanted Hart to pit the moment NASCAR allowed cars down pit road. They'd been racing for about fifty green flag laps, meaning everyone would be coming down for four tires and fuel.

"No adjustments," Hart called. The car was perfect. His team could complete the stop in 13.3 seconds or better.

"Pit road's open," Matt called.

"On my way."

SHE WAS LOST. Oh, she'd made it through Atlanta and found the race track with few problems, but she hadn't counted on the fact that she'd have to park. Parking lots required parking passes. Or cash. Most were full. Frustration consumed Kellie.

Her cell phone rang and she put the earpiece in her ear and hit connect.

"Are you there yet?" Charlie asked.

"I'm looking for a place to park," Kellie told him. "I've never had to do this part. This place is huge."

"Let me call you right back," Charlie said as he disconnected.

Kellie drove on and finally stopped at a light. She drummed her fingers on the steering wheel. This was a stupid idea. What was she supposed to say to him?

Her phone rang and she connected. "Hello?"

"Hi, Kellie, it's Russ. Charlie told me you're lost. Glad you're here."

"Really?"

"Absolutely. We've been waiting for you since this morning after your son called and let us knew you were on the way. He's kept us posted as to your progress."

No wonder he'd been calling her so often. Charlie's subterfuge ran deep, but she was so relieved that her welcome was to be a warm one that Kellie decided to forgive him.

"So exactly where are you?" Russ asked.

Kellie glanced up at the street sign and told him the name.

"You're not too far away. There's a tunnel. Here's what I want you to do...."

BY THE FINAL TEN LAPS, Hart had moved up to third. He was two car lengths behind the race leaders: Kyle Doolittle and Dusty Burke had been trading the top two spots for the last five laps. They were nose to nose, each refusing to back down. The crowd probably loved it. The rest of the field, especially the lap down cars, tried to get out of the way even if it meant they went down another lap.

"Eight to go," Matt called. "Donuts in front of you."

Out in third place by three car lengths, Hart simply held back a safe distance. If Burke and Doolittle wanted to rub tires down each other as they fought for the win, let them. Third was better than Hart had done in ages. He'd take it. He powered his way through Turns One and Two, hitting the backstretch and passing through some lap down traffic with ease. See, he could run with the chasers. Third place would be fine. Best showing in a while.

Static crackled. "Your fuel's good," Wally confirmed.

Hart breathed a sigh of relief. The biggest risk to the race leaders would be miscalculating gas mileage and running out of fuel. That had happened many times. Last year, a non-Cup contender had won a race, coasting in on empty, since that driver could take risks such as not pitting.

"Five cars front stretch," Matt called, and Hart wove his way through more of the field. Normally entirely focused on the sliver of the world he could see out his window, a vision of Charlie suddenly popped into his head. He was home and doing better. He'd be watching the race with Anita and eating pizza. Pepperoni was his favorite, Hart remembered. He'd call Charlie later tonight.

Hart smiled and then tried not to think about Kellie. Still, she was hard to forget. Typical male philosophy was that you went out and found a rebound girl, but Hart hadn't done that. He had no desire. He was probably a fool, but he was holding on, hoping she'd change her mind. He figured he'd give her two more weeks and then he'd go talk with her again. After all, two months was plenty of thinking time.

"Four to go," Matt called.

Hart entered Turn One, zipped through that and Turn Two and caught up with Burke and Doolittle on the backstretch. They were still fighting it out, driving as aggressively as they could without having NASCAR issue a warning.

As the three cars entered Turn Three, Hart saw that neither of the top two were ready to give up track position. "Bumper," Matt called, letting Hart know that a driver was closing from behind.

Wanting to keep his third spot, Hart accelerated, closing the gap between him and the front-runners as they rounded Turn Four and hit the front stretch.

"Three to go," Matt said.

Hart was only seconds behind Doolittle and Burke, who had begun to touch as they fought for position and championship points.

"Bumper cars ahead," Matt said.

"See them," Hart radioed.

Doolittle and Burke were fighting full out now, their cars battling as they headed into Turn Four and final two laps for the finish line.

"Kellie's here," Wally said in Hart's ear.

"What?" The jolt was enough that Hart made the beginner mistake of lifting his foot. The car decelerated.

"Spinning!" Matt said, and sure enough, just ahead as they came out of Turn Two, Burke had sent Doolittle into the wall. Not to be left behind—alone—in the points chase, Doolittle caught Burke on the rebound and both men went spinning. Thick gray smoke billowed.

"High! High!" Matt shouted.

Not again, Hart thought. He could not have his first meeting with Kellie back at the infield care center. He swung high and entered the smoke.

KELLIE CRANED her neck. Upon her arrival, she'd taken the extra seat on top of the pit box. She had a perfect view of Doolittle and Burke, and that of Hart entering the smoke.

The coincidence to her dream unnerved her and she dug her nails into her palm. And then she saw him, as car Number 413 cleared the wreck and coasted into the clean air of the backstretch. Hart was now the race leader. Someone handed her a headset and she strapped it on.

"Caution's out! Drivers have nets down and are fine," Matt called.

"You're good. Enough fuel," Wally added. "Get a good jump and this race is ours."

Kellie watched as Hart fell in line behind the pace car. "Is she really here?" he radioed.

"She's really here," Wally replied, and a giddiness Kellie hadn't felt for a while returned. He *did* still care.

"Don't let her leave," Hart called.

"Don't worry. I won't," Wally said. He gave Kellie a thumbs-up.

"Better not," Hart said, laughing.

"She's listening," Wally told him. "So's everyone else." A lot of race fans used scanners to monitor the drivers' conversations.

"Yeah, yeah," Hart said. "Just don't let my parents scare her away. You're going to have to meet them, Kellie, but I promise it will be fine."

Kellie glanced around. Meet his parents? As the pace car and Hart passed the finish line, she found herself oddly not nervous at all.

"PIT CAR on pit road next pass. We're going green white checkered," Matt called, and upon hearing those words, Hart wove his car from side to side, letting the pack behind him know that this race was his the moment the pace car pulled off.

Kellie was here.

Within minutes Matt was yelling, "We did it!" as up front

Hart could see the black-and-white flag waving, and he zoomed across the finish line first. "You're back!" Wally added.

No, Kellie was the one who was back. "Where is she?" Hart called. She'd finally come and he wasn't wasting another minute.

"Right behind me with Russ," Wally said. "Hey, whatcha doing?"

"Coming in," Hart said, turning his car down pit road instead of staying out for the victory lap. Normally his team would race out to meet him in the grass, but Hart brought his car in.

Hart had dropped his net a while ago. He'd flipped up the protective facemask. He had mere seconds before the media descended. "Send her over," he radioed, stopping out in pit lane just outside his stall.

He saw her immediately, climbing over the pit wall. Her blond hair was back in a ponytail and she wore a T-shirt and jeans. Hart didn't think twice about waiting for the official moment in Victory Lane. He killed the engine, yanked the helmet off, and slid from the car.

He held out his arms as Kellie ran forward. For a second he was as awkward as a schoolboy. "I'm really grungy," he told her.

"I'm not afraid of dirt," she said as she entered his embrace. "I think I owe you this. We had a deal, remember?" She placed both hands on his face and drew his lips to hers.

It was a kiss to rock his world. When he could focus, Hart was aware of media cameras beaming their reunion across the nation. "Media," he told her.

"Don't care. Not afraid of them anymore," she said, and Hart relaxed. He drew back but kept hold of her.

"Are you going to be here for every race?" he asked, for before his victory obligations tore him away that was something he had to know.

"I'm planning on it. If I have you, I guess you get me right back. I've been such a fool. I love you."

The words he'd longed to hear. "Just promise you'll whisper those last words over and over in my ear later."

"I'm planning on showing you," she said.

Hart whooped, grabbed her and spun her around. "Now that's what I've been waiting for. Come on. We've got a party to attend."

"You need to get back in the car," Cynthia said, coming up behind them. Hart knew she meant for the official climbing-out ceremony held for the media on Victory Lane. As he was already out, he really didn't have much desire to get back in, but duty called.

"Go," Kellie said.

"Wait for me?" Hart asked, hating to let her out of his sight for even a minute.

"If it takes all night," Kellie said, giving him a smile so full of promise that Hart thought he might burst from happiness. The emotion carried him into Victory Lane and the subsequent media interviews.

"So that's her," his mother said later as Hart's winner's tour took him up to Hampton Racing's corporate suite, his last stop before he could return to Kellie.

"That's her," Hart stated. "And she won't need your motor home this weekend. She's staying with me."

"Does she know what she's getting into?" Vivian asked, her tone serious as she searched her son's face. Hart knew she only wanted what was best for him.

And while once Hart had had his doubts, he didn't anymore. "Yeah, she knows exactly what she's getting herself into."

"Then you're a very lucky man and I can't wait to meet her," his mom said, smiling. "You two need some alone time now. Your father and I will call you and arrange something, say early next week?"

"Sounds great," Hart said as he moved away. Then he paused. He was lucky. He'd won the most important race of his life. Kellie loved him. That was the best victory of all.

EPILOGUE

"So, ARE YOU ready for this?" Kellie asked Hart. It was July, and the NASCAR NEXTEL Cup Series was off for a week.

"Like last year, I'm actually a little nervous," Hart said. "Aren't you?"

"Nope," she said, glancing around the living area of their motor home, her home away from home since February. So much had changed since she'd shown up at the track last October during the Chase.

Three weeks after Atlanta, while Ronnie McDougal celebrated his second NASCAR NEXTEL Cup championship in Victory Lane, Hart and Kellie had embraced the season's end by officially becoming engaged. She and Charlie had moved to Charlotte in December, and she and Hart had married in the Caribbean in January. Once the new NASCAR season had started in February, the family had been back on the road every weekend.

"You should do fine," Kellie told him as she gave him one last glance. He wore a polo shirt and jeans, and she marveled at how much she loved him. "Besides, it's only a Q&A. If I can do it, you can."

"You have gotten pretty comfortable with interviews over this past year," Hart said.

"I guess I have." Becoming Mrs. Hart Hampton had thrust

her into the media spotlight for a while, but Alyssa McDougal, Cynthia and Russ had all been there to help.

"You've gotten comfortable with everything," he said, grinning.

"I am okay in most things," Kellie answered. She was still nervous before every race. She still worried about Charlie and Hart. But she'd learned to control her fear. Love was the emotion she wanted to be consumed by. Fear confined and chained. Love freed and allowed one to soar.

"Hey, are you two coming?" Charlie called up the stairs. He was already outside in the North Carolina foothills ready for the night's events. "The camp director's on her way. Let's get NASCAR Night started. I bet all these kids are ready to change a tire and drive a simulator. I know I was."

"We're coming," Kellie said with a laugh. She, Hart and Charlie were back at the camp, something they'd decided to do as a yearly tradition, especially since this was where they'd all first met. "Oh, by the way, your grandmother called earlier while you were out helping Clyde and Clarissa get set up. Be sure to call her back."

"Will do," Charlie said.

Kellie's mother still lived in the Myrtle Beach house, but right now she was traveling with friends to Alaska. Charlie was doing well, too, and he'd made the transition to his Charlotte-based doctors with ease. Everyone was encouraged with his progress. So far, the treatments had worked. He'd turned seventeen and was ready to try a limited schedule for his senior year of high school.

"Come on. Let's go," Kellie said to Hart. She reached her hand out and Hart took it. "I doubt you'll botch up your Q&A any worse than you did last year."

He laughed and tugged, drawing her to him and pressing

her up to his chest. "I didn't botch anything up. Last year, I said I needed a wife. Looks like I got what I wished for."

"That you did. Although, thinking back, you said you wanted a family and would need a wife first."

"Semantics," Hart said, his nose and lips next to her hair.

"No, you said family," Kellie insisted.

"I got that. You and Charlie."

Kellie giggled. "Do you know how much I love you?" she asked suddenly.

"If it's half as much as I love you, then I'm a very lucky man."

"We're both very lucky, then," Kellie said. Her stomach fluttered slightly. She'd been victorious over her fear; because of that, she'd been blessed. Charlie had had a clinic visit this morning and things had been great. She'd even had her own appointment…. "Well, just don't tell them you need a baby."

She'd never been good at keeping secrets. Telling Hart here, where they'd first met, seemed like coming full circle. Very right.

"Why not?" Hart asked, his gaze searching her face.

"Because you're already going to have one," Kellie said. "You're going to be a daddy."

STANDING OUTSIDE the motor home, Charlie heard Hart's shout. Having overheard the news, Charlie shut the door. They could all celebrate together later. He watched as the camp director approached from the distance. NASCAR Night could wait a few extra minutes.

He leaned against the motor home and grinned. Sometimes holding out was the best thing you could do. His mom had held out for Hart Hampton.

And, no joke, life was exactly the way he'd wished.

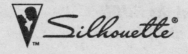